Dark River Passage

Torn from his frontier family during the turmoil of the Revolutionary War, a youth is adopted into a radically different culture—not once, but twice. A novel, based on the true story of William Walker of the Delaware and Wyandot Nations.

J. Larry Jacobson

To the Forrests,

In Christ,

TapRootBooks™
Chickasha, OK

J. Larry Jacobson

J. Larry Jacobson

International Standard Book Number
0-9778227-0-2
(ISBN-13: 978-0-9778227-0-6)
Library of Congress Control Number
2006901740

Cover design: "Emptiness Has a Claim on Death" used by permission of Seminole artist, Enoch Kelly Haney Contact: (405) 382-3369 or haney.studio@sbcglobal.net
Back cover art: "William Walker" by Jim Van Deman and "Crossing the River" by Ila Watson

For additional copies of this book, see order page at the back, or:
TapRootBooks
P.O. Box 2521
Chickasha, OK 73023-2521
405-222-4652

Printed in the USA by
Morris Publishing
3212 East Highway 30
Kearney, NE 68847
1-800-650-7888

Author's Preface

Some stories beg to be told. I ran across a reference to William Walker's captivity years ago and knew it was one that I wanted to write.

The information about his early years is sparse. An existing biography consists mostly of a handful of pages written by his son, William, Jr. For that reason, this book is what used to be called historical fiction and is now often termed "creative nonfiction." I've taken what is known about Walker and the history of the times and connected the dots. I've asked myself, what thoughts would a frontier boy have had about living with Indians? What longings are in the heart and mind of any adoptee, particularly one in a different culture? How did the known historical events in his geographical area affect him? How might he have participated in them? What did his family do in the way of rescue? How did their lives continue without him?

During the writing, I've been surprised at how the "dots" did connect. In the Endnotes, I've tried to help the reader identify what is historical and what is "creative."

Special thanks to friends Ed and Jerri Dexter for their support and suggestions, to Sara's sister, Fran Williams, who spent part of her vacation editing, and to Ed and Doris Williams for their enthusiasm. Much love to you all.

Also to Linda Poolaw of the Delaware Nation and Sheri Clemons, Wyandotte Nation of Oklahoma, for their kind help.

Special gratitude to Seminole Chief Enoch Kelly Haney for permission to use his painting on the cover. Haney's sculture "The Guardian" stands above the Oklahoma Capitol Dome.

Thanks to young artist Seth Cates for his preliminary work.

I'm very grateful for the artistry of Jim Van Deman, a member of the Delaware Nation, who designed the chapter headings as well as the portrait of William Walker. Also to Ila Watson, who painted the back picture, and to her husband Charles, for their continued friendship.

Dedication

With affection and love to Sara (who kept gently pushing me for years to write this book) for all her encouragement along the way. Also to our favorite family of kids and grandkids: Ginger, "J.J.," Wyatt, and Riley and their Native American ancestors.

~~~
~~~

William Walker
(artist's conception)
by Jim Van Deman

PROLOGUE (1785)

The young brave awoke just before dawn with the sounds of creation welcoming the sun. Before opening his eyes, he lay still and listened. From his pine-needle bed beneath a giant tree his ears absorbed the sounds—a multitude of birds singing to the Great Spirit. Only when a squirrel barked at him from the pine did he decide to join in greeting the new day.

Sitting up, he took the rolled deerskin-shirt pillow and shook it loose as he slipped his arms into the sleeves. The mountain air was chilly. He shivered, crossed his arms over his chest and rubbed his shoulders, gave a long yawn and walked to the clear stream that was gently rolling over smooth, worn stones.

The brave leaned over a clear pool of water in the granite basin and studied the reflection—a nineteen-year old warrior. One of his eyes was still swollen and bruised. "The kick in the head is healing quickly," he thought. He was disappointed there would be no scar as a battle trophy. It wasn't much of a fight, anyway, but he could embellish it a little for Catherine's benefit.

His shaved head with scalp lock in the center identified him as woodlands Indian. His face was deep brown-tanned but the eyes mirrored in the pool were blue. His braid was light brown. He smiled at the incongruity. "Guess a part of me will always come from these Virginia hills," he thought. "But I know who I am, where I belong, and where I need to be."

He plunged his face into the cool stream and raised it quickly towards the sky. As the droplets formed a beaded headdress, he lifted his arms and prayed: "Thank you Homendezue (Creator) for never forsaking me even when I could not find you in my heart. May my life be an offering to you, poured out for my people. Give me safe journey to the bark lodges."

William Walker mounted his horse, turned and waved goodbye from Laurel Ridge to the valley and Clinch River below, and set his face north towards the Wyandot Nation, across the "dark river"—the Ohio.

This is the story of an adopted son's spiritual voyage to fill a vacuum in the heart—of his journey from boy-captive to young manhood. It is also a tribute to Native American culture, the western frontier and the very real people with whom he lived.

ЖЖЖЖ

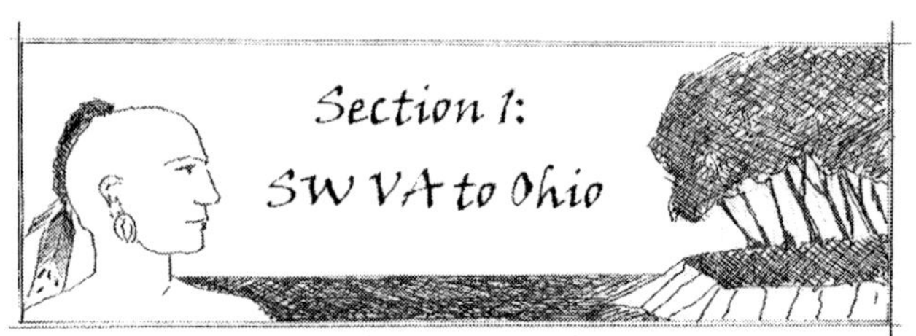
Section 1:
SW VA to Ohio

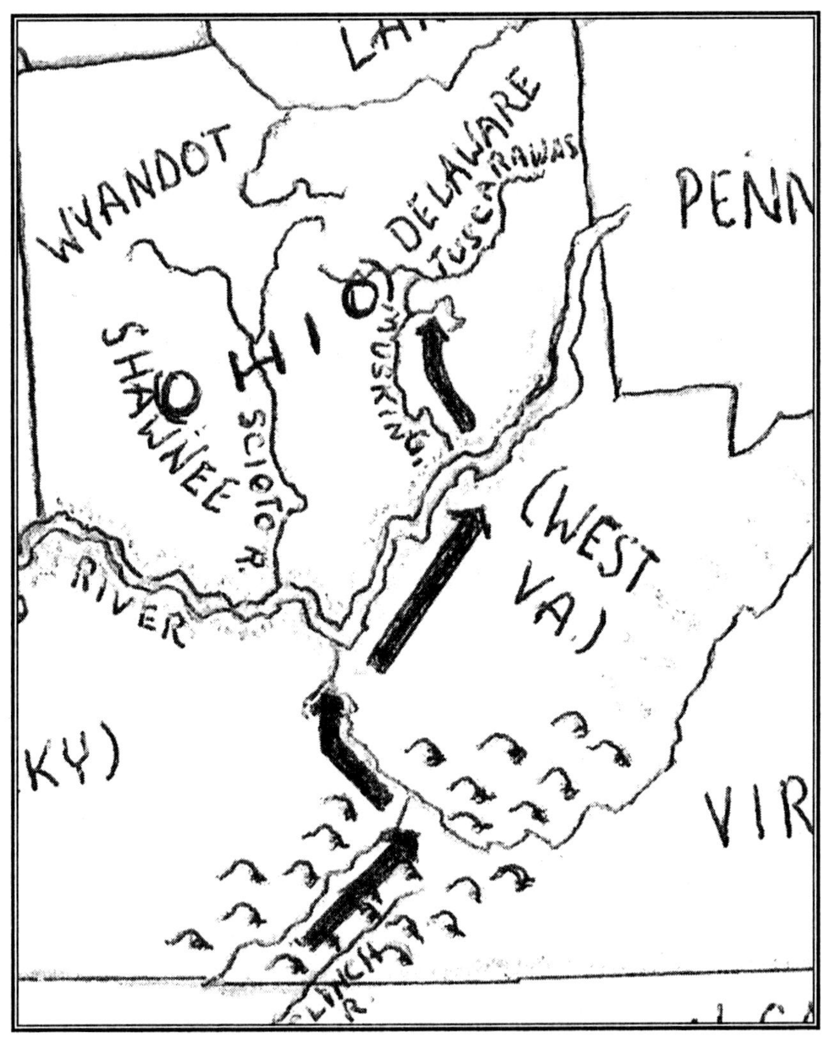

Route from Clinch R., VA, to Lenape villages in Ohio, following Tug Fork and Big Sandy trails, then by canoe up the Ohio to Muskingum R. Other trails by Scioto R. lead to Shawnee and Wyandot areas.

Chapter One:
Capture (1778)

"Faster! Faster!" William yelled—at himself—as he ran through the plowed cornfield in the direction of a blockhouse cabin a mile away, at the foot of the hill. Racing downhill on the sloped field wasn't easy but his eyes were on a tall clump of pine just yards away. "I can make it," he shouted, feeling the fear-pumped adrenalin pulsing through the bulging veins of his neck.

The thirteen-year old glanced back over his shoulder at his uncle staggering a short distance behind. Suddenly he heard a warrior's tremulous scream and glimpsed him standing over the man's body holding up a blood-dripping scalp.

Fighting panic, he willed his feet to move forward ever more rapidly over the plowed earth that separated him from safety. He was a swift runner but the clods broke under the pounding of his feet and the loose soil threw him off balance. He could only hope it would be as difficult for his pursuers—but a young Indian was gaining on him.

The hot summer sun had just slipped behind the mountain ridge west of the valley.

~~~

Twenty minutes earlier as the young brave contemplated this chase, his heart pounded in anticipation. He hid behind some brush and reached up to carefully spread the twigs of mountain laurel at the edge of the forest, staring through the small space framed by the branches. He'd been listening to the sounds as he advanced with slow and noiseless steps and now he discovered the source. He could see a boy about his own age riding a horse, coming towards him. He studied the rider's face.

The Indian boy spoke softly to Bigtree, his adult companion and teacher: "The horse is tethered to something. It looks like a huge iron spear digging up the ground as the animal drags it along behind him."

Over his shoulder he heard Bigtree whisper, "It is called a 'plow.' This is how they prepare the earth to receive the next seed corn."

The young brave crouched in hiding about twenty steps from the plowed field. Just as the horse and rider reached the edge of the forest, they made a right turn and went parallel to the trees. Mononcue was startled at a closer view of the man walking behind the plow, arms outstretched as he held the curved wooden handles. The man was without shirt and barefoot, wearing only deerskin breeches. The Indian boy
~~~

studied him. “Is that a white man?” he whispered in his native tongue to Bigtree, his mentor. “White,” to him, was the buffalo skull exposed to sun and weather for many days. “He is more the color of the juice of poke berries. Besides, his skin looks tan and cracked like old moccasins—same as an old chief’s.”

Bigtree carefully put his fingers sideways in front of his lips, a sign to Mononcue.

The face of the boy on the horse was similar brown-red to the white man’s but brighter and fresher looking. He had his hair tied back and braided into a single strand hanging over his neck much like Mononcue’s—not a shining jet-black but gold-tinted like the root tea his Indian grandmother made.

Mononcue was a quick learner, of medium build for his age but fast on his feet and bold to the point of being arrogant sometimes. His large eyes and long protruding nose took up most of his face. He was aware at this moment of his own single braid of hair from the center of his bald head. The braid hung between his bronzed shoulder blades and brushed against his skin in the light breeze.

His ponderings were abruptly interrupted when the plowing man began shouting loud and frightening sounds. Mononcue jerked his hands back, letting the branches hide his eyes again. He felt a sharp thump on his shoulder and glanced over at Bigtree’s disapproving frown at his sudden movement. But he had never heard such a voice as the plowman’s before. It made him think of the grunts his cur dog made when it was dreaming at night, only louder.

When he'd regained his courage, he reached again for the branches, carefully spreading them a little less wide.

~~~

Samuel had not really barked at his nephew, William Walker, the boy riding the plow horse. He had only spoken in his normally loud and boisterous voice. "Billy! Make that horse obey ye! Show 'im who's boss or he'll drag us both to the feed stall. Pull firm on them reins when ye turn 'im, hear me now?"

"I'm tryin', Uncle," William said, turning his head to look back and muttering, "Might as well be a mule." Then he put his hands over his eyes (which he often did when trying to decide his next move.) The boy gave the horse a hefty kick in the sides which must have felt like mosquitoes to the burly work animal.

~~~

Mononcue had never before accompanied the men on this long a trek. His companion Bigtree was much older, a warrior for twenty years or more. At his first battle he was only fourteen. He was now over six feet tall and was blunt and direct but very affable when he wasn't fighting. He had cut his earlobes, inserting several silver ornaments that stretched them nearly to his shoulders. A red jewel also dangled from his nose-ring which he wore with the other decorations, even in battle.

The warrior was growing impatient. He had kept his eyes to the ground and his body in a motionless crouched position for some minutes. He rolled his eyes up and glanced at his young apprentice who was still staring wide-eyed at the white man. Bigtree deftly plucked a stick from the ground and jabbed Mononcue's leg to get his attention. Without a word, the boy closed the branched window and twisted his upper body so he could see the older man. Bigtree nodded towards their rifles. Then his finger told Mononcue, "The big man I will shoot. Your target is the small one—catch him or kill him."

Mononcue signed with his hands: "Should we shoot them? The other braves are far from us at camp. We might bring other whites. This is a dangerous place!" His eyes were wide with both fear and excitement.

Bigtree squinted and stared at the younger brave. Without a word or sign he was speaking distinctly: "Is Mononcue a coward?" The younger boy thought of being shamed in front of the other hunters and taunted by the girls at the village. He glanced at the ground and nodded in understanding and submission to his elder.

His right hand moved spider-like towards the flintlock rifle lying at his side. He knew they would have only one shot each, but he had slung his bow with quiver over his shoulder, and a tomahawk rested in his waistband. Both braves slowly aimed through the branches at the man who was now walking away from them plowing the edge of the field. With the thrill of his first surprise attack Mononcue forgot his target was the boy. He had meant to argue with Bigtree about that, anyway. Both rifles sounded almost simultaneously—a flash of powder and an explosion that echoed three times from the Laurel Mountains around them.

Samuel exhaled a kind of shocked half-question—"Wha…?"—as his arms flew out in front of him and then fell limp and broken at his sides. Rifle balls had struck him in both, simultaneously. The force of the shots pushed him in between the plow handles but he was still standing, supported by them. The bone protruded from above the elbow of his left and his right arm had lost most of its upper flesh.

William's eyes were wide in puzzled confusion at what had occurred. He thought at first that the plow had somehow snapped in his uncle's hands. The man's face was splattered with blood, his arms spurting red even on the rear of the horse which was wildly struggling against the reins. Then William saw two figures burst from the woods and run towards them, tomahawks raised and mouths wide open in a startling, fright-filled scream.

"The cabin! Run!" shouted Samuel, awkwardly trying to move, his arms dangling and flopping at his sides.

William slid from the horse as it reared up again, vainly trying to escape the bonds that fettered it to the plow. In a second the boy caught up with his uncle and hesitated, trying to help.

Samuel motioned with his head, and William continued running as fast as he could, not looking back until he heard the scream and glimpsed the tall warrior standing over the prostrate form. The Indian raised his hand, lifting a bloody scalp—trophy of his conquest.

The second attacker—who had paused to watch the scalping—looked up just as William turned, and leapt into the chase again. William ran desperately, his chest and lungs expanding with rapid breathing, his head bursting with the pounding of his heart's blood.

When he had come to the field this morning the cabin seemed comfortably near. He could walk to it calmly in five minutes or less. It was a two-minute run, and yet he knew instinctively his situation was hopeless, that he did not have even fifteen seconds. He had never considered time so valuable before now. Hours he had wasted in boredom during the long winter months listening to old folks tell the same stories over and over again. Could he have borrowed a minute or two from those long sessions before the fire and used them now, how priceless they would be.

Suddenly the breath was knocked out of him and he was face-down on the ground. Mononcue had thrown himself headfirst into the middle of William's back, and now lay on top of him. The Indian boy moved to pin his captive's arms to the ground but William recovered in a moment. The adrenaline was flowing through his body and with all his strength he jerked up backwards, head-butting his opponent in the chin.

Mononcue bit his own tongue and fell back on his haunches in pain, not seeing the object that fell from William's pants pocket. Within that split second William was up and running again with all his might.

Again he was hit hard from behind—this time with much more force. The older brave had seen him escape from Mononcue and had taken up the chase. William felt his head jerked up by his braid and glimpsed a raised tomahawk. Oddly, his attention focused not on the weapon but on the Indian's earlobes. They were inches long, pierced and stretched around silver ornaments that dangled to the warrior's shoulders.

Mononcue—tongue still bleeding—ran up behind Bigtree and grabbed his wrist with both hands. Bigtree scowled at him and yelled in Wendat (Wyandot), "What are you doing? Turn loose of me, you mother's babe."

Still grasping the tomahawk, Bigtree jerked his arm and swung Mononcue to the ground astride William but the young Indian did not release his grip. He spoke to his elder firmly but with much respect. "Please, teacher. Don't kill him. Let me have him—I'll teach him a lesson for smashing me in the face!" He really wanted to save William's life but didn't know why—maybe because he was about his own age.

To Mononcue's surprise Bigtree immediately dropped the tomahawk. He did not intend to kill the boy, but was angry the capture had taken so long. "You are right, young one. We need to replace the many braves who have been killed. This one will make a good warrior!"

Bigtree pulled William's head around where he could see his eyes. William could see his nose-ring with the red jewel pendant. It frightened him by hanging so close to his own face. "You!" the Indian said in English, "do not talk or shout. If you do, my tomahawk will be inside your head. Understand me?"

"Yes," the boy answered with quavering voice.

Bigtree motioned for Mononcue to take a leather thong from his belt and tie the captive boy's hands in front of him. The three of them lay still on the ground for a few minutes watching the house some yards distant. There was no sign anyone had heard the commotion and behind them the plow horse was now calmly eating grass. At Bigtree's sign they half stood up, and crouching, moved across the field into the forest.

William's mind was racing at the speed of the events happening to him. He was not panicked at all but tried to make sense of his situation. "They are not going to kill me," he reassured himself. "I will just be taken to the Indian villages to live." Somehow, the fact that he was alive was comfort enough and the thought of leaving his home and family wasn't something he could dwell on at the moment.

It was dusk as they entered the forest, Mononcue leading the way with Bigtree behind him. One end of a strap was tied to Bigtree's wrist; the other end tightly bound around William's hands. The boy's hands were in front of him as he stumbled along trying to keep up with Bigtree's steps, sometimes encouraged to go faster by a yank on the strap. It was already getting dark in the woods but the Indians moved swiftly towards a creek-bed and waded up it through the shallow, cool water.

William was barefoot—customary for him—and the soles of his feet were hardened. Even so, it was tricky walking over the stones in the creek, especially trying to move at a swift pace. All his senses seemed to be working overtime. He licked the black earth from his lips—acquired when he was knocked to the ground—and noticed its taste. His feet felt the slickness of fallen leaves and in his nostrils was the musty odor of compost along the banks.

A flock of geese honking loudly almost landed on top of them in the twilight, coming in for the night to a sandbar where the creek widened and forked. Bigtree muttered something that sounded to William like a curse, maybe because they didn't have the time to harvest any.

Once he thought he heard his mother's familiar warbling whistle calling to him from the blockhouse. Maybe not, he thought—probably just a night bird's call.

Then he knew he heard a horse whinny. No, no, he thought—don't let it be brother trying to find me. He will just be killed like Uncle Samuel. "Please God don't let it be Alex," he whispered.

In a moment they reached a clearing between the trees and the mountain. As they approached the rock face he could see two horses partially hidden behind a cleft, reflected in the bluish light of a three-quarter moon rising.

)()()()(

Tough as they were, William's bare feet were cut and bruised. "Now," he thought, "I'll at least be on a horse." Then he saw there were only two horses. "Someone's going to be walking," he said to himself. He'd heard of captives having to walk until they fell and were dragged behind a horse. He briefly imagined himself in that condition.

Bigtree took hold of the strap tied to William's hands and led him over to a gray horse, grabbed him by the britches and tossed him on its back. Mononcue grasped the horse's mane and swung a leg over, taking his seat in front of William. Bigtree lifted the boy's hands—still bound together in front—and Mononcue ducked his head. William's arms were now around the Indian boy's waist.

Neither boy was comfortable with this close proximity. Mononcue complained in his own tongue to Bigtree: "Wait. Why do I have to have him tied on my back? What if I have to dismount in a hurry or reach my gun or tomahawk? How can I ride with him there?"

Bigtree turned his head away and swept his hand through the air at the boys. He spoke in Wendat, then English, so William would hear it: "Shut up and follow. Maybe you will learn something too, and grow up someday." He quickly mounted and started off up the mountain trail. A cloud obscured the moon.

The trauma of the evening and the slow plodding of the horses finally took its toll on William. He nodded off to sleep and his head fell against the Wyandot's back, who gave him a violent shove away. The third time Mononcue let him alone. Soon he too was asleep as the horse obediently followed the lead pony.

An hour later (though it seemed a few seconds to him) William felt himself falling through the air, landing with a heavy thump on the ground. When the horse stopped, he had slipped off its back, taking Mononcue with him.

The Indian boy was startled awake and began yelling, "Wauh! Wauh!" as if he'd been attacked. He was scrambling to free himself from William's tied hands, reaching for his tomahawk and continuing to yell.

The other four warriors in the camp, some of whom had also been dozing off, were running around grabbing their guns trying to assess the situation and determine the direction of the attack. It took a few minutes for the storm to calm.

Bigtree and the two guards who were awake when he arrived were all rolling on the ground laughing hysterically. “This is too good,” he said, through guffaws and cries. “A mighty Wendat warrior, the hope of our future, is pulled down and paralyzed by a sleeping white boy with no weapons. While his hands are bound! It’s too good, it’s too good…!”

Mononcue finally freed himself from William and gave him a shove to the ground with a grunt. He was angry and saw nothing at all funny about anything.

Bigtree finally composed himself and took the Indian boy by the arm. “Better get away from him before you get so embarrassed you injure somebody. Don’t be ashamed. Every brave falls off…his…horse…someti…”—he lost his composure again, “O! Yah! Yah!” and the other men all joined in with boisterous laughter.

As Mononcue stomped away, Bigtree knelt down beside William when he was sure the other warriors were preoccupied elsewhere. The boy was still confused and flinched in fear when he saw the scalp on the Indian’s belt. Bigtree took the boy’s chin and turned his face toward his own, though William still looked down at the ground. “Indian boys have pride. His pride has been broken. It will mend like a broken arm—maybe good, maybe not. Better stay away while he’s mending.”

William listened but had no intention of being around the Indian boy anyway. “I heard you call him ‘Mononcue.’ And you are 'Bigtree.' How is it you speak English? What about the others? What tribe are you from? Where are we going?" He looked at the scalp again. "Why did you kill my uncle but not me? What are you going to do with me?" A stream of questions gushed out of him, formed in his thoughts during the past hours.

Bigtree put his hand lightly over the boy's mouth. "Too much questions. We are at war for our land. White settlers are enemies just like soldiers or other Indians we fight. I am sad the man I killed was your—hutenoro'—your uncle. But, I know what it is like to be taken by not your people. Happened to me."

William lifted his eyebrows and asked, "Americans?"

"No," said Bigtree, "Watayurunoh—the people of the caves—the Cherokee."

William was surprised. "Other Indians? Were you a boy taken from your home, like me? "

"Not your age, no. Some older. Want to hear about it? I'll tell you—I'd like to hear it again, too," he laughed. "Not now. First we walk some more, while it is still night. I'll answer your questions later when there's time. You will not be hurt—just adopted into a good Dasayane family. This is their hunting party. Mononcue and Bigtree are Wendat people, the Dasayane—the Delaware, our nephews. They tell us to come hunt with them. Mononcue's first hunt. So he, like you, learns to become a man. Do you understand?"

William nodded, still trying to sort out the events that had wrenched him from his family. He felt numb about his uncle's horrible death and, strangely, he was sorry for the Indian boy. He felt sad about how the men had ridiculed him. He knew how it felt to be mocked and made sport of and he hated that feeling. He also felt guilty that it was his fault the Indian boy had fallen from his horse. For a moment his hands went up over his eyes so he could think. "One more question?" He looked at Bigtree.

"That's already one," he replied, "what's the other?"

William looked at the ground. "How do you say, 'sorry' in the Wendat tongue?"

Bigtree grunted in surprised disbelief. "Hume'dat. But it's not something a brave Indian warrior would likely say," he chuckled.

"Nor most white men," said William. Then he muttered to himself several times, "hume'dat... hume'dat...hume'dat."

The braves seemed anxious to leave as soon as possible. William could hear them talking and sometimes gesturing towards him. Nearby, one was saying to another in the Delaware tongue, "We need to get started. It's already been quite a while since Bigtree arrived with the captive. Somebody might be coming."

"Maybe," said the other. "But, we shouldn't leave without the other hunting party. They should arrive before long. Bigtree was surprised that nobody seemed to hear them shoot at the settler."

"I know," said the first, "but it wouldn't take them long to figure out they were missing—it was late evening. They would have found the man within the hour. I'm uneasy about how long we've waited here."

~~~

In fact, circumstances had conspired to delay the discovery of William's capture. No one at the cabin had taken much notice of the rifle shots. William's older brother, Alex, about sixteen years, had gone inside and said to his mother, "Uncle Samuel must have got a deer! We'll eat high-on-the-hog for awhile."

Mary replied, "Maybe. More likely jist a rabbit—but that'll make some tender stew. I'm tared of them tough turkeys yore uncle keeps bringin' in. He's partial to 'em I reckon."

It had been a long time since there was any danger in the area. In fact, William, his mother, and Alex had gone to the Clinch River valley while his father was away fighting the War for Independence. They thought it would be safer to stay with their father's sister and her husband—Ann and Samuel Cowan—than at their home in Rockbridge County, nearer the war.

By the time they looked for and found Samuel's body laying in the field it was too dark to mount any kind of search party. Alex found his uncle's gruesome corpse and suddenly became the man of the house, breaking the news to the women.
~~~

His mother, Mary Walker, cried out uncontrollably, "No, God, no! Not William too. Oh, God. Maybe he's hiding in the woods—or maybe he's injured. Alex, go look for him again."

Alex tried to comfort his mother. "Ma, it's too dark and dangerous out there now. I tried callin' him but I wasn't sure if the savages were still around or not. You know they take young captives to adopt for future warriors. I'm sure he's alive and William knows how to survive in tough weather and all. We need to gather up some of our stuff and go the two miles over to Moore's Fort. We'll mount a search party as soon as y'all are safe at Moore's. I'll bury Uncle Samuel tomorrow."

~~~

William and the Indian raiding party were only about six miles away waiting in the forest. Suddenly another group of six Indians arrived and were quickly surrounded by the others. There was a commotion as they exchanged news of the day's events, one holding up another scalp.

Bigtree walked over and pulled William up by the hand. "You come and see this. I think you'll be surprised." He took the boy by the shoulders and led him over to the group of Indians.

As he was pushed into the center of the circle he saw the reason for the excitement—it was his own Aunt Ann Cowan. She was a small plumpish lady with fiery red hair and a pioneer woman's spunk, fending off the braves' mock attempts to touch her. In between swats, she looked up and saw William, who ran
~~~

and threw himself into her sobbing embrace. "Billy! Billy! I didn't know for sure you were alive. Oh, Lordy! Thank you Lord."

The boy looked up at her face, disheveled and streaked with tears. He squeezed her tightly. "How did they capture you Auntie? Weren't you at the cabin?"

She started to answer when one of the braves pushed them both towards the outskirts of the camp, pointing towards the woods. Bigtree walked past them and said, "We are ready to walk, now—long ways to the river. We will take you to our villages and it is a long, long walk. Drink some water,"—he offered them a container made of deerskin. "Eat this," he added, giving them each a piece of buffalo jerky. "You will need the nourishment."

Ann was surprised at his soft-spoken English and shocked at the size of his earlobes and the silver decorations. His nose ring looked ominous to her—but William encouraged her to eat and they both hastily and thankfully complied.

)()()()(

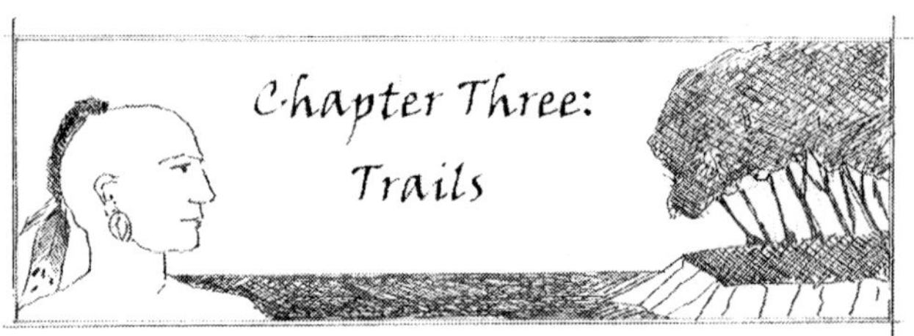

As soon as the two raiding parties finished comparing notes on their exploits, they swiftly made preparations to continue the night trek. There were only the two horses, which Bigtree and another older brave rode. William's hands were again tied together in front with a strap attached around Mononcue's waist, who shook his fist at the captive and said angrily in his own tongue, "Stay awake white dog. Pull me down again and I will gut you and leave you for the wolf!" The final word he spat out through snarled teeth, with particular venom—a'narishkwa'!

Of course, William couldn't understand the details but figured out the intent. Something inside him however, still compelled him to try and make amends. He was as tough as any frontier boy and had fought his share. But the Indian boy was the only one in present company who was near his own age. He deflected his glance from Mononcue's eyes and said as sincerely as he knew how, "Hume'dat (sorry), Mononcue.

Hume'dat." He caught the Indian boy off guard, who immediately turned his back and tried to hide his initial reaction. William, though, had caught a glimpse of the look on his face which changed briefly from anger to surprised puzzlement.

Then as quickly as he had turned away Mononcue spun around again, pulled the tomahawk from his belt and gave a war shriek. William jerked his head to one side, avoiding the swinging hatchet that sped by his ear with a "whoosh." He grabbed Mononcue's arm with his bound hands and the two boys fell to the ground in a wrestling match.

The warriors gathered around to watch and cheer, seeming to enjoy it if either wrestler got an advantage. Fortunately for William they soon rolled into briars which not only tore their skin and clothes but prevented Mononcue from being able to swing his weapon.

Bigtree stepped in to break up the brawl, angrily scolding them in two languages: "Stop this. You are delaying our already long walk." He pulled them to their feet then shoved them both back into the thicket letting the thorns scratch and pierce their skin for added emphasis. Neither was seriously injured but they got back up very carefully. It was fortunate that neither triumphed over the other—both boys kept their pride intact. Mononcue led his captive forward but did not yank on the leash as he had been doing before the fight.

The night walk was worse than the earlier one. The forest was thicker, darker, and every insect and animal was on the prowl. The warriors walked in single file, captives in the middle. The only relief came once every few hours when they were allowed to stop and rest. During those breaks he and his aunt were allowed to sit together and even talk in low voices.

"Are mom and Alex alright?" William asked her.

"Yes," she said, taking his hand. "He was taking your mother and me over to Moore's fort for safety, shortly after we discovered you missing and your uncle..." Tears came to her eyes and she wiped them with her torn sleeve. "Alex walked out to the plowed field and found your uncle with a tomahawk still wedged in his back. On the way back to the house he saw something shiny in the sun and found your grandpa's old gold watch he gave you on your birthday. Wonder why the Indians didn't get it?"

William smiled slyly. "Must've been where I head-butted the younger one."

Ann continued: "On the way to the fort we was met by your Uncle Sam Walker a'comin' to check on us. He said he jist had a feelin' we should join 'em over at the Moore's fort. Afore we could tell him the details of the attack th' other group of Injuns was all over us! They killt your Uncle Walker too but not 'fore he was able to put up enough of a fight to give Alex and your mom a chance to get away. I'm shore they made it to Moore's fort—it was less than a quarter of a mile. I couldn't know for shore but I didn't hear no shootin' or yellin' from over that-a-way. I was starting off with 'em but one of the Injuns knocked me from my horse and several surrounded me. Oh I am so thankful you are alive! Please don't fight with 'em any more."

William answered, "I think we should try to get away during one of these breaks. They are as tired as we are and want to rest. If you don't think you can make it I'll go alone and try to bring back help."

"Don't try it, Billy." she cautioned. "You'll only git yourself killt. They know this area better'n you do. 'Sides, we're a-travelin' on foot. A rescue party'll be on horseback and likely catch up to us sometime tomorry. I doubt they'll attempt it in the dark. Our best chance is to cooperate and pray for a safe rescue." William agreed only to think about it some more. She made him promise not to try anything without letting her know—and then, they were walking again.

Hunger and thirst were becoming a problem by late morning. The Indians had made several "by-hunts" looking for raccoon, beaver, squirrel or anything edible—without luck. Occasionally they would find a creek but mostly dry beds it was so late in summer. The heat was nearly unbearable in the mountains, especially for Ann, and the humidity sapped their energy in the forests. Finally, late the second evening, several hunters brought back one big raccoon which they quickly skinned and butchered. Bigtree brought a large chunk on his knife and offered it to Ann and William. "I'm sorry it is not cooked," he apologized. "We can't take time or chance of building fires. But it will give you energy. We still have a long walk ahead of us."

William had no trouble taking his share and biting into it, squirting blood over his face. It was tough and stringy meat but he was famished. "Eat some, Aunt," he said, blood running from his mouth. "You need the strength." She ate.

"It may be awhile before we get more game," said Bigtree.

William could see Mononcue standing nearby, talking with Bigtree. After a few minutes, he walked towards them but squatted down a few feet away chewing something. A few more minutes passed, then he stood and moved closer to William and Ann. He had a large leaf holding half-a-dozen orange-red persimmons which he held out to the captives, motioning toward his mouth and saying in English, "Eat."

"Oh, thank you," said Ann, "it will help me get rid of this taste of raw meat."

William looked at Mononcue who nodded once, turned his head and spit out a seed, hitting a tree. William bit into a soft persimmon and sucked down some of the sweet juicy pulp. He separated one of the flat slimy seeds with his tongue and shot it out of his mouth at the same tree. It rapped against the bark and he looked up to see Mononcue smile for the first time. The night walk soon continued as before but somehow it seemed a little easier.

It was still a forced march, and under very difficult conditions. Both captives were accustomed to the hardships of the frontier but ill prepared for this journey. Ann managed to tie her dress between her legs like pantaloons. William was still barefoot and suffering cuts and bruises. His aunt's moccasins were nearly worn out. At one stop, Bigtree brought over some kind of crushed leaves with a strong medicinal smell like wild eucalyptus. They both rubbed them on their feet and were extremely grateful for the relief it brought.

Ann asked, "How far are we gonna walk?" They had traveled all night and day and it was close to dark again.

Bigtree looked at the horizon. "Maybe six days maybe five. Depends on the weather, enemies, animals, rivers—who can say? But, I've come here to hunt many summers and always got back home for dinner and dancing. We've been away from our towns—our women and children and old ones—for nearly three weeks. When we get tired we think of that—dinner and dancing. We make it fine. Best thing is don't give up."

She felt faint at the thought of walking six more days. But they were hardy Scotch-Irish stock, not used to easy lives. If they had no choice but walking they would walk. When Bigtree moved on to speak with another brave she turned to her nephew. "I'm going to do my best, how 'bout you?"

"Nothin' else to do," he answered, "until rescue comes."

"Well, we will walk and God will be with us."

"How do you know that?" he asked, "He wasn't there with my uncles was He?"

Her optimistic expression was overcome with a look of exhausted sadness. "I know it seems that a-way—that God's nowhere around sometimes."

"Yeah," he said, "like God is just leanin' against a tree somewhere with His hands in His pockets, careless about everything and everybody else."

"Honey, I know there's lots o' bad in this old world. You jist have to remember what you larned in Sabbath school."

"What's that," he asked, "to set down and be quiet?"

She smiled. "No, that 'we know that all things work together for good, to them that love the Lord, and are called according to His purpose.' That's Romans chapter eight, verse twenty-eight."

He couldn't think of anything to say in reply but he did think about what she had just said. But when he tried to figure out how terrible things could all come out for the good, he could only hear his father saying, "Will, two wrongs don't make a right."

"Auntie," he added, "I'd give anything right now if I could talk with Pa."

She put her arm around his shoulders and shook her head. They rested a few more minutes before Mononcue came back and took hold of the strap on William's hands, tugging it to let him know it was time to move.

A few more hours and the trail began to get gradually steeper. Bigtree came alongside them on his horse and called it to their attention. "We are soon going to come to the big mountains. I know it's getting harder for you to walk," he said to Ann. "Will you ride the horse?" he asked.

"Oh," she said, "I couldn't...well, it would wear out the horse to carry us both."

Bigtree dismounted, saying, "I meant I will walk and lead the pony—you ride." He stood and waited until she got up and pulled herself on by its mane.

They'd been walking a couple of hours when their environment changed. "The fog is getting pretty thick," William remarked. He called to Bigtree, "How can you see where the trail is?"

Bigtree pointed ahead. "Right now, I can still see the top of the tree line in front of us. Where there is a break we know it's either the trail or a creek or ravine. Of course if it's not the trail we may take a tumble or get wet. But, we'll go slow so that won't happen. Better not talk much. We will be in Cherokee country when we cross the ridge."

"Then, that would be Kentucky I guess," said William.

"Anyway," Bigtree added, "they think it's their country. We've hunted there for many years. Southern Indians think they can claim anything they want."

As dawn began to break they reached a high point on the ridge. The fog dissipated enough that they could see the gap where they would cross, avoiding having to climb the higher mountains. William could see the warriors ahead pointing at the sky and talking excitedly. Within the hour dark clouds rolled in over the surrounding peaks. A booming thunderclap was followed quickly by a wide bolt of lightning hitting a tree down the hillside from where they stood.

Ann's pony reared up in fright but Bigtree managed to pull its head down and hold it steady.

Mononcue was now leading William ahead at a fast run, following the other warriors. Descending into the gap, William saw a wide-mouthed cave. They all—warriors, captives, horses and riders—were swallowed up like Jonah in the whale. Just in time. Torrential rains began to roar through the valley. The lightning continued with booming flashes that reflected against the walls of the cave, revealing painted murals childlike in simplicity of herds of buffalo and spear-carrying hunters.

Bigtree explained, "These are not our people. They were here before us all. But the buffalo came first. How can anybody say, 'These hills and forests belong only to me'?"

)()()()(

Hunting was sparse during the next two days, as it had been from the beginning of the "long walk." After the thunderstorm, the weather had been more typical for late August—hot, dry, and humid. Still, nothing like the day they had spent in the cave witnessing the fury of the skies. Side hunts had harvested another raccoon, a couple of rabbits and squirrels, and a snapping turtle which made a delicious stew with wild carrots and onions and gingerroot flavoring. There was no large game to be found but everyone got at least a bite of meat each day and plenty of persimmons and blackberries.

Until now they had avoided contact with any other humans—Cherokee or soldiers. Either would have meant a ferocious battle, captives likely dying first. There was no rescue party either—a fact that became more and more depressing to Ann as the days passed. The boy had not spent time thinking about what might happen to his aunt, not choosing to deal with it until it became a reality. For himself, he had always been curious and adventuresome. He imagined an Indian brave's life filled with excitement—fighting, hunting, listening to awe-inspiring stories. He had been well prepared on the frontier for that kind of life.

They had nearly reached the end of Kentucky territory when one of the lead warriors stopped and crouched. Like a line of dominoes, the others imitated his sudden signal. The word came whispered down the line, "Watayurunoh (Cherokee)." Warriors had been spotted just below the trail, resting by a small spring of water. Then another word was passed from mouth to ear, "kwutash (six)."

When Mononcue passed the word to William, he held up six fingers and said "waza'"—translating into Wendat—and William repeated the gesture, also saying, "waza'." He counted eight warriors in their own group.

Mononcue untied the strap around William's wrists and motioned to the captives to quietly and slowly crawl into the brush beside the trail. They both knew that escape was nearly impossible at this distance from settlements and capture would mean a horrible death. The lead brave signaled the others to move slowly forward so they could locate the Cherokees below them. (William wondered how an Indian could sneak up on an Indian—and smiled at the thought in spite of the fear taking hold of his body.)

Each warrior carefully drew an arrow from the quiver on his back and readied his bow. The enemy was holding steady below, mostly resting. Two of them got up to fill a cask with water at the springs. As tension mounted on the trail above, each (including Mononcue) held his arrow in the loose bowstring and awaited Bigtree's leading shot.

Unseen in all of this, a rabbit was growing nervous in its hiding place beneath a fallen tree near the trail. A split second before Bigtree's arrow left its bow the hare jumped out from under the log and dashed through rustling leaves.

The two warriors by the water instinctively fell on the ground, arrows zipping over their heads. Of the four resting at the base of trees, two were hit squarely in the chest and killed outright. Two arrows hit one of the others in his leg. The fourth, partially hidden by a tree, received only a superficial wound in one shoulder. That meant that three of the four Cherokee were instantly armed and ready for battle, charging up the hill towards the trail with wild war shrieks. Bigtree and his men, knives and tomahawks raised, ran to collide with their enemy.

William couldn't stay in the brush any longer. With the first sounds of alarm, he crawled closer to the trail in order to see what was happening. He shivered, his skin tingled and a chill ran up his spine. He couldn't seem to get enough air in his lungs and he felt weak as he watched the clashing of bodies below him.

He saw an Indian charging towards Bigtree. The Wyandot caught his opponent's upraised arm with knife in hand; they clinched and fell in a struggle on the ground. Six Delaware plus Mononcue engaged the other two Cherokee warriors. The odds were not even but the Cherokee fought like ferocious, cornered bobcats. William saw one Delaware go down with a wound spurting blood from his neck. Another cried out in pain when a knife was plunged into his side while he and a comrade wrestled with an enemy. Mononcue caught the combatant around the waist and tried to take him down but the Indian knocked him off with a blow of his fist to the boy's head.

As Mononcue lay temporarily addled, William's heart nearly leapt out of his chest. Between him and Mononcue the warrior with the shoulder wound was crawling through the grass towards the Indian boy, tomahawk in hand.

William started to put his hands over his eyes—but instead sprang up, gave out a loud shrill warrior's howl and ran impulsively down the hill towards the wounded Cherokee. William was lunging as fast as he could and without a second's pause on the way down grabbed a two-foot piece of a broken tree limb.

As the warrior began to stand to his feet, his back to William and oblivious of the boy's yell, William hurled the heavy oak limb crashing it squarely into the back of the man's head. The warrior fell like a tree across Mononcue's legs, tomahawk in hand. The boy had raised himself up just in time to see it all. William reached for the tomahawk and plunged it into Cherokee's skull just to make sure. Then he bent over and put his hands on his knees, panting for breath.

The sight and sound of the white boy distracted one of the other Cherokees who was immediately dispatched by his opponents. Bigtree had been victorious and the Delaware braves also overcame the third.

Mononcue placed his hand over William's heart and said words in his language that the captive boy could not interpret, but understood. They were even, now—each had saved the other's life and all within the week. It seemed like they'd been together for a lifetime.

Ann came flying down the hill as soon as the fighting ceased and threw her arms around her nephew. Again she sobbed in terror and joy that he was alive and safe. Her display of affection embarrassed him, but he was glad that she also was saved from the battle.

When they'd caught their breath, Bigtree spoke: "We have lost two Dasayane braves, our brothers and nephews. It has been a great victory—the Watayurunoh are the most powerful nation of all the Original People. Now we must bury the dead quickly and go before more of them come along the warrior's trail. We may not be able to defeat a larger hunting party than this, and we are now weakened by the loss of our braves." They dug shallow graves with knives and hatchets and buried the dead quickly but reverently, friend and enemy alike, side-by-side in the wilderness, covered with stones. The survivors bound up their wounds and moved out, avoiding the trail for the remainder of that day and night.

The next morning as they emerged from the woods William could not contain himself. "Oh, wow! Wooweeee!" he exclaimed at the sight. The warrior's trail had taken them to the edge of the great, beautiful Ohio River, stretching as far as he could see in either direction. The banks were steep but the riverbed was shallow in front of them.

Ann had a beaten, dejected look on her face. She knew once they were across the Ohio—which some called "that dark and bloody river"—there would be little hope of rescue. The Indian towns were not far away.

Bigtree led the way and his horse was only knee-deep at the middle of the river. "Mononcue, can you take these straps off my hands, now?" William asked. "Let me go so I don't drown. I promise not to to escape." The Indian boy obliged, warning William again in Wendat of the consequences of trying to escape—death by burning. The cool stream felt great to William as he waded and swam across. It was the first relief from the heat in over a week. "The only thing I hate about it," he said to his aunt, plodding along beside him, "is I still had dirt on me from plowing in our field. Now it's all gone down the Ohio."

"You have somethin' from home far more valuable and lastin'. You carry on the inside everythin' you've learned of the Walker's beliefs and ways. Don't forget those, William. Don't ever let 'em be washed away. They're what makes you, you."

Just as they neared the shore Mononcue threw two handfuls of mud over William's head, then laughed so hard he slipped and fell back in the muddy water himself.

The warriors were consulting in a little huddle and Bigtree emerged. He walked over to the Ann and the boys who were scuffling good-naturedly.

"You look serious," she said.

"I have some news that may be sad for you," he answered. "The Delaware are from two different villages. You are the trophy for the first group and William is claimed by the second. I'm sorry but you and your nephew will be split up soon."

Ann put her hand to her chest. "But, why?" she asked. "Cain't you do somethin'? You and Mononcue are responsible for William bein' here." Her voice had a sharper tone than she intended but anger had been building along the trail.

Bigtree responded in a softer tone, "I can do nothing."

"But," she continued, "will you then protect him? He knows you now and you have been kind to us both. Please forgive my outburst. I am really thankful for all your considerate help."

Bigtree explained, "Mononcue and I are of the Wyandot nation—or as the French say 'Huron'. The Delaware were once a part of the mighty Algonquins, the first people to come to this land. We all used to call them our 'grandfathers.' Now they are few and asked to live on part of our land. We now consider them our nephews and often hunt and fight together. However, this is their hunting party—we are invited guests. Any plunder belongs to them unless they voluntarily offer it to us. We must continue on north for another day or two. I'm afraid we will not see you again for a long time. I wish you good luck and I will pray for you to the Great Spirit." With that, he turned and motioned to Mononcue who followed him as they left the others on the bank.

William and Ann both looked at each other. A great emptiness seemed to take over inside each of them. For the first time they felt totally without friends or helpers. The other warriors had left them alone in deference to Bigtree but now—who knew what they would do to them? Ann tried to hold back the tears, sensing that William was watching her for courage.

It was happening too abruptly for him to comprehend it all. He would miss their talks and her encouragement but he felt he'd miss Mononcue even more in spite of their earlier conflicts. And yet—who knew? "Maybe somehow things are working out with a purpose," he thought. "And maybe we'll meet again as friends someday—who knows where."

Mononcue and Bigtree mounted up on the horses. "We're going to Sandusky near the Great Lakes," he said, pointing north. "You will be at Newcomerstown in about one day. There are some there who speak English. Eskoyeh. Goodbye. May the eye of Hamedisu' (Great Spirit) watch over you!"

Mononcue repeated after his mentor, "Eskoyeh. Goo-da-by-ye." He grinned at William, obviously proud of his accomplishment at attempting English. William waved as they turned the horses north.

ӾӾӾӾӾ

Chapter Five:
Challenge

The six Delaware warriors said farewell to their Wyandot "uncles" and were ready to take the last leg of the journey to their respective towns. The captives were led along the Ohio River bank for a ways.

"Do you think you can walk another day, Auntie?" asked William, worry-lines showing on his forehead.

"I am exhausted and hungry," she said, "but I don't think we have any alternative."

After about twenty minutes however, they saw ahead of them a large tributary flowing into the Ohio. Just as William was wondering how they would cross it, he saw a group of Indians on the opposite bank about 20 yards away. They began shouting loudly and waving to the warriors with Ann and William. They in turn shouted, waved and pointed to the captives. A strong brave came up behind William, clinched him in a bear hug and lifted him up so they could see him better. The four other Indians all cheered with great enthusiasm.

There was deep water at the mouth of the tributary and the Indians brought out three large birch-bark canoes from under the brush and paddled across. Three Delaware braves took Ann in one of the craft—the other three Indians and William knelt, sitting back on their haunches, in the second.

The tallest of the young men (the one who had lifted William up) was next to the boy. He nudged him and pointed at the four Indians who had guarded the canoes. "Nohseyodi," he said. One of the other braves added, "You say 'Seneca.'"

There was other discussion among them and apparently a disagreement about how to translate into English what was said. The tall warrior finally raised his hands in frustration and gave up. From their gestures the boy guessed they were telling him the Seneca were friends and allies. He remembered hearing something once about the "Five Nations" of tribes who formed a confederation in the northwest. While he was trying to piece all the information together in his mind, a warrior pushed the canoe off the bank and they were moving swiftly through the waters of the Muskingum River.

For the first time since his capture William was able to relax. The breeze felt good in his face and his trail-weary legs welcomed the inactivity. He breathed deeply, smelling the aroma of the pine trees on the bank, his hands resting over the smooth bark rim of the canoe. He closed his eyes and listened to the sound of paddles splashing in a lazy rhythm and the waters hitting the bow of the boat. Crows cawed noisily, chasing a blue jay from their nesting area.

He was about to doze off when the canoe began to buck and jerk as if it were a wagon on a path full of ruts. The river was narrowing and the water's force was pitching the canoes around like acorns. He clamped his fingers tightly on the boat's frame and he was trying to keep from being thrown into the river. He was thankful he no longer was lashed to an Indian in case he did have to swim. He wondered about escape but quickly put the thought out of his mind. The river was too dangerous. At that moment the canoe was thrown violently against a protruding rock and William bounced out into the raging white water.

He fought for air but got a mouth full of water. He had never experienced anything like it before; he was totally helpless in the river's embrace. He was pulled under, thrown against rocks, pushed powerfully down the current past the canoes. When he did bob to the surface he was able to gulp air but only for a split second. Down again it shoved him, throwing him around without turning him loose—like a dying rabbit in a dog's jaws. He tried to beat against the water but could barely move his arms. Finally, he felt brush scratch and entangle him in debris piling up against a huge fallen tree at the side. He was trapped underwater but found he could bend his head back just enough to break the surface for air.

The next thing he remembered was a warrior pulling him out of the logjam and carrying him over his shoulder. The motion of his rescuer's walk forced water out of William's lungs. He threw up the residue of river water and his chest filled again with oxygen. The concerned look on the warriors' faces turned to relief as he was laid on the bank where they waited. Ann was on her knees at his side, stroking his hair and weeping with thankfulness and praising God. William glimpsed one of the warriors also raising his head and hands toward the skies, speaking aloud as if to an invisible presence.

He wasn't much to look at. The current had ripped off his shirt and shredded his breeches. He had cuts and scratches over most of his head and body. At a flat rock beside the river some braves set about building a fire. Others went into the woods and soon returned with several squirrels that they skinned, gutted and skewered on sticks slanting over the flames. The squirrels were plump from acorns and the hunters removed the fat and melted it in a small clay bowl from the canoe. They allowed the tallow to cool and later rubbed it over William's scratches and scrapes. It had a strong wild smell about it.

Safely in the canoe again one of the Indians got William's attention and made a level sweep with his hand towards the river ahead. He took it to mean they had smooth sailing the rest of the way. At least he hoped that was a correct interpretation and went to sleep in the peacefully rocking cradle of the vessel.

He didn't even stir when the canoe was steered to one bank and anchored among the brush and was unaware of the sight of two deer walking along the river, headed towards the brushy area but stopping to lick salt deposits along the bank. For nearly a quarter of an hour the braves waited like statues in the canoe, bows and arrows ready for the deer to come to drink. They were rewarded for their silence by the sound of fleeing hooves of both buck and doe as they fled in panic from the surprise attack, only to drop within a few yards of their pursuers, the life-blood gone from their flailing bodies.

It was the best fortune the hunters had found on this trip, and so near their own homes. They paused to thank the Great Spirit and the river for their providence before field dressing the game and loading the meat on the canoes. They continued on the journey while William was still completely unaware of this brief adventure, and the west fork they had taken of the river known as Tuscarawas.

By early evening he awakened as the motion of the canoe ceased again. He could see they had arrived on the banks of a village. As he rubbed his eyes he realized he was alone with half the warriors—the other canoe with his aunt was no longer with them.

They banked in a small inlet and within a few minutes there were hundreds of Delaware coming out of the village to meet them. Small Indian boys arrived first, outrunning the others.

Dozens of little girls and other Indian young people followed them. Older women and warriors and gray-haired men—several hundred villagers in all—surrounded their canoe with shouts and loud congratulatory undulating sounds and wild gestured greetings. When the braves brought William out of the canoe the noise level increased excitedly. And as they brought the slain deer out of the canoe, the shouts were even louder for the fresh meat than for the captive boy.

As one of the Indians led him by the arm towards the village, small children darted in and out touching him and giggling at each other. He could see the houses—some large log structures covered with bark, scattered among smaller bark-covered rounded houses. He'd heard the men back home talk of the "long houses" built by some of the tribes. He was led through the village to a point on a hill about a quarter of a mile from the last house. When he turned around the sight amazed him. It looked as if the whole town—maybe four or five hundred people—had formed two parallel lines stretching from the center of the village to a few feet from where he stood.

A boy that looked about fifteen years old came up to him. "You are gonna run the gauntlet," he said. The boy looked "Indian" enough except for his blue eyes and brownish hair—his skin was a little lighter tanned than others were—and he smelled like he'd missed last month's bath. Raw tobacco juice ran down both corners of his mouth and he spoke in "perfect" backwoods English. "Do ya know what the gauntlet is?" he asked.

William stammered, "Eh, well I have heard the word. It's some kind of test isn't it?"

The other boy smiled, "Yeah you could say that. I had to run it about nine months ago after I was captured in Pennsylvania." He spat on a nearby rock.

"I—I'm William, what's your name?"

"Big Kittles—anyway that's who I am now. Up to last year I wuz Billy Spicer. Too many 'Bill's' around, I guess, so I got a Indian name now. See that big log house way down thar at the end of the two rows of us Indians?" William put his hand above his eyes to shade them. "Well," Big Kittles continued, "You gotta run like a long-legged lizard down through them rows never mind all them that's tryin' ta hit ya with a stick or club or everwhat they holden on to. If'n ya make it through the bearskin door of that thar Council House you's safe and ever'body'll celebrate how brave ya are. If'n ya quit they'll kill ya as unfit to be a warrior sure as you're born. Now git ready. Yur about to be shoved into runnin'."

With that, Big Kittles walked behind the new captive, put both hands in the middle of his back and pushed him forward as hard as he could, yelling, "Go, Will'am, go!"

William took three off-balance steps and fell flat on his face as the crowd began to yell and chant at the tops of their voices. He felt sharp stinging blows to his bare back and legs and could hear Big Kittles's voice shouting to him: "Git up, Will'am, git up now and run like that lizard. They'll kill ya. Git up!" William struggled to his feet amidst the blows from broken tree limbs and began to run—faster than he'd ever run before.

Through the blur of faces, William could see differences in some of them. The little children were laughing and swinging small sticks at his feet and legs, mostly missing as he sped by. Sometimes he caught sight of an older woman who looked with pity at him and didn't hit him hard or maybe missed him on purpose. The meanest hits were from boys his own age or older. He learned quickly to try and dodge their attacks because most of them had large tree limbs, some even clubs. Fortunately it was harder for them to swing the heavier instruments and if he dashed with a burst of speed they would miss. He had succeeded in avoiding several of these older boys but they tended to group together in the lines so it was inevitable he would catch some of their torture.

Twice more he was knocked to the ground by such whacks. The third time he was close to giving up. "I can't make it," he said to himself. "It's still too far."

He was only on the ground a few seconds but it seemed like an hour. His back, buttocks and legs were being pelted with blows—then, a strange thing happened. Someone took his hand—he was being raised to his feet and helped to run again. He thought he recognized the man—and puzzled, he ran.

He ran "like a long-legged lizard", eyes straight ahead on the large opening of the Council House. A warrior swung at his head with a club but William bobbed and stooped, feeling the breeze from the weapon as it swung past his ear and missed him. All along the line he was jumping the low swings and ducking the ones aimed at his head and shoulders. Once in awhile he caught one in the back but he was moving so fast the blows did not land solidly before he was gone.

One tall boy in line ahead of him had a determined look and a large club. As he ran near enough to see his face, William lunged and caught him in the neck with his forearm, knocking the Indian boy down. He could hear laughter behind him as he sprinted on towards the big door now just twenty yards away.

The final dash was easy. Most of the determined ones had scattered towards the front of the line. Now only a few old grandmothers were left and they barely tapped him with their sticks. He fell against the bearskin that covered the Council House doorway and stood panting and bleeding as a great roar of victory went up in his honor from the crowd. He had earned his place as a warrior. Someone placed a brave's deerskin around him and he was led to one of the smaller houses.

The walls were made of cornstalks tightly bound together and covered outside with bark. A woman gently washed his wounds and rubbed them with bear grease. Whether it helped the healing or not he couldn't guess but at least it kept flies and mosquitoes at bay.

Big Kittles burst in the house in a few minutes. "You did it! You're a big man now, just like me. How's it feel ta be a Indian warrior with honor?"

As sore as his body felt, William gave a kind of weak smile. "It's better than being burned at the stake, I guess."

"Will'am," the older boy said, "this is your new ma. She's Moonshower, and she's a nice lady. Her son was killt in a skirmish this year in Virginy, so they've decided you'll take his place. She'll treat ya right, and do most of the work, cookin' and all. She's even made ya some new clothes. But don't cross her—she's got a temper like a messed-with mama bear." He turned and spoke to Moonshower who reached under a blanket and pulled out a breechclout and belt and shyly handed them to William. "That's about all you'll need for now. She'll be makin' some winter clothes in the next month or two I reckon."

That night Moonshower gave him a bowl of yellow-squash stew and a handful of chestnuts she'd been saving. She spread a blanket for him over a platform built along one side of the wikwames (little house). It stood about two feet off the ground and was covered with long pieces of bark. He drank the stew quickly and curled up on his right side on the blanket trying to find a comfortable position where some part of him was not cut or bruised. Just before he dropped off to a restless sleep, he saw again the blurred face of the man who had helped him to his feet in the gauntlet. Half-conscious, he thought to himself: "I know you—why can't I think of your name?"

)()()()()(

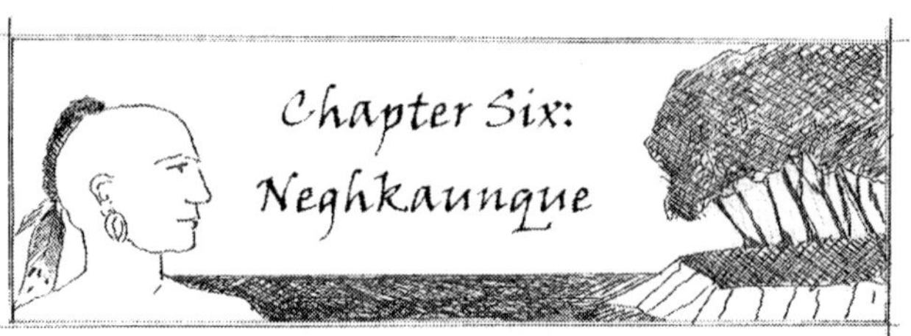
Chapter Six:
Neghkaunque

For a few moments he thought it was his mother Walker pushing on his shoulder and trying to wake him up. As he began to regain consciousness he felt like he was still in a nightmare. Every bone and joint in his body was aching. He dozed off again and dreamed he had come in the door of his log cabin in Virginia and found his mother tied up and gagged in the corner. He tried to run to help her and couldn't move his legs. Then he yelled out "Ma!" and woke himself up. He opened an eye and saw Moonshower bending over him with a bowl of cornmeal mush with maple syrup on it and some jerky. With a lot of effort he finally managed to roll over and slowly, very slowly, sit upright. He felt better after eating a few bites of the hot food. He could smell the smoke of many fires and similar meals being cooked outside the wikawans (houses) and long houses.

When he tried to stand up his legs trembled and wobbled beneath him. He stood still a few minutes and gradually tried walking. He could take a step—then another—like a tottering old man. He opened the deerskin covering the entrance to the wikwames (little house) and quickly let it fall again as he shut his eyes at the already bright sunlight outside. Big Kittles, who had slept in another corner, ran up to meet him and hollered in his ear, "Mornin' Will'am. How was yur night at th' boardin' house? Wuz the featherbed to yur likin'?" He mischievously slapped William on the back, who recoiled and grimaced in pain before trying to backhand him in the mouth.

Big Kittles ducked and backed away laughing. "Big brave man is a little unhinged today I sees. Hope yur mood don't last all day—yur my assign-mint. I gotta larn ya all I knows as quick as a flea kin leave a killt dog. You ready ta figger out how ta be a real live Lenape Indian?"

"Here," said Big Kittles, handing him the breechclout and belt, "Better go put these on and git outta them filthy britches o' yur'n." William noticed Big Kittles's own well-worn trousers. Then he glanced at Moonshower. She was sewing a new pair of moccasins, paying no attention as he changed into his new suit of woodland clothes.

When he and Big Kittles stepped outside it looked like a huge anthill to him. Little shorthaired brown dogs were running everywhere, yapping at everything (or nothing). Women were busy about innumerable chores and chatted with each other while they worked. He saw them carrying skins of water to their bark-covered homes, which were either corn-straw huts with dome roofs or long domiciles housing several families. Some women were grinding corn into meal with wooden pestles—or chewing deerskin to soften it, or sewing it into a garment. Some were frying bread in clay pans over the fire, or cooking fish.

Small children were running to and fro laughing as they chased one another around the camp. Older men sat and smoked with each other and watched the children play, while some of the younger braves were heading out to fish in the river. Some had poles over their shoulders and others were carrying three-pronged spears.

The girls his age seemed to be helping the women but they kept their eyes towards a bunch of young boys playing pasaheman (Lenape football) in an adjoining meadow. "They need the practice," said one of the girls, and they all laughed because they'd won the "boy vs. girl" match earlier. Several of them glanced at William but turned their eyes away as soon as he noticed. One of them was not so shy and walked to meet the two boys as they strolled through the village.

She spoke to him in the Delaware tongue, looking him square in the eye. William thought she was the prettiest of them all. He looked at Big Kittles for help. "She says she thinks you ran fast yesterday and she's mighty glad you're courageous." Just then a grandmother snapped her fingers and called out to her to get back with the other women. As she turned away she looked over her shoulder, tossing her black braids, and smiled.

William looked at Big Kittles and remarked, "I may like it here."

"Your day's startin' off better'n yesterday—that's fer sure. By the way, her name's Dancing-Fire—case ya need ta know."

"Where is your cabin?" William asked his friend.

"Oh, I don't live here permanent," Big Kittles replied. "I'm staying with you fer awhile. I belong to the Wyandot's—they's the ones what took me. I'm jist loaned out fer awhile to help the Lenape.

"Who's Lenape?" William asked. "That's what the Delaware call theyselves. It means "the people."

"But I thought they were called Dasayane."

"Well, that's what the Wyandot call 'em. But if the Delaware is with other Indians they say 'Lenni Lenape'—it means something like "original people."

William scratched his head, "I thought that's what the Cherokee call themselves."

"It is. So do the Wyandot—Wendat jist means 'the island people'—this whole creation is the island. I guess we's all jist people. But you would also be in the Little Turtle clan—that would be the same whether you were with the Lenape, Wendat, or several of the tribes."

"Which means…?"

"Well, best I can 'splain it, groups of families belong to different clans. You can tell by the totem in front of your area of the village—see that thar turtle carved on top of that pole near your wikwames (little house)? Then over thar's the wolf and thataway's the turkey clan. Sometimes they's called tribes and has they own chief. Their leaders all sits together in the Council when it meets in the Big House."

They had neared the meadow where their peers were playing stickball. One of them came out of the group and walked over towards them. He looked a couple years older than William did, and had broad shoulders and strong arms. While he was still a few yards away, Big Kittles informed William,"That thar's John Killbuck, jr. See that thar bruise on his neck? That's whar ya forearmed him in the giblets yesterday."

Killbuck raised his arm and gestured threateningly at William's head. William flinched but showed no expression on his face and neither did Killbuck. He was a proud young warrior who didn't take kindly to being shamed or bested, especially in front of others. He turned to Big Kittles with a scowl and spit out some words, shook a fist at William then turned and walked back to the group of Indian boys.

"What was that about," asked William with a blank stare. "Well seems like ya got ya a duel."

"Wha—what?"

"Yeah well a kind of a duel—a contest I guess you'd call it. Stickball. Like a game—only it's serious business. The Great Spirit decides who wins. We do it lots ta settle a dispute. The Wyandot play it a lot—we teached it ta the Lenape (Delaware). They're more peaceful usually, but when Wyandot teams play, sometimes thars a bloody fight at the end. We call it the 'little brother of war.' It'll be his team against yur'n."

William was still looking confused. "What, what? I don't have a team—I don't even know how to play it! I haven't been here one whole day and I'm bruised and stiff and sore."

Big Kittles looked down and dug some dirt with his bare toes. "Yeah well life's tough ain't it. Ya don't have ta a'cept the invite—but if'n ya don't you'll be considered as a rotten dead wolf the rest of your worthless life. So you better get teached fast er put on a petticoat and go he'p the little girlies."

William felt like his head was spinning. "How much time have I got and how can I raise a team even if I knew how to play it?"

"I'll help ya gather yur team and the rules is simple. Main thing is don't touch the ball with yur hands. As to time why don't ya jist ask him?"

"Who—you mean Killbuck? You gonna translate?"

"No need. He speaks better English than me, if ya kin imagine. He speaks French, too. Larned it from a mission school."

"You mean he has been to school—a mission school?"

"No but his father has. Used ta be one right on Lenape soil when the priests was there—'fore they come to Ohio. Killbuck junior larned English and French from his pappy. He jist don't like ta talk it to a white man if he ain't sure it's perfect."

Two Indian men approached while the boys were talking. They were dressed in decorative deerskin breeches and jackets with colored embroidered designs of animals and plants. William saw them coming and thought they looked like men of importance and gravity.

Big Kittles looked at the ground as he greeted them with respect and said to William, "This here's Wicocalind—Chief White Eyes—and this is Captain Gelelemend." The latter extended his hand to William. He spoke in a commanding voice and a decidedly British accent, "I am also known as Captain Killbuck. Chief Wicocalind and I are both friends of the Americans. Welcome to Newcomerstown!"

Wicocalind (White Eyes) also extended his hand and confirmed his companion's statement. "Not all our leaders agree," said Wicocalind, "but the two of us hope you Americans win the War against England. In fact it makes me very proud to tell you I am a lieutenant colonel in the American army."

William blinked in surprise. Perhaps his shock contributed to his bravery as he blurted out, "My father is also fighting in the Revolution. If you are our allies why am I being held captive here?" He crossed his arms over his chest, faced flushed with built up anger. "Why did your warriors kill my uncles and kidnap my aunt? Why cannot I go home?"

White Eyes (Wicocalind) and Gelelemend (Killbuck) both were speechless for moments. Big Kittles dug the ground with his toes again. Wicocalind regained his voice and answered William sympathetically. "You must understand that the entire Lenape nation is divided at this time. Only a few months ago I debated strongly with the Council and barely stopped them from declaring war against the Americans. Some are still killing and taking captives. Officially, we have been neutral because of the surrounding Indian nations that are fighting for the British.

"The Wyandot have allowed us to settle on the land but would crush us if we chose sides against them and the British. We have just signed a treaty, however, that places us on the American side and General McIntosh has agreed to build a fort on the Tuscarawas River to protect all the Lenape villages. A part of that treaty recommends to Congress that we be the principle tribe in a fourteenth state once independence is won.

"I'm leaving tomorrow to guide General McIntosh across the Ohio territory to attack the British at Detroit and I believe the red coats will be vanquished in a very short time. When I return I will do everything I can to help you return to your people if that is your desire. We would be happy for you to stay with us or visit us any time."

William couldn't believe his ears. Captain Gelelemend (Killbuck) said in his gruff British tone, "I see you have already gotten acquainted with my son. I saw him speaking with you and Big Kittles. He looked even angrier when he left you—hope he didn't make any threats."

Big Kittles looked up and joined the conversation. "He throwed down the glove and dared Will'am ta meet him on the stickball field. Poor Will'am didn't even know nothing' 'bout stickball 'til then." The Captain and Chief both enjoyed the thought with a hearty laugh.

"John junior is just a little proud and headstrong," said Gelelemend . "Don't worry about it—I'm sure Big Kittles will train you well before the contest takes place." He patted the boy on the shoulder as they started to walk on.

When they were a few yards away, William turned and cupped his hands over his mouth, "Thank you Chief White Eyes—and good luck on your mission tomorrow with the army!" The Chief acknowledged his good wishes but put his fingers to his mouth. William hunched his shoulders and lowered his head, realizing he inadvertently had given out information that not everyone needed to know.

A big smile had returned to his face and he felt hope beginning to fill him again. "The Chief said I could go home when he returns." he grinned at Big Kittles. "That's the best news I have had for the last two weeks!"

"Well," Big Kittles replied, "if you got Chief Wicocalind 'n Cap'n Gelelemend on yur side, yur halfway thar. But don't count yur chickens afore they's a bird in the bush."

"What in Sam Hill does that mean?"

"It jist means to not git all excited or you'll be mighty disappernted when it don't come ta pass. It's in the Bible."

"It is not," replied William scornfully, "at least I know what's not in the Book."

"Well that's fine as flour, laugh at me now. But jist take it ta heart, yur ole buddy tole ya. Always happens ta me—let a fat rabbit come my way and a snake'll jump out and eat it ever durned time."

)()()()()(

Oneida Nation Illustration
Indian Lacrosse (Faulkner)

It was an early October morning when Moonshower built the first fire of the season inside the bark wikwames (little house). William woke to the sweet aroma of burning cedar wood and watched the smoke curling up towards the opening at the center of the roof. He guessed it had been a little over two months since he'd arrived at Newcomerstown. He was adjusting well to Delaware life, feeling stronger and more confident each day. However, he watched daily for the return of Chief Wicocalind (White Eyes) and Captain Gelelemend (Killbuck), anxious to hear news about the War and hopeful of his release to return home. They had been away about three weeks. Every passing day brought him that much closer to leaving for home.

He continued to lay on the bark platform and studied Moonshower for a few minutes. She had treated him with such kindness though he'd hardly even spoken to her. He noticed she was singing softly and stroking a pair of worn moccasins—

he'd seen her carrying them around before. It dawned on him that they must have belonged to her deceased son. When she saw him get up she quickly put the shoes under her blanket on the platform. William walked over to her and she greeted him with the usual smile, offering him some scheechganim (ground corn) from a pan near the fire. William looked into her sad dark eyes and pointed to her blanket.

"Whose moccasins?" he asked. She pretended not to understand him. "Moccasins," he repeated, pointing at his feet, and then for good measure added the pronunciation he'd pick up from Big Kittles—"machtsin."

The sad look returned to Moonshower's eyes as she reached under the blanket and pulled out the soft worn shoes. "Ehoalan,"(beloved) she said and held them to her heart.

"Your son's?" William gestured toward the shoes and the fishing spear by the door, and she nodded. Impulsively he put his arms around her and felt her tear fall on the side of his face.

Later he asked Big Kittles to tell him more about her.

"Don't know a lot," he said. "Jist what they tell me. Her husband was a drunk and wife-beater. He made her live outside the long house so he could keep an eye on her. Then after their son was born he upped and left her for a Cayuga woman. That boy was all she had. When he didn't come back from battle she jist holed up in that wikwames I reckon. Been there 'bout a year when you come along and maybe brung a little life back to her."

He changed the subject abruptly: "Well, you've been ketchin' and throwin' at stickball fer 'bout a month—ya feel 'bout ready ta face up ta Killbuck's dare he throwd at ya?" He handed William the stout hickory bat with the thong-webbed pocket on one end. William hesitated. Big Kittles continued, "Ain't nothin' to it I tell ya. Jist run around tryin' to ketch that deerskin ball and throw it to a teammate or try and hit the goalpost with it. Meanwhile, watch out fer your opponents."

William rubbed his chin. "Why try to win it if the Great Spirit is gonna decide it anyway?"

Big Kittles looked at him with disgust. "Well He shore ain't gonna pick no winner what acts like a loser before the game starts," he argued. "Don't worry," he added, "I already got us a hell of a team. A lot of them braves don't like Killbuck's strutin' around like a turkey cock. They been waitin' fer a chance ta pluck a tail feather or two.

"I done put the word out that in two sunrises from now the dispute gonna be settled 'twix you and him."

William's mouth fell open but he knew the time for argument was long passed.

Two afternoons later there was a festive atmosphere all over the village. Special ceremonies would take place in the Council House or Big House as some called it. It was the largest structure in the village, solidly built of huge horizontal logs. William discovered it took him nearly twenty-five steps to walk the outside length. "I figure it's at least fifty feet long," he announced to Big Kittles. The roof stood nearly three times his height. "Are we allowed to look inside?"

"I dunno—but we'll be goin' in there purty soon."

He led William to a group of about a dozen Indian boys standing nearby. All of them were painted with distinctive red-and-black markings on their faces and bodies. Big Kittles greeted them and introduced them to William. "This is our team," he said proudly. William had played with most of them while he was learning stickball but the language barrier had prevented much interaction otherwise. "They think you've larned the game and are good enough to play with," said Big Kittles. "Eh! Eh!" they shouted, two of them raising William's arms in the air.

"First," continued Big Kittles, "we go to the ceremonial dance in the Big House. 'Member, now, this is a very serious time—like goin' ta church back home I reckon, not that I ever staked a claim on a pew or nothin'. But it's a spiritual time, hear? This here dispute 'twix you n' Killbuck calls for big prayers ta be say'd."

At the appointed hour people began filing in through the bearskin covering over the Big House doorway. They were dressed in their finest—women wearing dresses made of blackened buckskin or black cloth from the traders. There were red clan symbols stitched in several places on each dress, with red fringe on the bottom. The men wore their best deerskin tunics and leggings with a few decorative feathers in headbands. Moccasins were decorated with black porcupine quills and colored beads. William noticed Dancing-Fire enter with the Wolf clan and sit down. She was especially eye-catching with her long braids hanging down in front of her, over the winter red fox fur shawl that covered her breasts and shoulders. Her eyelids were painted light red, with a small red circle on each cheek. She wore a knee-length skirt made entirely of turkey feathers, carefully sewn in rows that overlaid each other. Her leggings were adorned with painted shells.

Big Kittles elbowed William to get his attention and pointed at the large center post with a carved face on the east, another on the west. Each face was painted half black, half red and gazed through slanted eyes with long furrowed brows, flat noses, and slightly open mouths. Big Kittles wasn't much help for William but an old man sat beside them. He explained in the Lenape tongue to Big Kittles who did his best to translate for William. Each of the three clans—turtle, wolf and turkey—was seated on deerskins laid out over the dirt floor at reserved areas around the sides of the interior, men and women in separate sub-groups. Two large stone areas in the center were piled with firewood directly under the smoke holes in the roof.

As men began to shake rattles made from turtle shells and two others beat drums with sticks the old man whispered to Big

Kittles, who then leaned his head close to William's, saying, "He says the center pole kind of joins the earth to the Great Spirit above. The two carved faces represent Broken Nose, spirits that watch what we do here and take the prayers to Ketanetuwit—that's what the Delaware call the Great Spirit. The rattles and drums say it is time to start the fires."

Just then two women entered carrying small wooden sticks on an oak base. "He says the women are the ashkahsuk—whatever that is. Sacred helpers, I guess." They handed the sticks to two of the men who attached leather thongs on them and began a sawing motion that twirled the sticks with increasing speed on the oak base until a small swirl of smoke began to rise. As the wood began to glow, the men placed the sticks under cedar branches in both fireplaces. The cedar snapped and sparked and exploded into flame.

With the fires burning, each clan brought out its prayer sticks and began chanting and singing. An old man stood near the ridgepole, his eyes following the smoke spiraling up through the roof as he prayed to the Great Spirit. The ashkahsuk swept the floor repeatedly with turkey-wing brooms. Each clan then stood and began a slow stomp-dance around the center pole, still chanting and praying solemnly to the beat of the drums.

At the end, the two teams of stickball players—Killbuck's and William's—were brought forward and stood on either side of the center pole between the fires. The ashkahsuk men brought a handful of black-painted pebbles and another of red ones and gave them to the women who favored one team or the other. Moonshower took her place near William's team. Another dance began as the women scattered the black stones and stepped on them rhythmically, tenderly holding the red ones to their breasts—or vice-versa depending upon which color represented "their" teams. When the dance ended each participant was served from large bowls of corn-meal mush which they ate with reverence.

Big Kittles nudged William. "It's time ta start the games. Only thing is, I'm thinking' you need a Indian name. I'm passin' the word around; from now on your name is Pemsit. How ya like that 'n?"

"Doesn't sound very tough—what's it mean?" asked William.

"It jist means, 'Man Who Walks.' See? Walk-er!"

The crowd of people filed silently out of the Big House but burst into a cacophony of voices once they were several yards away. The excitement of the game was in the air. Men, young and old, surrounded the two teams of players—at least a dozen on each side. They began to escort them towards the playing field. The women and children—all chattering enthusiastically with each other—followed them closely.

William saw a group of men exchanging beaded wampum belts and surmised they were making bets on the players or teams or both. As he looked over the Indian braves on each team, Big Kittles said, "These here are the strongest and swiftest runners in the whole village. You skeert yet?" William just shook his head. He felt some hesitancy about his role in this—many were several years older than he was. But he also knew he was as tall as most of them. The work he was used to doing in Virginia—plowing, sawing and chopping wood—had conditioned him well. Besides that, he could knock a squirrel off a limb with a rock at twenty paces. He was ready to play this game with fire and fervor.

He saw Dancing-Fire watching from the crowd and waved but Big Kittles poked him again. "Now 'member," he said, spitting on an anthill, "all ya gotta do is ketch that ball in the pocket on yur stick, run and throw it as hard as ya kin ta one of us what has more red paint than black—or try ta hit that thar pole what has a fish on the top. If'n ya hit the fish ya git extra points. Game lasts 'til sundown—or 'til ever-body's daid."

The ashkahsuk women who served during the Big House ceremony brought out the bat-sticks, which they had already consecrated by prayer. Each player was given a three-foot long hickory stick, curved at the end with a long net attached from the crook to midway down the handle. A shaman religious leader carried the deerskin-covered, fur-stuffed ball to the middle of the field, between the two posts at either end. The crowd grew quiet. As the players took their places around him, he gave a shout and threw the ball high into the sky—and quickly got out of the way.

The spectators immediately broke into shouts and yells as every Indian player raced to capture the ball on its descent to earth. William tripped over somebody and sprawled headlong into two other players. At least half the boys were knocked down in the initial scramble for the ball and as it came within reach, Killbuck with smooth motion swept it up into his net and speed away. William and the others were on their feet again, chasing him as his lean frame and agile legs carried him swiftly towards the team pole. Two of the "black-paint team" Indian boys ran at him from an angle and delayed him long enough for others to block him with their bodies. He was able to make a strong throw of the ball across the field to a teammate who headed back towards the pole.

As he passed the ball on to a fellow-player, William stretched his body in a flying leap and intercepted it with his net. He fell to the ground but was able to get off a quick shot at the opposite post, missing it by only a couple of inches. A "black-paint" team member quickly scooped up the ball and threw it with speed back to Killbuck. This time he leapt into the air with his right arm raised behind his head and threw the ball with tremendous force into the middle of the post. Groans and victory shouts rose up from the audience and players alike.

The ball was thrown into the air again and William managed to stay on his feet as he competed to catch it but was outrun by another boy. The ball was thrown from one to another, changing teams several times within the course of a minute. The action was fast and adrenalin flowed as the game progressed. Big Kittles got control of the ball and got a shot off to William who again had the goalpost in his sights. As he ran and drew back to throw the ball he caught a glimpse of Killbuck running alongside him. Suddenly his legs went out from under him and he rolled on the ground in excruciating pain. Killbuck had struck him across both shins with the length of his hickory stick, transformed into a vicious club.

William was aware of the other players watching him, not to mention the whole village on the sidelines. He determined not to let Killbuck get the satisfaction of seeing him wince with pain. He sat up, gritted his teeth and rubbed his shins a time or two, then a teammate took his hand and pulled him to his feet. The pain was so sharp he thought he couldn't stand—but he did, by sheer will-power.

The shaman came and briefly scolded Killbuck, then threw the ball into the sky. The game was on again.

William continued to play but he was clearly not able to run as fast or jump as high as before the foul. Nobody ever made a more noble effort. As the sun neared the horizon, fatigue was telling on most of the players and the game slowed somewhat.

William made one last determined catch and threw the ball as straight as he knew how—and smacked the top fish on the post. Killbuck's team had won the game but most of his teammates joined with Big Kittles and the others as they surrounded William with shouts of "Hoh!" and "Eh! Eh!" Some were yelling, "Pemsit! Walk-er! Pemsit!"—as "the man who walks" limped off the field.

Moonshower greeted him at the door of their wikwames with beaming pride, and as he lay down to sleep he felt for the first time that he really belonged. He slept like a stone—but dreamed of his mother and father back home.

He awoke late the next morning to the sounds of Moonshower yelling angrily at Big Kittles and throwing an iron pot as he dashed out the door, carrying a half-cleaned fish.

)()()()(

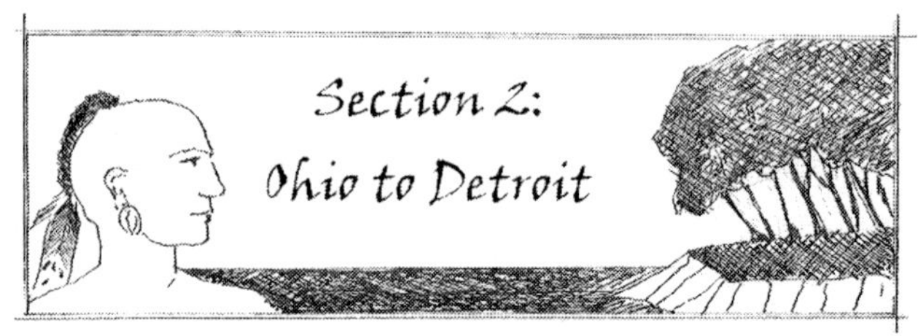
Section 2:
Ohio to Detroit

(1778-1780)

John Walker rode up into the clearing of his log cabin late this evening, finishing three months of living in the woods and mountains looking for the Revolution. It had been nearly four years since he was in a good battle and he was hungry for one. He was also glad to be home again. A man ought to check on his own family once in awhile, he thought.

As soon as he saw the horse and rider, Alex came running from the shed splashing a trail of milk from a bucket he carried. "Paw! Paw!" he yelled—and the ranger turned and spread his arms wide to receive the strapping 16-year old. "Now you've spilled most of the milk," his father pretended to scold, frowning. In his bawling voice he added, "Your ma will have your hide hanging in the loft when she sees that!" Alex squinted his eyes and shook his head. "Ma's gonna be too excited to worry," he replied, and yelled out, "Ma! Paw's home!" as she flew out the doorway and jumped off the creaking porch into his arms. They kissed and held each other tight, Alex grabbing them both around the waist and half-dancing through the yard. Three brown hounds added their yelps and howls to the mix, jumping and nipping at the happy humans.

John Walker had been a Virginia ranger since he was nineteen and had been fighting somebody ever since. As a ranger he had volunteered to roam the frontier on his own time and resources, protecting settlers where there was no organized militia or army. He had battled with Indians allied with the French, Indians allied with the British, and Indians warring against the Americans. His Scotch-Irish blood well suited him for the dangers of the frontier. His strict Presbyterian training gave him a certain "devil may care" attitude about life and death—whatever will be will be. At least that had been true during his first forty-three years. Lately, he'd found himself wondering whether he ought to settle down more. Nothing brought him more real happiness than this cabin and these three—Mary, Alex, and William. "Where's William," he asked as his eyes searched the clearing.

Mary looked up into his eyes with tears in her own. Alex broke the silence. John thought he looked like he'd grown a good six inches since he'd last seen him. "Father, William is not here. He has gone…"

John Walker interrupted him. "He's gone to help the Cowan's with their fall planting?"

"No, father," Alex continued sadly, "the Indians have got him. I wanted to go after him but they hit us again on the way to get help and killed Uncle Samuel and your brother. They took Aunt Ann, too."

"Damn those savages!" his father yelled. He walked over and slammed his fist against the top rail and kicked at the hounds, sending them scattering under the porch. "Damn 'em all to hell!" Then he sat down on the steps. He removed his bearskin cap, sighed heavily and brushed his hair back over his head. Mary put her arms around his neck and continued to sob.

Alex tried to apologize, "I…I'm real sorry…I should've gone after him. I just thought I could round up some men fast and then they hit us again. I should have gone after him right then."

John looked up at his son, grasped the boy's forearm and pulled him over closer. "You did exactly the right thing, Alex. If the Indians had meant to kill him they would have done it right here. He's still alive—I'm sure of it—and you're still alive. If you'd tried to do anything on your own you might have gotten yourself and your brother killed. I know Indians. William's alive and we will find him. Do you have any idea what tribe they may have been?"

Alex rubbed his head. "We didn't see the ones that got William. And it was getting dark when the other group attacked. There was a tomahawk stuck in Uncle Samuel's spine—would that tell us anything?"

Mary looked stunned and asked, "Didn't I tell you to get rid of that horrible thing—to burn it?"

Alex avoided her eyes and continued to speak to his father. "I did get rid of it, Paw, but I buried it. I know where it is."

"That's good, son. There's a slim chance it may lead us to William. Is it close by? Take me there and let's take a look at that hatchet."

As they walked towards the forest Alex asked, "How do you know Indians so well?"

"You don't remember all those stories I told you when you were little? I was just a few years older than you are now when I became a ranger in Augusta County. A year later I was doing some hunting with a fellow ranger and we stopped to cook some venison for the journey home. A band of Cherokee braves jumped us. He was killed—I was only knocked out. When I came to I was tied to a tree while the Cherokee were sitting around the fire eating our venison. They kept looking at me and poking burning sticks in my direction—I really thought they were going to set me on fire before the night was over."

"Oh, yeah," Alex said, "I remember that part. How'd you ever get loose from 'em?"

"They kept me alive and took me to their village in Georgia. I was with them several months but they had signed a treaty with the British to release any prisoners taken in battle so they let me go. They actually sent an escort of braves to make sure I got home in one piece. I learned a whole lot about the Indians from those three months—but I'll tell you I was plenty scared for a while. I'd just as soon not go to that school again."

Alex had never considered his father as being afraid of anything. He had resented his father's strictness—especially when he'd been away for long stretches of time. It always seemed to him that his father was trying to make up in a hurry for all the discipline he missed administering between his frequent treks to the wilderness. Still, he loved his dad with all his heart, admired his tremendous strength and courage, and missed him terribly when he was gone. There was no doubt in his mind that with his dad in charge they would bring William safely back home.

The boy stopped at one of the oldest trees in the forest—an oak that was at least six feet in diameter. He took his bone-handled hand-made knife from its scabbard and began to dig near the north side of the tree. About two feet below he brought out the weapon and handed it to his father.

John took the tomahawk and brushed the dirt away from its wooden handle. It was decoratively carved and painted. He turned it over a couple of times and studied the patterns. "See that double curve design with the rounded lines going towards, then away from each other?" He used a stick to draw the design in the dirt—)(. "That's typical of the Iroquois-language tribes. The ones that frequent this area are Wyandot and Seneca probably and they often hunt together. Tribes that stem from the Algonquin race—Delaware, Miami or Shawnee for instance—generally use curved lines like this." He scratched in the dirt—( ). Which direction did they go?" Alex answered, "I trailed them that way for a long ways."

"North," said his father. "I'll bet they're Wyandot or Seneca from across the Ohio—that 'dark river' which settlers seldom cross. If so, it would make rescue more difficult."

"Why?" asked Alex.

"Because those tribes favor the British. We don't have treaties with them now. If he were with the Delaware for example, we might get the Continental Indian Agents to intervene for us. The Delaware are neutral so far as the War is concerned but their villages are on Wyandot controlled territory. We might be able to get them to bargain with their "uncles" for William's release—if that's where he is, I mean—with the Wyandot. Course, we don't have much to go on—the Shawnee could have taken him. Better bury that tomahawk again or your mother will be upset. We'll know where it is if we ever need to see it again."

Alex was glad to get rid of it. The two of them walked silently back to the cabin while John mulled over the best strategy to take. In the back of his mind he felt the matter was nearly hopeless. Without a definite location in the middle of a War and attempting to enter Indian territory in Ohio that was unsettled by whites was an extremely tall order. There was no doubt he would take action very soon—he was not the type to sit around and worry—but not until he was resolved it was the best choice that would most likely return William alive and safe.

"What are we going to do?" asked Alex.

"Well, I will probably ride north tomorrow morning and see if I can find the Indian agent at Fort Pitt who deals with the Delaware. I think you'd better take your mom and head back east to Rockbridge County—much safer there right now. She's still got people that will take both of you in."

Alex was not happy but said nothing. His father looked at the boy's squared jaw and tanned face and saw his own father's features. He had a sudden realization that he'd almost lost out on seeing the boy grow into a man. Sadness came over him at the passage of time and the lack of any remedy. "Alex," he said, lifting the boy's chin to look him in the eye, "I know you want to go with me. I would give anything if it could be so but I don't know what would become of your ma. Somebody's got to stay and watch out for her."

Alex pulled his face away from his father's hand. Angrily he replied, "She's not my wife. Why do I always get stuck with the chores and guarding the house?" John had never allowed any backtalk from the boys and without thinking, he smacked Alex across the face with the back of his hand. He instantly regretted it, but tried to justify his actions. "Don't talk that way to me—ever again!"

Without another word, Alex stomped away back towards the house. His father had only been home an hour and there'd already been a confrontation. Alex was fuming as he detoured out to the cow shed to be alone. "I'll see that mom gets safe to Rockbridge County," he told the red-bone hound trailing him, "the Cowan's have been talking about going. Then I'll enlist in the Continental Army. If dad wants to search for William by himself I'll go fight for somebody else's freedom."

After a supper of cornbread and red beans John threw a few more logs in the fireplace. Alex went to bed on his usual straw-filled tick in the half-loft over the main floor. Mary pinched out the coal-oil lamp beside their bed and she and John snuggled under the heavy patchwork quilt. With his arms around her, she felt safe for the first time in months. He didn't tell her he was leaving again until early the next morning.

)()()()(

William, of course, was unaware of the concerns and attempts being made by his family to rescue him. He'd been with the Delaware for a little over three months. He missed his family from time to time but generally was pretty much preoccupied with understanding the culture and geography of his present situation. Besides, it was not all bad. As an adopted member of the tribe, he was given all the rights and privileges of any other person—perhaps more. He had quickly been accepted and was especially loved—maybe even "spoiled" because he'd been a captive. He was not closely watched anymore, but free to roam about at will.

He was still somewhat of a child at thirteen years and like most Indian children was seldom scolded or punished harshly. But as a young man he would soon be expected to help hunt and fish—living in the forests many months out of the year—which he loved. His mother and other women of the village did all the manual work of cleaning the wigwams, dressing game, making and washing clothes, fetching water, caring for the livestock, even building bark huts and houses.

He was surprised on this particular day when young Killbuck approached him without his usual scowl. "William!" he hollered across the village path. "A bunch of us are going hunting for the next few weeks. Want to come along?" William was suspicious and hesitated to respond. He could picture himself with Killbuck's skinning knife in his chest lying in some secluded woods, wolves gathering to partake of the carcass. Killbuck could almost read his mind. "Don't worry," he said, as he walked close enough to put his hand on William's shoulder, "I'm not going to kill you. By the way, you played a good stickball game the other week. Especially for a beginner and a pup. We'll call it even—bruise for bruise—agreed?"

He stuck out his hand and William took it warily. "I don't think your neck was sore for as long as my shins were—but I'm willing to forget it if you are."

"Good," said Killbuck. "Now, what about it? It's time you did some hunting to repay all you've been eating. Go get your stuff—you'll need winter clothing. I'll bring you a good knife and a tomahawk. See if Moonshower has a pair of snowshoes you can use. We may need them before we return. It's November—winigischuch we call it—snow month."

William nodded, turned around and ran back to the hut. As he burst through the hide-covered door Moonshower saw his excitement and surmised what was happening. She stooped and pulled from under her blanket a full deerskin coat she'd been sewing for a week. "Schakhokquiwan," (a coat) she said as she displayed it with pride. Then she motioned outside and added, "Winigischuch."

"Yes, I know—the month of snow."

He accepted the beautiful and heavy coat with much appreciation and made an attempt to thank her, saying, "Anischik," hoping it was the correct word. She nodded and smiled as she helped him put it on. Then she pulled out two leggings with leather laces to the knees that attached to his belt. Under her sleeping platform she had a pair of winter moccasins and a fur hat for him also.

William felt like a little child at Christmastime, and he even jumped up and down whooping like a...well, like an Indian brave. He felt greedy asking for more but he had seen the snowshoes hanging on a side pole near the doorway and pointed at them. She seemed happy for the reminder and quickly handed them to him.

"Anischik, anischik! (Thank you!)," he repeated, gave her a bear hug and ran outside to join the hunters.

Dancing-Fire approached him before he could reach the hunting party. He was embarrassed that the other boys would see them together and felt tongue-tied as she walked up. Her black eyes took him captive again and she blinked her eyelids and smiled with the whitest teeth he'd ever seen.

She held out both hands holding a small, carved wooden box and said, "miltowagan" (gift—without obligation). He opened it and saw a beautifully hammered silver amulet on a string necklace. He felt stupid repeating one of the few words he knew, "Anischik"—thinking there might be a better way to say "thank you" to a girl that is not the same as to your mother. Then she turned and walked gracefully away.

Big Kittles was with the eight other boys—all between the ages of thirteen and sixteen—with Killbuck the oldest. "Hey, Will'am," hollered Big Kittles, "Whadja git?" William self-consciously opened the box and showed him. "That thar's a good luck piece. We gonna be gone a perty long while. Trade ya some jerky fer it." Before William could answer, the boy pulled a chunk out of his pocket, brushed off some dirt and straw, and handed it to him. "I reckon I kin spare some. We gonna live off'n everwhat we kin kill so hope that silver charm works and you're handy with that thar knife," he said, pointing to the scalping-knife Killbuck was handing him along with a well-worn tomahawk.

Killbuck said, "This is a good temahikan (tomahawk)—probably killed lotta white men. Let's go walking, Pemsit."

William took the hatchet firmly in his hand without hesitation, ignoring Killbuck's pointed remark. He was more interested in getting on with the hunt. He put the amulet around his neck and the tomahawk in the one side of his belt and with the snowshoes slung over the back of his new deerskin coat, he felt like the best-dressed hunter in the village.

"Where are we going?" William asked Big Kittles.

"Down to the salt lick," he said, "there's most always some kind of game thar." The small band of hunters split up into three canoes on the Muskingum River from the edge of the village and drifted for a few hours. Killbuck was in the same canoe with William and Big Kittles, a fact that made William uncomfortable. The captain's son finally motioned to the braves in the following canoes to paddle onto the riverbank where they would set up camp. That consisted mainly of clearing brush, digging a pit and lining it with stones and gathering wood. They wouldn't make fire until later—they wanted what was left of the evening hours for hunting. "A hot fire would feel mighty good 'bout now," said Big Kittles, "but it'll be whole lots warmer if'n it has some kinda meat roasting over it."

"You can leave your snowshoes here at the campsite," Killbuck instructed in English and Lenape. They had no fear of enemies in this area—the Wyandot and their allies controlled it. Enemies, white or Indian, had seldom crossed the Ohio River to pester anyone. Pitting their courage against the elements and forest animals was their only challenge and for the time being the weather was mild for November.

Killbuck handed William a bow and quiver of arrows. "You can use these. I have my rifle."

"I don't think they'll do much good in my hands," said William, "haven't had any time to practice using arrows."

"Can you shoot a rifle?"

"Oh yeah—if I don't have to load on the run."

"Well if you wound a grizzly," Killbuck said, handing him his flint-lock, powder horn and bullet pouch, "I'll toss you the knife so you can finish it off."

The gesture surprised William. He thought he would just be watching the others and learning Indian hunting methods.

As he took the rifle, talking came to a stop. Quietly and carefully they stepped into the woods, their moccasins treading gently on fallen leaves. Not a twig snapped as they spread out in a semi-circle. When Killbuck motioned, they all crouched behind the cover of trees and waited. One of the boys began sounding a high-pitched noise—"ree-eeek, ree-eeek." In about fifteen minutes they heard the crunching of brush and leaves. Then the familiar throated gobbling of a tom turkey. The boy gave one more screech and sat quietly waiting. The turkey never slowed his gate as he burst into the open just a few yards in front of them.

"Shoot, William." Killbuck whispered.

He barely had time to raise the barrel and click the hammer before the bird began to flare up and turn. The woods echoed with the rifle's explosion and feathers circled the spot where "tom" was flopping around on the leaves.

The braves erupted in exclamations of joy—Hoh! Eh! Eh!—as they danced around the dying fowl, slapping William and each other in anticipation of a good meal that evening. Killbuck put his foot on the bird's head, apologized to it and thanked it for the offering of its life. Then he pulled it by the legs, breaking its neck. He tied the legs together and draped the game over William's shoulder. It continued to flop around for some minutes as they walked further through the woods.

Overhead they heard the honking of Canadian geese flying low and circling nearby as the hunters leaned against trees for cover. William realized he'd forgotten to reload the rifle. The braves remained quiet until the geese landed on the river and floated past where they were standing.

Killbuck leaned over to William. "Watch and I'll show you an old Indian trick with these kaak (geese)," he whispered. As soon as the geese were out of sight around a bend in the river, Killbuck stripped off his clothes and walked out into the cold November water. Without a shiver he moved until the river was up to his neck. He moved with hardly a motion with the current, only his head bobbing above the surface, until he came to the bend. Then he submerged and swam underwater towards the flock of geese heading to a sandbar.

Though he was momentarily out of sight, the boys soon heard a great commotion and saw the flock rise and fly with speed in the opposite direction. At the same time, they could hear a lot of loud squawking and the beating of wings on water.

"I-ee," cried Killbuck, "help me!" When they ran around the curve in the riverbank they could see him standing chest-deep in the river holding two very lively geese by their legs, one in each hand. Killbuck had swum underwater and grabbed the geese by their legs. Then he didn't know what to do with them.

He yelled again in both languages, "I-ee—help me. I can't kill them because my hands are full—but they're killing me!"

Several braves stripped and swam across the sandbar where they struggled to cut the necks of the huge geese without slicing Killbuck's wrists and arms at the same time. Eventually the screeching stopped and their wings stopped beating the braves and the water.

After swimming back across he stood shivering on the bank, his chest and arms covered with cuts and scratches. He said to William in a quavering voice, "I never tried to grab two at once before."

William tried to be sympathetic but couldn't help commenting: "A few more old Indian tricks like that, you won't have to worry about ever being an old Indian."

Killbuck dried off as best he could with leaves. He dressed in his heavy deerskin clothes but was still shivering for a long time until they got the fire going back at the camping grounds. Other braves were cleaning the turkey and geese, placing the meat on skewers over the fire, while carefully saving the shiniest black goose feathers and largest colored tail feathers of the turkey. Those would become proud decorations for the hunters' village attire, hopefully impressing some of the girls. The smell of roasted flesh was a refreshing one. Sometimes it was a long time between hunts and with many mouths to feed in the village they never seemed to get their fill.

"We'll eat tonight," one said, "and wait for a fat deer or buffalo to take home." Killbuck was the hero for sure to this hungry band of hunters.

Later as William tore a large turkey leg away from its thigh, Big Kittles squatted beside him. "How long's it been since ya et this much real flesh?"

"More than a month," William replied. "We didn't have a lot of game at home during this summer. Killed a pig at the end of last winter and that's about the last time I remember being satisfied with enough meat."

"Well, if'n we're lucky we'll bag a bunch more 'fore we hast ta carry it back. Canoes will make it some easier."

Before dawn the next day three of the boys went out scouting to find game and returned just as the sun was sending a splinter of red-orange glow over the hills, reflecting in the Muskingum waters. They were as excited as they'd ever been and shared the news with enthusiasm. "Sisi'lija! Sisi'lija!" they shouted and one of them came over to William, put his curved forefingers over his ears and butted him with his head, grunting.

Big Kittles said, "Guess you kin figger that fer a buffalo cain't ya?"

Killbuck came over and talked with the excited scouts, then said to William, "I didn't think there were any buffalo around here. They've thinned out a lot in recent years. We usually have to go to Kentucky to see very many."

"What are they saying exactly," asked William.

"That there's two or three big sisi'lija grazing just down on this side of the river. Not far from the salt lick. We're going to need that rifle—did you reload, yet?"

William handed the gun to Killbuck. "I think this calls for an experienced hunter," he said.

Killbuck refused to take it. "You're the only one here who has shot anything in the last two days. You are the one with experience."

They walked behind the three scouts in single file through the woods, stepping as gently as possible and being careful not to snap any small tree limbs as they went by. After a couple of miles the lead boys stopped and motioned the others down. William could barely see through the trees and brush to a clearing a hundred yards down the riverbank. Several large brown figures moved slowly back and forth, their heads bobbing up and down as they fed.

Killbuck pulled what looked like a small bedroll off the back of one of the boys and unrolled it. With as little motion as possible he put the wolf-skin over his back, the beast's hollow face over the top of his head. "Buffalo will run if they see us coming near but they are not afraid of a few wolves. We have several of these furs with us—would you like to join us, William?"

"Well, yeah," he replied, trying not to act too childishly eager. Several other boys unrolled furs they'd been carrying and placed one over those selected, including William. He imitated Killbuck as he got down on hands and knees and began moving slowly forward, knife in hand.

Killbuck looked back at him and said, "Be sure you don't drag the barrel of that gun and get it full of dirt. Or accidentally cock the hammer. I don't want a hole through this fine fur I'm wearing, especially in its butt."

They made their way slowly, slowly towards the huge animals. Part way they came to a dry creek bed feeding into the river at an angle and they were able to follow it for a ways. They moved a little faster with the added concealment of the creek bed until they were ready to crawl carefully up the side. They peered over the edge enough to see a large shaggy bull just within gunshot range. There were two other rifles in the group besides William's gun. Two boys also had bows and arrows. They watched Killbuck for a signal to fire but suddenly the bull raised his head and loped lazily a few more yards away. Killbuck shook his head under the wolf skin. They would have to get that much closer.

The boys slowly moved back down in the ravine of the creek, crept forward a ways, then emerged on the crest to take a look. Now the smaller cow buffalo had walked between them and the bull. They wanted the larger animal for its size but also so the cow could continue to reproduce. There was little choice. Killbuck motioned the riflemen to prepare to fire. They stood up in unison, aimed and slowly pulled the triggers as three shots rang out almost simultaneously.

The buffalo cow's forefeet gave way under her, throwing her headfirst into the ground. The bull and the younger buffalo began to lope away, then to run faster down the riverbank when the bull suddenly slumped to the ground, rolled, stood up and fell again. Killbuck's arrow had sped past the cow's nose by a handbreadth to lodge in the bull's neck, which was now spurting blood profusely. The Indian boys raced down the river with knives drawn ready to finish their kill. The cow was no problem but those who reached the bull had a fight on their hands as its stubby black horns flew at them from every direction, it seemed.

Eventually the blood drained from its veins and the poor creature wobbled along on its feet a few more moments, then fell with a tremendous thud to the earth. William looked at his scalping knife in his hands, both covered with blood as he'd plunged it over and over into the buffalo. He'd gotten his share of being pitched to the ground a few times by its ferocious head-tossing. Somehow he felt pity for it now, this magnificent beast, felled by a few puny humans. He understood something of the reason for the Indian's custom of stopping for a ceremony of respect before claiming their prize.

Half the braves circled around the dead cow and the others around the bull. They paused in silence as Killbuck led in a prayer, which Big Kittles tried to interpret for William as he offered it: "Oh Ketanetuwit (Great Spirit, Creator) we want to thank You and our brother sisi'lija for this provision of nourishment. It is not for us hunters only but for the hundreds back at the village, some elders who are old and feeble and many women and little ones. They depend on us to sustain their lives through Your power and gifts of bounty. May we be worthy of what You have granted us today."

The trip was cut short by the overabundance they had acquired and, as the buffalo were field-dressed, the braves took every care to save the parts. Even the tongue and organs would become meat, the hide for warm coverings and stretched to make drums, the tendons for thread, the inedible parts for bait in fishing or trapping. They would carve the horns and use them to carry powder. Hoofs would become decorations or be made into musical rhythm instruments. Virtually nothing would be left but the bones. All this, and more, would have to be prepared and transported to the canoes and paddled on to the village. It wasn't far, but it would require all their remaining strength.

When they finally banked their canoes along the village shore hordes of children ran to greet them and became the excited shouting messengers of good fortune to the whole town. Hundreds came to greet the victorious hunters and help them carry the welcome spoils up to the bark lodge. But there was something missing in their cheers and William sensed there was an underlying melancholy not being expressed. He understood when Big Kittles relayed the message, "Wicocalind—Chief White Eyes—is dead."

)()()()(

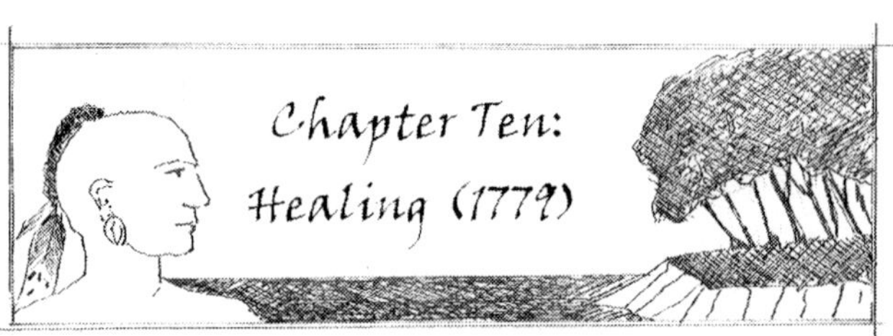
Chapter Ten:
Healing (1779)

The winter months had seemed gloomier than usual to William. With the hope broken that he would soon be home in Virginia he found little that interested him. Even Dancing-Fire had quit waiting for him to join in the village feasts and celebrations. Big Kittles had about given up on talking him into participating with the other boys in any kind of game or hunt. Moonshower tried making a variety of meals, even borrowing things from other women if she thought it was something he might like. Nothing brought him any happiness.

On this day someone outside the hut called to him. He recognized John Killbuck, jr.'s voice as he stuck his head through a corner of the bearskin door. “William, I need to talk to you. Will you go with me to the forest?”

He was reluctant to go, thinking this was another attempt to cheer him up. The truth was he didn't want to be happy—and the kinder anyone was to him the angrier he became.

“Please,” said Killbuck, “This is not about you. I need to talk with a white man and it's either you or Big Kittles. I'd rather talk to you." William got up off the platform and walked out of the door, a little annoyed at the interruption.

When they got to the woods Killbuck began to pour out his heart. "I think I'm going to be in big trouble. Since Wicocalind (White Eyes) died, father is losing influence in the tribe. There are rumors being spread about him—ugly things that are not true. They say he is taking money from the Americans while the Lenape starve; that he is a drunk or that he sleeps with white women when he goes with the Americans."

William listened without saying anything. Killbuck continued, "Now father is planning a trip to the Continental Congress. He is sure the Americans will give us the supplies they have promised for four years —clothing, food and trade goods. Taimenend—your Col. Morgan the Indian agent—has even arranged for a visit with Gen. Washington. Do you know that Wicocalind even named his son after the General?"

William expressed the thought that these things should help Gelelemend's (Killbuck's) reputation in the tribe. "Maybe," said young Killbuck, "but the worst part is this: they plan to leave me, my half brother Thomas, and even eight-year old George White Eyes in Philadelphia."

"Why would they do that?" asked William.

"Because they think that leaving the sons of three chiefs to attend school at Princeton will convince the colonials we are committed to the American cause."

"Whose idea was that?" William asked.

"Well, apparently some of the leaders in Philadelphia suggested they pay for our education as a way of making up for Wicocalind's death. I don't think he died of smallpox like they said. I think some Indian-hating whites killed him. Nobody has told me this except the spirits. I am not afraid to fight any warrior, white or Indian. I am afraid of being stabbed in my bed while I sleep."

"Let's sit down and talk," said William motioning towards the bent trunk of a tree that formed a kind of low bench. "I don't think you would need to worry about being murdered at Princeton. You would be welcomed as an honored guest. There are many good whites who want friendship with the Delaware and other nations."

Killbuck replied, "It is not the good people that worry me. Do you know about Cornstalk, chief of the Shawnees in Ohio? How he went to Ft. Randolph on a mission of peace two years ago? How he and two other chiefs and even his son Elinipsico were brutally shot and mangled while they were 'safe' in their beds? Chief Cornstalk and Chief Wicocalind had just returned from another peace mission to Ft. Pitt when this happened. I have heard that the murderers were from Virginia, a place called Stone Bridge, I think."

William put his hands over his eyes to think. Finally he spoke, "Rockbridge is where my people the Walkers are from. I have also heard the stories. It is true that some people of any race do evil things to others—even their own relatives sometimes. My aunt, who was captured and taken to another of your villages, told me that all things work together for good if we love the Great Spirit. I don't know if I believe that but if it is true then something good will come out of all this killing someday. Maybe people will just get tired of killing and decide to love their own lives if no one else's. Maybe if you go to Princeton you will learn more how to convince white settlers to live in peace with your people, even to work together. I don't know. Maybe we could all just play a game of stickball and let our shins heal."

Killbuck smiled and put his hand on William's shoulder. "I hope you're right. Thank you for walking with me, Pemsit. If you do pray, ask the Great Spirit to give me courage for this. And by the way, I really meant to break those shins of yours," he joked. Then he looked serious again. "I am very worried."

While they talked, the Council was assembling in the Big House to discuss the growing resentment at the lack of trade from the Americans. With White Eyes' death, power was divided between Captain Killbuck (Gelelemend) and Captain Hopacan (Pipe)

Killbuck had just explained eloquently his plan to meet with the Congress and Gen. Washington, speaking assertively in his naturally gruff voice. "Chief Wicocalind trusted the Americans and he was not wrong. I will return with a signed document giving us protection from the British and their Indian allies. I will bring horses loaded down with trade goods and supplies. But that is not all—we do not want to be children that need to always nurse at the nipple of Americans or any other people. We will trust our sons to their care—that they may acquire the knowledge of the white man's wealth and power and bring that wisdom back to us. We cannot live as our ancestors lived, but we can be a great and mighty nation again! Enemy nations have accused us of wearing petticoats and trading the tomahawk for a grubbing hoe. That is because we prefer to live in peace with all. But now let us throw off the petticoats and stand up as men! Who will go with us to Philadelphia?"

Twelve chiefs stood who had traveled from other villages to join the Council proceedings. Captain Pipe and his majority walked out—but not before he uttered his angry prophecy: "You will fail, Gelelemend, and all who follow you. You will lead Lenape to murder their brothers and mothers and nephews before this is over. The Americans will send you home naked and we will put your petticoat on you again. Then we will fight beside the British and crush you all."

The next dawn William walked with Big Kittles to see young Killbuck and the others who were boarding canoes for the trip down river. Young Killbuck showed none of his hesitation of the day before. "Jump in!" he called. "Maybe Gen. Washington will shake your hands, too. When you next see me I will be dressed with cravat and long black coat and you will think I am from Pennsylvania. Big Kittles, you may have my old loincloths—they are much cleaner than yours."

Big Kittles just puckered his lips and spit a long brown stream of tobacco juice into the water.

When the canoes were downstream, Big Kittles turned to William. "I been sorta concerned 'bout ya fer a week er two. You got a black cloud over yer haid?"

William didn't look him in the eye. "Maybe."

"Well, I got jist the thing fer ya. This is yer first winter here so I reckon you ain't had the opportunity of the sweat lodge cure have ya?"

"Not interested."

"'Course ya ain't interested—if'n ya were ya wouldn't need it. Nobody in their right mind is interested in sweatin' jist ta be sweatin' lessin' he's a hound's tongue in August. It's when ya ain't interested that it brings the interest back ta life." He took William by the arm and continued, "That settles it. First thang tomorry mornin' I'm a gonna take you down to talk at the medicine woman." William shook his head but Big Kittles talked louder, "No, ya caint say no cause I'm yer guide sent here by the Spirit and the Wyandot. Ya do what I says er I kin report ya to the big guys."

At dawn the next day William buried his face in the blanket and tried to go back to sleep but the shaking continued. Big

Kittles was determined to help his friend, even if he was a little rough in doing it. “Get out of here!” William said angrily—but Big Kittles persisted until he got him up from the sleeping platform. William agreed to go with him in hope he'd get rid of him eventually by humoring him.

When they reached the medicine woman's wigawan Big Kittles called out “Ohum” (Grandmother), and an elderly wrinkled, stooped woman emerged from the opening. Big Kittles said something to her that William couldn't understand, (though he had learned quite a few Lenape words from ordinary daily listening to conversations.)

The old woman nodded and took William's face in her hands, looking deeply into his eyes. In spite of missing most of her teeth—the remaining ones were badly stained—she had a compassionate look and gentle touch, he thought. She stroked his forehead, felt his earlobes, put her hand over his chest and paused as if in prayer or deep thought.

Big Kittles translated her words: “She feels you have lost yur spirit. It kin not talk to yer mind and heart. She thinks it leaked out of yur wounds and injuries and cain't find its way back in. Jist as I tole ya, she says you should spend some time at the pihomoakan—the sweat lodge. She'll make the preparations right away.”

William still had no interest in this but couldn't work up enough energy to fight it. So he just gave up.

About mid-morning several women were heating large stones in the outdoor sacred fire pit. They carried the stones on forked sticks into a small rounded, igloo-shaped mud hut built beside the river.

The interior floor was strewn with soft cedar boughs and the red-hot rocks were placed in the center, in a circular shallow pit. A single post stood between the fire and the pihomoakan (sweat lodge), beyond which no one was allowed to go except the women helpers and the participant. On top of the post was the skull of a buffalo.

Big Kittles emerged from Moonshower's bark wikwames leading William, who was wearing only a large buffalo robe flung about his shoulders. When they approached the sweat lodge, other women and some of the girls took bark buckets filled from the river into the pihomoakan (sweat lodge), where the medicine woman used a sacred gourd dipper and doused the stones. The boys could hear the sizzling as water hit the rocks and turned immediately into steam, filling the "cave" with a heated cloud of heavy mist.

One of the helpers began a slow thump-thump-thump on a drum to signal the beginning of the cleansing ceremony. An old man took burned cedar branches and smudged William's body under the robe.

The medicine woman closed the entrance temporarily and lifted her hands and eyes while seated on the cedar boughs.

"Ketanetuwit!" she prayed, "Great Spirit, our Grandfather beyond the sky! We search for you and seek your healing and guidance. Touch our wounds with your sacred invisible fire, both inside and outside. May the boy who enters here be more a man when you have spoken to his heart."

As she left the lodge, William got down on his hands and knees and started crawling through the small entrance of the steam lodge as instructed, "to get closer to Mother Earth." Once inside he removed the buffalo robe and let it drop from his shoulders and sat on it.

At first he felt suffocated by the thick hot humidity. Sweat began pouring off his body and he thought to himself, "If this is the purpose it's sure working." He covered his face with his hands and tried to think—but only thought, "I can hardly breathe." He felt uncomfortable on the floor and shifted his body around, trying to find a better sitting position. It was perfectly quiet inside—he was alone and the others had left him with the solitude of his own thoughts.

These kinds of practical thoughts distracted him for a while, until at some point he felt himself begin to relax. The sweat seemed to be washing over his body, taking with it the tenseness of his muscles and poisons from inside. "My head is clearing up," he thought. Then thoughts began to come like pictures flashing through his mind: the cabin in Virginia where he was born; playing with children of other settlers; his mother teaching him to chop wood; his father riding away to war.

But other images, darker ones, also flared up and disappeared: a younger brother being buried during a rainstorm; his own lengthy childhood illness and terror that he might be buried alive; a brush-arbor backwoods sermon about the fires of hell, the elect and the damned; the dread he often had that his father would never return. He ducked in terror as he thought a demon-like creature was trying to tomahawk him and take his heart. He felt he was in the middle of a nightmare and couldn't wake up. After a long while the images stopped and he again was able to relax a little.

Big Kittles had said, "When you're ready you have ta pray. That's the mainest thang is ta git in touch with the Great Spirit. You believe in God don't ya?" William remembered his words and tried to pray. He still felt that God, if He existed, was somewhere far away.

He prayed as best he could. "God or Great Spirit if you care about me why do I feel so alone and full of fears? Why did you let my family be split up?" He felt angry as he prayed. "Why hasn't my father come and rescued me—he always says how much he knows about Indians. It's been most of six months and nobody has come. If I were Alex, Paw would have come for me. Why am I left alone?" As he prayed, the anger turned to great heaving sobs.

He felt dizzy and laid back, wrapping himself with the buffalo hide. It was easier to breathe now but he felt faint. Now faces appeared in his mind, one after another: Bigtree, Mononcue, Big Kittles, Moonshower, White Eyes and Killbuck.

Suddenly he saw a hand reaching out to him and an unknown man's familiar blurred face—the same man who helped him to his feet when he fell, running the gauntlet. The man took his hand and raised him to a seated position. His lips did not move but William heard a firm voice coming from somewhere within himself: "You are not abandoned. You are greatly loved."

He had no way of knowing how long he'd been inside when he finally crawled out into the bright sunshine of the winter afternoon. Big Kittles led him past the post with the skull and gave him a push into the icy waters of the Tuscarawas River. It was like coming alive again.

)()()()()(

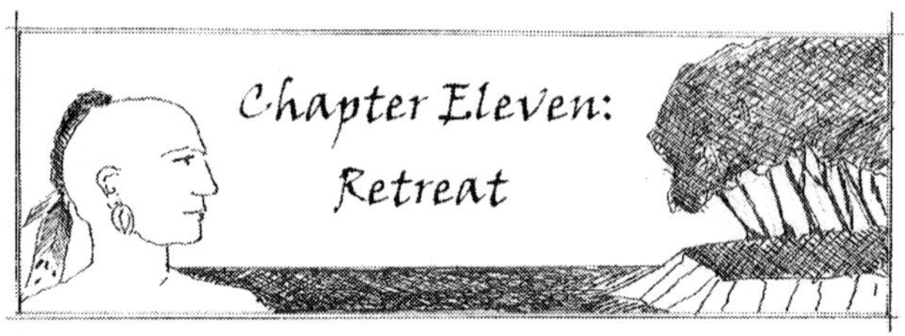
Chapter Eleven:
Retreat

John Walker had made several trips north and back home to Rockbridge County in the past five or six months. Unknown to him he had just missed the Killbuck delegation at Ft. Pitt which arrived three weeks after he left.

Walker had talked with everybody he could find that knew anything about the Indians across the Ohio. They all advised him to wait until summer when supplies would be more available and reinforcements sent to Ft. Laurens near the Delaware towns on the Tuscarawas.

Col. Morgan told him, "The Indian nations are divided, some supporting us and some the British. The Delaware in particular are split within their own ranks and pressured by both sides. They are facing dwindling supplies and little opportunity for bartering for what they need.

"If you think your son is with the Wyandot, I would suggest you wait until hostilities end between us and the British. It is only a matter of time before the Wyandot confederation is defeated and they will be forced to come to terms. At that time they will be much more open to an exchange of hostages. Meanwhile, they treat adopted children with great kindness and affection.

"A delegation of Delaware will be coming to Philadelphia soon but I can't say exactly when. If you like, I will be happy to see if they can find out anything for us. The trouble is, the part of the nation that favors the Wyandot cause will not be those who are coming here. If the Continental Congress does not do anything to relieve the need, all the Delaware will turn against us. I'm sorry but no one really knows what is going to happen in Ohio."

Walker was not one to be easily distracted from his goals especially when they affected one of his sons. But with no more definite information than he had, he was compelled to take Morgan's advice and head back to Rockbridge for the time being, mulling over the possibility of other methods of rescue.

Meanwhile Alex was also busy looking for his own way out. He'd had several conversations with cousins and other relatives in the Rockbridge area, determined to look for William. As the eldest son he was used to making decisions on the many occasions his father was away. He was a hard-worker and never left a job half-done. His father's voice echoed in Alex's subconscious, "If something's worth doing it's worth doing well. Don't put off 'til tomorrow what you can do today." He felt responsible for losing William because he didn't come to his rescue sooner.

One day his cousin James dropped by. "Hey Alex, let's go hike over to Jump Mountain. Bring your gun—we might see a rattler, er better yet a Indian." At seventeen, James was only a year older than Alex was but tended to think that put him in charge. Alex started to make an excuse but James insisted. "Hurry up! Time's a wastin'."

They had climbed to the top and taken in the wide and verdant view of the long valley and forests just bursting into spring. Halfway down, they stopped to catch their breath.

"You remember the story of Jump Mountain?" James asked and Alex shook his head. "They say that two Indian tribes fought a pitched and bloody battle in the valley, the Cherokee and Shawnee, I think. Too bad they didn't kill each other off.

"An Indian princess climbed the mountain to watch the fight and saw a knife plunged into her lover's heart. At that, she just ran to the edge of the cliff and jumped plumb off. What d'ya think of that?"

"That's a hell of a story," Alex said, "would you do that for your lover? Would you jump?"

"Shoot, I don't even have a lover and if I did I wouldn't." He pulled a small medicine bottle out of his pocket and took a swig. "Take a drink," he said to the other boy. Alex shook his head but James pushed it up to his mouth. "I said take a drink!" He obliged just to get his cousin to back off.

James continued, "Hey you wanna find William? I know a way you can get into Ohio to the Indian towns—shoot, I'll even go with you."

"Alright what's the pitch?"

James gulped some more whisky. "They's a Col. Bowman been goin' around lookin' for hunters and farmers to join an expedition across the Ohio River. He's wantin' upwards of 300 men to join forces with George Rogers Clark in Kentucky and hit the Wyandot-British center at Dee-troit. He figures that will break the Indian alliances in Ohio, drive the British up into Canada and punish the Indians for attacking our settlers along the frontier.

"Along with dividin' up horses, weapons and furs, the plan is to take Indian women and children captive to trade for American prisoners. That might be a way you could find out about William and maybe get him back in the bargain. You need to do this Alex; you're a crack shot. Besides we could have some real adventure on this kind of journey."

Alex thought a minute. "You know, we thought the Wyandot may have taken him—I found a tomahawk that dad thinks came from them. Where can we find Col. Bowman?"

James jumped up and let out a whoop. He grabbed Alex's arm and they ran down the mountain, got their horses and sped off for Lexington. They left a letter at the Walker's cabin: "James and me have gone to get William. Don't worry—got a good plan. Alex." He made sure he left before his folks got home.

In town they were told that Bowman had left hours before for Kentucky, disappointed with the number of recruits he'd found. "If we ride fast we can catch up to them before dark," said James. "What are we waitin' for—let's light out of here now!" They whirled their ponies whose hooves soon were throwing up dust and clods of dirt for as far from Lexington as anybody could see their "smoke".

When they arrived at the campsite late that evening Col. Bowman's men welcomed them enthusiastically. Every added man that could shoot a rifle brought them that much closer to success. They signed up even before the venison finished roasting over the open fire.

Next morning a rider came from Clark's camp with a message, and Col. Bowman gathered the volunteers to make an announcement. "Men there's been a change of plans." Audible groans came from the crowd of men sitting down or leaning on their rifles.

"Now don't get your bowels in an uproar," the colonel bellowed. "We'll still be fighting Indians but George Clark has decided against a march on Detroit at this time—not enough of us. Instead, we're going to head straight north for a short three-day march to Chillicothe (Chalahgawtha) the capital town of the Shawnee. They're the ones who've hit the Kentucky settlements so often lately. They think they can hit us and run back and hide across the Ohio. Well by God we aim to show 'em different!" The volunteers erupted with wild shouting, a few swinging each other in a do-si-do. Except one.

"I thought we were going to Detroit," said Alex later in the tent.

James shrugged his shoulders. "Fightin' an Indian is fightin' an Indian. There's not nearly as many warriors in Chillicothe. And they been doin' more damage to our people than anybody. Time they was cleaned up, I say."

One of the other men in the tent spoke up: "They gonna be a hornet's nest, though. When we killed Cornstalk we done in the only peace-loving chief the Shawnee had. And now the battle's gonna be at their own doorstep. They'll be mad as frog legs on a hot skillet!"

Col. Bowman lined up the men shortly after daybreak. "Here is the plan, boys. We're taking the horses as far as the mouth of the Hocking River—should be there in a few hours. Then it's overland on the west side of the river north about twenty-five mile. Should make that by nightfall then we continue almost straight west another thirty miles. We'll surprise them because any visitors usually come from the south via the Scioto River. We'll arrive tomorrow night on the outskirts of the town but we'll wait 'til daybreak to attack. Let's wipe them out and take some women and children hostage to exchange for our captives later.

George Rogers Clark will have to share some glory with us. Grab some grub and mount up!"

Alex and James made a dash with the others for the boards laid out across stumps by their camp. They both snatched some day-old fried biscuits, stuffing several in their mouths and pockets. A tin cup full of coffee (made with parched corn), a couple handfuls of grits and they were on their horses headed towards Ohio.

By afternoon they left the horses at a blockhouse for safekeeping and began a march along the river. Before dark they took a left turn and headed west. They marched most of that night and the next day, resting only a few hours. Shortly before night the column halted and Col. Bowman invited the men to crawl to the crest of a hill and peer carefully at the scene spread out below.

Wigwams interspersed with a few log structures sprawled out between them and the Little Miami River—Alex figured at least two-hundred dwellings plus the long Council house. The wigwams were pitched in neat rows from north to southwest and the sight caused adrenalin to begin flowing fast in their veins. Alex's hands were trembling not from fear but from the electrifying anticipation of being in his first battle.

Some women were carrying pots and baskets and children were playing with their dogs or stick toys. What the volunteers didn't know was that these plus a few young boys and old people were the only ones in the village. Upwards of a thousand braves were away at a council gathering.

Col. Bowman gave the silent signal for them to retreat a little ways back down the hill. He wanted to attack with full daylight and it was now dusk. The expedition bivouacked in the edge of some trees for the night.

Some whisky was passed around and about midnight the colonel began talking loudly, barking orders. "Move that pile of gear," he said, "spread it out so the enemy can't see it. Get off that log," he yelled, kicking at a man with his boot. "I said get some rest! You can't fight like men if you don't rest." He seemed to have no perception that anyone could hear him beyond the little clump of trees.

At dawn they again crawled up to the top of the hill to spy on the village. James whispered, "Looks like a piece of cake, don't it? What bothers me is where the Indians is. There's smoke curling out of some wigwams but not many. Only a few of the outdoor cooking fires are smoldering."

"No dogs," added Alex. "What does that mean?"

Just then the colonel gave the command to "Charge! Give no quarter! Remember what they've done to your family and friends in Virginia!" One-hundred fifty hunter/farmers went screaming down the hill into Chalahgawtha.

Rifle fire began to pour out of the Council House where the remnants of the village quietly holed up when they heard the commander's voice during the night. Some of the volunteers began pumping bullets into the log Council House but others stayed out of range and looted anything they could carry from the wigwams and cabins. Soon they were trying to carry away everything from weapons and furs to pottery.

On command, some men took smoking logs from the fires and pitched them into the sides of the wigwams. In a very short time the whole village was ablaze except a dozen or so dwellings near the Big House.

Shooting from the Council House had wounded eight or ten of the expedition. Col. Bowman lost control of his army and sounded retreat. The Shawnee horses penned up at the corral were confiscated, enough for each of the volunteers, and the men made as hasty a withdrawal as possible cumbered with their load of spoils.

Alex and James did not manage to get in the lead this time but were not quite to the rear. Within fifteen minutes they could hear hoof beats behind them as a dozen or two Indian youths managed to catch stray horses and overtake the frontiersmen. Shots again sailed over their heads and some hit their mark. Men began to fall from their horses near the boys, until Col. Bowman turned the column around and drove off the enemy.

This happened again and again—a few Shawnee boys stalking more than a hundred invaders. When Col. Bowman continued to allow the killing, several of his commanders took matters into their own hands and ordered the men to dispose of their loot and attack the Indians in force.

As they chased the Shawnee, Alex felt as though a hot knife had been jammed into his right leg. His horse was running at full gallop when he leaned over the side to look. An Indian boy leapt from a large bush, caught him around the waist and pulled him to the ground. The wind was knocked out of him and he lay looking up into the scowling face of a very young warrior. Alex sprawled completely helpless, blood coming from a bullet wound in his leg.

The Indian raised a spear—hesitated—and lowered it. His angry look vanished and he said something. Alex's hand was lying on a smooth round object that had fallen from his pocket. On impulse he grabbed William's gold watch, held it up, and tossed it to the Indian boy. The Shawnee caught the shiny object in midair and examined it in the sunlight, then turned and disappeared into the trees.

With the enemy gone Colonel Bowman barked, "You men split up and find your ways home. The expedition force is dismissed." James wrapped Alex's leg, helped him hobble to his horse and headed south. Alex tried to recall what the Indian had said. All he could think was it sounded like "bone."

)()()()()(

Chapter Twelve:
Connections

"It's been great fall weather," said William to his friend Big Kittles, "I don't remember one any better. Look at the fish I just caught," he said, proudly holding up a string of catfish. "They're really biting today!" Big Kittles looked disdainfully at the six large cats and replied, "It ain't how they're bitin' that counts but how ya present the bait."

As they walked up from the riverbank they noticed a group of about ten warriors riding up through the village. They were met by Chief Hopacan (Pipe) who had them dismount and led them into his large two-story log house.

"Them's Shawnee warriors," said Big Kittles. "Wonder what they's a doin' here? Must be important if they's havin' a sit-down with the big chief hisself."

William took exception to the remark. "He's not the big chief—Killbuck is." Big Kittles shook his head, "Well, I dunno. Long as Killbuck's away at Ft. Pitt, Chief Hopacan and Wingenund (Well-

Beloved) pretty much run the show. Hope Killbuck gits back with winter goods before winter gits back."

"I hope he gets back before Hopacan and Wingenund convince the Lenape to fight for Britain against the Americans," said William. "I think they'd do about anything to make that happen. Killbuck, jr., told me they were out to get his father."

Big Kittles looked worried and spoke more softly, "Better not talk so loud when yur a-talkin' 'bout them chiefs. Ain't good medicine, ya hear?"

As they neared the center of the village, William saw several boys talking with a disheveled-looking white man. When he saw William and Big Kittles approaching he grinned and stuck out his hand. His hair looked like it hadn't been cut or washed for several months and his smile revealed a few missing front teeth. His worn deerskin shirt gave off an odor that even made Big Kittles wince.

As they shook his hand he introduced himself, "Howdy lads. I'm Simon Girty, better known as 'Katepacomen' to the Five Nations. I'm acting as their interpreter. Been with 'em for many years. 'Scuse the appearance—been on horseback and campin' for many moons, rallyin' the tribes."

He made a sweeping motion with his hand and added, "These here Indian boys are real warriors they are. In spite of their size they just fought off a band of frontiersman that outnumbered 'em about six to one. Don't let their innocent looks fool you—they are real warriors."

He turned to the boys and exchanged information with them, then looked back at William and Big Kittles. "They want to know why you are here with the Delaware. What'll I tell 'em?" The two boys explained briefly their situation; Girty relayed the story to the Shawnee boys. "They want to know if you will help them fight off the Shemanese—that's what they call Americans—if they attack again."

Big Kittles was quick to reply, "Jist tell 'em we are Lenape warriors and as mean as they'll ever want ta find."

The older Shawnee braves were just coming out of the chief's house with Hopacan (Pipe) and they walked over to the little group standing with Girty. Chief Hopacan looked at William and spoke, Girty interpreting, "The Chief says there is going to be a big council gathered at the Delaware capital at Coshocton a few miles from here. He'd like for you to go along and begin to learn to interpret for them. I'll to be your teacher."

Seeing William's surprise, Girty added, "You've been here long enough that you understand a lot of conversation. I'll just help you translate it back into English. It's a pretty important job to both the Indians and the whites. Anyway just say yes for now because you ain't got no choice but to go with them, hear?"

William nodded his head and the chief seemed pleased. "The gathering takes place tomorrow sometime whenever everybody arrives. It's only a short walk from here," Girty explained.

As they walked away, Big Kittles said, "Know who Girty really is? He's probably the most hated white man on the whole frontier. The settlers consider him a traitor and a renegade."

"Why?" asked William, "Because he was an adopted Indian?"

"Not only that," said Big Kittles. "He's led a lot of successful raids against the settlers. He's went back to 'em once and tried to work with the military. Turned tail and come back to the Shawnee. Cain't hardly trust 'em, even some Injuns don't. Least-wise that's what they say."

William answered, "I'd like to know who 'they' are. Everybody's always tellin' what 'they' say. Could be 'they' don't know everything about him." Big Kittles's only reply was a disgusted grunt.

That evening William heard shouting and ran out of Moonshower's hut to see canoes banking at the river. Captain Killbuck and his twelve chiefs had returned from their visit to Ft. Pitt for supplies. The shouting soon died down as the onlookers grasped the fact there were no additional canoes with supplies.

Killbuck looked glum and spoke few words. "The Americans have promised to send supplies soon." He knew that his friends at Ft. Pitt could hardly find food for their own army in the field.

The crowd at the riverbank began walking away, one by one, until only William and Big Kittles were with the Captain.

"Where is your son, Killbuck, jr., and his friends?" William asked, respectfully looking at the ground.

"They are living with Col. Morgan and enrolling in school at Princeton," Killbuck replied. It was the only smile he would show for a long time.

The next day the Council was convened at Coshocton for Killbuck's official announcement although everyone knew essentially what he had to say. As always, the Americans "promised" but never delivered. Wingenund spoke after Killbuck: "We have heard the promises before but we have never been in such need before, either. Winter is coming. The Great Spirit has blest us with a friendly summer but game is not plentiful. The beavers work building bigger mud houses at their stick dams. Winter will be long. The rabbits and raccoons have extra thick coats, now. Winter will be hard. The bears we have killed are fatter than usual. Winter food will be scarce and storms will come. We know that Mother Earth promises and it happens. The Americans only promise. There is one answer—we must open trade again with the British!"

Killbuck tried to speak but Chief Hopacan stood up a moment sooner. "The Shawanee warriors who came today brought tragic news. Cowardly Americans have ransacked and burned Chalahgawtha while the warriors were away. A small group of young boys—some of them are here with us—held off the invaders and protected their women and elders. They even chased the Americans back across the Ohio River, these brave boys! We can no longer claim to be neutral and see our uncles and grandfathers attacked by these aggressive Americans. I say we vote now to alliance with the Wyandot and British!"

The Delaware had not always followed their Shawnee uncles but the news of the burning of their capital was frightening. The tribes had felt fairly secure from attack across the Ohio. By the time the vote was taken Killbuck had left the Council and was on his way back to Ft. Pitt. The other chiefs and captains voted to follow Chief Hopacan (Pipe).

William had attended the council and listened attentively to Girty's translation of the speeches. He felt confused, sad for the killings described and scared about what would happen to him now. He was walking alone outside the Council House when he saw one of the Shawnee boys showing something to the others. He walked over to them and a boy held out the object in his hand for William to see. It was a watch—just like the gold watch that he had dropped in the plowed earth that Aunt Ann said Alex found. The Indian boy let him hold it. He popped open the case and saw the inscription: "To William from Grandpa Walker."

He was trying to make sense of all this when a Shawnee chief walked up and put his hand on the Indian boy's head. He spoke to William, "This is my son. Two years ago he was fishing and I started down to the stream when I saw a frontiersman in the woods with a rifle aimed at the boy's head. Unseen by the man, I also took aim at him but before I could fire he lowered his gun. Then he saw me and I lowered mine. We talked—he told me his name was Daniel Boone. I thanked him for sparing my son's life and let him go, though I knew he had escaped from our people. When my son was chasing the attackers from our village, he pulled one of their wounded from a horse and was ready to spear him. Later, he told me, 'I looked at his eyes and he was just a boy like me. I thought of Boone and put down my spear. Then he threw me this handsome gold watch.' He said to him, 'Your life is returned for Boone.' "

William asked the warrior, "What happened to the American boy? Is he safe?"

The warrior spoke with his son and translated, "He says he watched the boy being helped by a friend. The friend bandaged his leg and put him on a horse and they left. That's all he stayed to see."

"Alex is alive," thought William, "He was here in Ohio and he is alive." And he heard again the message of the sweat lodge vision: "You are not abandoned."

ⵋⵋⵋⵋⵋ

Chapter Thirteen:
Laughter

William had learned a good daily Lenape vocabulary though he was still hesitant about expressing himself in the language. His newfound confidence and optimism made him feel more like getting out in the mornings and joining the activities around him. He was up and outside by first daylight.

He saw Dancing-Fire walking near her wikawames carrying a basket and thought about hailing her but was too shy. He hadn't made any effort to see her during the time he was so depressed.

She glanced up, saw him, and immediately came over. "Pemsit," she said, "Walk-er, why have you ignored me for so long? I thought if I waited you would come by."

He wasn't sure he understood everything she said but struggled to answer her in Lenape: "I—have not—eh, I can't—feel well—some yesterdays—ago." He raised his eyebrows with a questioning look.

Dancing-Fire laughed heartily. "I guess I know what you mean. I'll try to talk slower for you," she said, "I just mean that I missed seeing you." William blushed and looked at the ground. "You look more like an Indian every moment. Well," she continued, "I have to go to the river and gather some berries." She walked a few steps past him and then looked back. "Aren't you going to offer to come with me?"

He looked surprised and couldn't think of what to say. She helped him, "Just say, 'May I carry your basket for you?'"

William stammered, "May I basket carry you for?"

"Of course," she said, "it is polite of you to offer."

As they strolled and looked for blackberries, Dancing-Fire did most of the talking. William thought about how beautiful her black hair was. And how smooth her brown skin. He had noticed it during the summer months when she could display more of it. He was daydreaming about that when she said, "Don't you think that's right?"

He was embarrassed again and stuttered, "Eh, if you say it is, I know."

She giggled again. "I was saying that I heard the Council voted to become allies with Britain and the Wyandot. I think the War will end soon, maybe before there's any action from us. Don't you think that's right?"

"Yes, yes," he said with firmness, as if he'd been listening all along to her observations.

He watched her stoop down to pluck some fruit from the low vines and his mind again wandered. "She is so graceful and her hands are dainty," he thought. She put a berry in her mouth and then put one to his lips. He swallowed wrong and it lodged in his windpipe. He coughed and hacked for a long minute before he could get it out.

"I'm sooo sorry," she cried, patting him on the back and brushing his hair back from his eyes. "Are you all right, now?" All he could think of was how stupid he felt.

"Let's sit down here a minute," she suggested, smoothing some leaves. "Catch your breath. Want to learn some more Lenape words?"

"Yeees," he rasped.

She took his hand in hers and said, "nachk"—then pointed to his mouth.

He pointed to his mouth and repeated "nachk."

"No," she laughed and pointed to her hand again—he got it right that time. She continued, tossed her black braid over her shoulder and placed his hand on it—"milach." He repeated and she moved his hand to her cheek—"wonanno." She put her hand on his cheek—"wonanno." Her finger gently touched his lower lip—"wscheton." She moved his hand to her leg and William began feeling strange. At one and the same moment he wanted to sweep her up in his arms—and also to run away like a frightened antelope.

Then it happened—three children, all giggling in the bushes beside them. And a little boy with one hand over his mouth was pointing with the other and saying, as William later understood, "Machtumbunk, machtumbunk. (Dung, dung.) You are sitting where I pooped this morning!"

~~~

That evening when he entered the wikwames he was surprised to see Moonshower had a visitor. "This is Joseph Sabosh my new friend. He lives in the Gnadenhutten village of the Moravian Lenape just a few hours walk from here." The man seemed pleasant and friendly to William. He dined with them on machxitachpoan (bread-and-beans) and stayed late talking incessantly with Moonshower. William stayed outside as long as he could but she begged him to come in out of the cold. He lay down on his side of the fire thinking, "Is he going to spend the night? Any night but this one. Not after my time with Dancing-Fire. It will make me crazy." His worries were not long lasting. When the moon was halfway up in the sky the man left, walking home.

By the time William was out the next day Big Kittles had already heard the gossip started by the children. He was discussing it with a boy named Tschimamus (Rabbit) but they became very quiet when William joined them. He suspected he was the topic of their conversation and confronted them about it.
~~~

"Yes," Big Kittles admitted, "we heard about your tryst at the latrine yesterday." They both broke into wild laughter.

William took a swing at both of them and said angrily, "Shut up. It wasn't my idea."

Tschimamus tried to stifle his joy. "Sorry, William—don't be so touchy. We all have a hard time with the girls." William knew that Tschimamus had a reputation in the village of being a heart breaker. He was handsome with an extra-long black scalp lock and wore a gold earring and an eagle feather when he "dressed up" for festive occasions.

"Look," William said, more calmly, "I need some advice. Haven't had a girlfriend before. It's hard trying to be romantic in two different languages. Teach me some things to say, Tschimamus—you know how to do this."

They talked it over and Tschimamus finally pounded his chest. "I know what would be good with Dancing-Fire. At the right moment—after some small talk—look her in the eyes and put her hands on your chest and say with as much sincerity as you can, 'kschipsin.' Practice saying it sincerely—'kschipsin.'"

William obliged. "Not sincere enough," said Tschimamus, "make your eyes talk. Can you even make them moist a little? Try it again. Say, 'kschipsin.' She will understand."

William did his best. "Now what exactly am I saying?"

"It is a very romantic word that girls love to hear. It means something like, in English, 'I am falling in love.' But it's much more than that—it conveys a physical feeling that comes from deep within. Try it again. There. That's it!"

William could hardly wait to surprise Dancing-Fire and knew she would be walking down to the river again that evening if it didn't rain, to fetch water or berries. All he had to do was stay busy during the morning and afternoon and wait for the right time. Maybe he'd even invite her to dine with them if Moonshower didn't mind.

Late in the afternoon Joseph called from outside the doorway of the wikwames and Moonshower went with him for a walk. When they returned William was still inside waiting for the right hour to strike. Joseph said in English, "Moonshower tells me you have become her adopted son who has made her very happy. Where are you from?"

William was surprised at how well he spoke. He was obviously a well-educated man but his hands were big and rough like those of a farmer. The boy gave him a brief history of his life in Virginia and Joseph listened intently.

"Are your people believers?" Joseph asked.

"Well—no, we go to the Presbyterian Church."

Joseph smiled, "That's close enough—but better not mention that around here. The Scotch-Irish are some fierce enemies of ours and they are mostly Presbyterians."

William tried to apologize but Joseph waved him off, "It's alright. My people have had their share of hatred. Since I've become a believer I have traded the rifle and tomahawk for the hoe and spade. At our village at Gnadenhutten we are all Christian Indians."

"Lenape?" William inquired.

"Yes—our Brother David thinks we can live a purer life away from alcohol and killing if we are dwelling separately from the world. We only want to live in peace and love each other. You should visit us sometime."

"Thank you, I will," said William politely, though his mind was on something else at the moment. "If you will excuse me, there's a chore I need to take care of before night." Joseph nodded and shook his hand as he left.

Dancing-Fire was carrying a keg to bring up some water for supper. They walked together and chuckled about the children. William looked over his shoulder to make sure they weren't following this time, hoping the lateness of the hour would avoid "the little village mice" as he called them. They stopped at the river's edge while he took the keg and filled it, being careful to wade out past the cattails where it flowed more freely. After they talked some more about the river, the moon and stars and the wind whistling through the trees, he felt the moment had come. Taking her hands and placing them on his chest, he said as sincerely as he knew how—"kschipsin."

~~~
~~~

Joseph was still at the wikwames when William and Dancing-Fire came in for supper. Joseph said, "What is wrong, William, you don't look as happy as you did."

"Joseph, what exactly does 'kschipsin' mean in English?"

"Oh," replied Joseph, "that's what's wrong. You have an *itch*."

ⲘⲘⲘ

Col. Morgan had predicted some months before that Indian allies in the northwest would turn against the Americans if supplies and trade were not forthcoming. Apparently his words had fallen on deaf ears. The government seemed more focused on their enemies than on their friends. The winter of 1779-80 that almost brought Gen. Washington's troops to their knees at Valley Forge was as severe—perhaps more so—for the Delaware in Ohio.

"I somehow like the snow," said Dancing-Fire as William leaned over to smash the river ice with his tomahawk. "It's must be close to the month you call December. To us it is mechakhokque," she stated, still teaching words to her friend. "It means 'when cold makes trees crack.'"

"Yes," said William, "I've heard a lot of them cracking the last few days. I like snow but not all this ice," he said, chopping harder at the frozen river.

Several of their friends came walking down the riverbank. Tschimamus held up a couple of skinny squirrels. William waved at them, "I see you've finally trapped something."

"No," Tschimamus replied, "we found these two frozen. There are a lot of hungry creatures in the woods and rivers now. There was a dead wolf with cubs just outside the village. Wild animals are coming to us for food—they don't know how scarce it's getting for us. Want me to break that ice for you?"

"No, thanks," William said, annoyed at the suggestion he wasn't man enough to do it alone.

Tschimamus started on down the river but looked back and shouted, "Hope you've gotten over that itch."

Dancing-Fire giggled but tried to hide her mouth in the collar of her deerskin coat.

When William looked up at her he noticed how wan she looked, and thin. "When did you eat last," he asked.

"I had some venison jerky and hominy," she said.

"I asked you when," he insisted.

She looked down at her moccasins. "Maybe a day ago."

"Why didn't you tell me? I would have tried to find something around our wikwames." He put his arms around her and felt her shivering. "Let me get this bucket filled with water and we'll go get by the fire and find some food," he said, finally making a small hole in the ice.

The falling snow was drifting several feet deep as they made their way back to the Long House where a number of families were gathering to save firewood. Dry wood was also getting hard to find except for an occasional dead tree that was still upright. As they came through the bearskin door they were greeted by about twenty others of all ages. The elderly were huddled around a large fire burning at the center, blankets draped around their shoulders. A number of dogs were sleeping as close as they could to the stones around the fireplace.

Only the children seemed to be having a good time running around the sides of the building, playing a version of "tag." Women were preparing what food they had. They'd already skinned the muskrats and added them to the large black pot hanging over the fire on a pole suspended by two forked sticks. Most of the stew consisted of lots of wild white potatoes and a few other kinds of vegetables. Whatever roots a family had stored in the ground by their wigawan (house), they shared. William's friends came in last—Big Kittles and Tschimamus and others from the ball teams.

When everyone in the Long House had eaten their small bowl of stew, they gathered close around the fireplace in a tight circle. Dancing-Fire cuddled up to William to the glee of some little boys nearby. A small girl called out, "I know who likes William!" Everybody laughed and William just looked down and grinned.

The same little girl said what every child was thinking: "Muchomes (Grandfather). Tell us a story!"

An old man named Tauwatawik (Wilderness) began to speak in a very weak, quiet voice. A hush came upon everyone in the circle, some leaning forward to catch the words they had heard many times before. Every time the stories were told was a brand new experience, because the circumstances were entirely different each time.

Tauwatawik spoke: "Long ago the wisawanik (squirrel) was huge—not like the skinny ones we cooked tonight. No! He was great and walked all over the place. He traveled through the valleys and up the mountains—everywhere—looking for smaller animals to eat. He would eat all kinds, frogs or bears, even snakes or turkeys.

"One day when he was really hungry he saw a two-legged creature walking along..."

The little girl interrupted him, "He was running, Muchomes. You always say he was running."

The old man cleared his throat and continued, "He saw a two-legged creature walking—then running along." A wave of chuckles went through the audience. "Well, he was so hungry he snatched up that person and ate him all up except for one hand which the giant squirrel held in his giant paw.

"While he was chewing, all of a sudden a giant person was standing there, right there! The person had a bright white light shining and shimmering all around him. When he said anything it sounded like thunder from the clouds and the earth shook and trees fell down it was so loud. He was the Creator!

"Now, giant wisawanik, you have done a terrible deed. You have eaten up my child. From now on you will be little and you and your children and grandchildren will be eaten and the shameful thing you did will be remembered by the mark under your forearm.

"Well the squirrel was scared and trembled in fear. He wanted to hide the evidence he carried, so he put the man's hand under his own arm. This must be a true story because for a long time now, I have hunted and cooked many wisawanik and I have seen the hand under his arms always. We cut that piece off before cooking Mr. Squirrel."

The fire was warming their bodies as the stories warmed their hearts. Shouts of "Hoh!" came from around the circle and "Kange wulit!" ("Good story!") Now it was a little boy who yelled, "Tell us another one, please. Quick, while I'm warm!" Everybody laughed and relaxed a little and forgot for the moment the frozen night and the gnawing hunger in their bellies.

An old woman pulled a worn shawl around her and began to speak. "Once upon a time there was a good-looking woman." She was sitting next to Dancing-Fire and without turning her head, she rolled her eyes towards the girl. Her friends giggled and gently pushed her and William. "The men all liked her looks but she wouldn't have any of them. Even the animals thought she was beautiful.

"There were three animals who decided to have a contest to see who could win the woman's love. They were the beaver (ktemaque), the skunk (shkaa'k), and the owl (gokhos). The owl was chosen to try first to charm the beautiful woman. He went to sing to her but she said, 'I won't have you because you are ugly, your eyes are too big.'

"The owl went back the said, 'I couldn't get that woman.' So the skunk went to see the woman, to try and charm her with his colored fur. She said, 'I won't go with you because you are ugly and you stink.' So the skunk said, 'I couldn't get that woman to like me, either.'

"The beaver went over to try and charm the woman with his flat tail. But the woman said, 'I won't have you because your teeth are wide and your tail is too flat and big. That tail of yours looks like a paddle used to stir soup.' When he reported that he also couldn't get the woman, they had a Council, the three animals. 'What can we do to get that beautiful woman,' they asked. The beaver had an idea and said, 'She goes to get water 'way over at the creek. There's a log there that she walks on. I'll go chew it in half, so when she steps there it will break. She will fall in the water and we can go save her and be heroes.' They all liked that idea very much. So he did it, chewed the log almost in half.

"Then when the woman fell in the water she wished the beaver was there to help her. She started singing, 'Pe pe kwan sa, pe pe kwan so, Ni ha noliha ktemaque.' (I like the beaver.)

Anyway, the beaver, he said, 'No one would like me because my teeth are too wide and my tail looks like a stirring paddle.' And he went away. So the woman sang, 'Pe pe kwan sa. Niha nolina shaa'k.' (I like the skunk.) The skunk said, 'No one would like me because I am so ugly and I stink.' So he went away. Then she sang, 'Pe pe kwan sa. Niha noliha…"

When the old woman paused to catch her breath, all the children shouted, "Niha noliha gokhos!" (I like the owl!)

The storyteller continued, "But the owl said, 'No one would like me because I am ugly. My eyes are too big.' So the woman floated away down the creek. With nobody to help her she finally drowned."

Shouts and giggles from the crowd. Dancing-Fire and William both got teased and pushed, again. Joseph was also there with Moonshower. Someone said, "Let Joseph tell one of the stories of the Moravians."

"Yes, yes!" they shouted, "tell us a story from the Moravians!"

Joseph cleared his throat and began. "This is a story that was first told to our people many moons ago on a frozen night like this, around a big big fire," he gestured, "like this one. The story came to us from a Huron warrior—a Wyandot ancestor. A Lenape brave rescued him from the icy waters. He said he heard the story from the Black Robes who had lived among them, time before. The Moravian missionaries also know this," he added.

"It is a story about a man with my name, Joseph. Now when he was young—eh, about William's age—Joseph made his brothers angry because he was his father's favorite son. His mother made a special coat for him with many colored cloths and dyed skins. One day when they were taking care of their horses some warriors from another tribe came along and wanted to buy him. So they sold him to them. Then they killed a goat and put blood on his coat and tore it. They took it to their father and said, 'Joseph is dead. See the bear killed him and carried him away. Only his coat was left.' The father wept for many days because of his son.

"These Indians took Joseph with them—he was maybe twelve or thirteen years old—but they didn't keep him. The chief of another tribe came and saw him and wanted to buy him. So they, too, sold Joseph to the chief. He went to live with him and became his servant. He carried the chief's arrows and watered his horse. He cleaned the chief's game and served his meals. He was so good to the chief, the man began to think Joseph was his own son.

"But the chief's wife looked at what a handsome brave Joseph was becoming and she tempted him. 'Come and lay with me in the wigwam while the chief is gone,' she said. 'No! I cannot do that,' he said, 'the chief trusts me with his own life. How could I do that?' He tried to get away from her but she tore off a piece of his coat as he ran out the door. Then she showed it to the chief when he came back and cried, 'Your servant Joseph tried to lay with me in your wigwam, but I ran.' The chief was so angry and he sent warriors out to find him and kill him. But Joseph ran away and hid in a cave in the forest for many days. There were some other men the chief was mad at who also found the cave. One night Joseph told them a dream he had, that they would be caught and one would be allowed to live. Sure enough, it happened.

"Then another night the chief had a dream and couldn't understand it. He said, 'I dreamed about seven fat buffalo and seven skinny buffalo. The skinny ones came and ate up the fat ones. Who knows what this dream means?' Several braves and elders tried to figure it out, but nobody could. Then the servant who had been in the cave remembered, and told the chief, 'I know a man who can interpret dreams from God. He can tell you.' So, he went out and got Joseph and brought him to the chief.

"Joseph said, 'The Great Spirit will tell me what it means.' Then he said, 'There will be seven fat years and seven lean years. Store up food now for the lean years.' It was true and the chief promoted Joseph and put him in charge of all the food in the nation. He put venison in bags and hung them in the trees where bears could not get them. He dug pits and kept the potatoes and wild onions in the ground.

"Well, when the lean years came, the years of famine, the tribe had plenty. Even Joseph's brothers came and begged for food. He forgave them and gave them food and a lodge to live in with his father. He said, 'You were bad to sell me—but the Great Spirit meant it for good.' He works all things for good when we love and worship Him, the Creator."

The whole room was very still. There were some tears running down cheeks. An old man said, "That is not a Lenape story but it is a good one. Good story!" And they lay down and slept a peaceful sleep. (But not before Dancing-Fire's grandmother came over and escorted her to the women's side of the Long House.)

)()()()()(

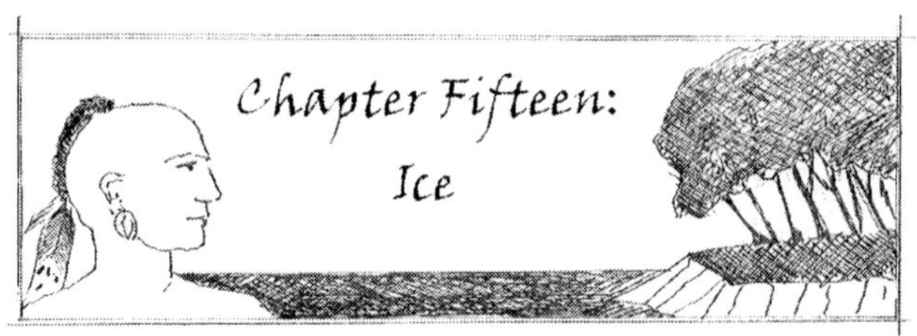

Snow continued to fall into the third week of the blizzard. William, Big Kittles and Moonshower had moved back to their wikwames from the Long House in order to try to stay warmer. The boys searched for twigs and branches every day and usually found enough for a sufficient, though small fire in their diminutive quarters. It was impossible to keep enough fire burning at the Long House to warm everyone there.

This particular day the search for fuel took them farther away from the village than usual. It was impractical to walk far without snowshoes and with them it still took much longer than in good weather. A normal fifteen-minute stroll might take an hour. If the hunters went very far they risked not returning before dark and that might mean death by freezing. The villagers had been without sufficient food for at least two weeks. Many people were living on bark stripped from nearby trees. The root crops buried in the fall had been completely devoured two weeks before.

Frozen animal carcasses were so deep under drifts they couldn't be easily found.

"Can you see anythang more'n a inch in front of ya?" shouted Big Kittles.

William was walking right beside him but yelled, "I can't hear you over this wind—talk louder!" They were both leaning into a belligerent north gale that was slinging tiny arrows of sleet against their faces.

"Wait," Big Kittles screamed again, "One of my snowshoes just fell off!" They both got on all fours to retrieve it and found it caught on a twig under the snow.

"Start digging," William said, "Maybe there's a bigger branch attached to it." They aggressively dogpaddled the loose snow and followed the branches down to a limb bigger than they could put their fingers around.

"Hoh!" said Big Kittles, "we got us a treasure fer sure! This is gonna make Moonshower grin tonight." After more digging, the boys hoisted the log up over their shoulders and started walking away from the wind.

As they came up over a small ridge, they walked within two steps of a doe and her fawn, gnawing bark off a tree. When they came to a halt, the animals did not run but continued trying to get food. The doe simply looked at them out of the corner of an eye and trembled as she ate. William watched them and shook his head, knowing if they dropped the log the deer would be gone before they could draw an arrow.

"Good thing for you we're looking for wood right now and not meat," he said.

"I 'spect you gonna be roasted 'fore long, Miz Deer. Sorry we caint feed no pets, neither," said Big Kittles.

They dropped their firewood in front of the hut and had to push the snow away from the entrance again. It was falling so fast and thick the bearskin doorways were covered every few hours. Inside, they heard Moonshower coughing. She was still lying on her bark platform, covered with a blanket from feet to neck. William ran over to her side, shocked at what he saw and heard. Her complexion was a kind of dark yellowish shade and she had a hacking cough. She shook convulsively from the cold.

"Don't worry, g'ichke (my mother)," he said, "we found firewood for you." It was the first time he'd ever called her that. Somehow what seemed wrong to him in English was appropriate when he spoke Lenape.

He touched her forehead and realized she was burning with a fever even as she chilled. "Big Kittles," he said, "Quick! Go find the medicine woman." William ran outside to get a handful of snow to bathe her forehead.

In a short time Big Kittles returned with the old woman, who looked extremely tired. "She says it's all over the village," Big Kittles reported, "same dang thang—fever 'n hackin'. They ain't much she kin do—doctorin' herbs is hard ta find in this blizzard."

The medicine woman mostly prayed and chanted, dropping pinches of tobacco on the fire every once in awhile as she shooed away the evil spirit that was attacking Moonshower.

Big Kittles explained, "She says we're lucky ta have a fire goin'—some don't even have that much."

The woman fanned Moonshower with a turkey feather.

Two braves arrived at the doorway and the old woman left on another mission of mercy. William went over and sat quietly on his bark platform. "God, I haven't talked to you much for a long time. I thought you had abandoned me but I know you didn't. Moonshower is all I have now and she has been good to me. Please don't let her die. Thank you, amen."

A number of elderly and some small children had died during this storm already. Their relatives faithfully wrapped the bodies in animal skins and placed each on a high platform at the sacred place, awaiting a time when the weather would allow thawing and eventually a ceremony over the bones. Their remains would then be reburied in order to allow the deceased's spirit to leave the site and journey to the afterworld.

The boys decided the best thing to do was go hunting for something to boil in the pot while they still had a fire. "Wait a minute!" William exclaimed. They both shouted in unison, "The doe and fawn!" They tracked the animals a short ways through the forest and discovered the fawn frozen at the foot of a large tree.

"I'm kinda glad we didn't have ta kill it," said Big Kittles.

"Yeah, I guess the Great Spirit meant it as medicine for Moonshower. Any longer and a wolf would've had it."

It wasn't long before the hindquarter was roasting over their fire and another chunk of venison boiling in the pot. The rest they shared with several families around them.

The next day Moonshower was up and moving about slowly. Her fever had broken sometime during the night and her countenance was ruddy.

"Thank you, God," William whispered, his faith growing stronger and stronger.

A moment later they heard the mournful wailing of grief from a wigawan a short distance away. As the boys ran in the direction of the death-song, they realized it was coming from a house they knew well. When they bolted through the door, they saw Dancing-Fire's grandmother weeping aloud in disconsolation, kneeling over the pale body of the beautiful, frail young girl.

William felt numb with confusion as he walked behind the warriors carrying her body, blackened with charcoal, through the snow into the forest. He leaned against a tree as the men tomahawked four saplings and forced them deep into the drifts to support the bark platform. They'd made it from Dancing-Fire's bed because of the scarcity of materials. They wrapped her in a blanket and lifted her up to the top, then cleared away the snow underneath so predators couldn't reach the body, placed about eight feet above the earth.

All was done in silent reverence.

William did not pray or weep—he only watched, then walked away as Big Kittles assured him, "We'll come ever day and clear the new snow so she'll be safe."

As night came he ate nothing even though Moonshower brought a bowl of the roasted venison, expressing her appreciation for the new strength she found in the broth. She sat by his bed and stroked his hair as he turned towards the wall and sobbed, exhaling with great sighs of desperation.

Moonshower thought it best to leave him alone for the next few days but the fourth night she called Big Kittles over and began to speak with William. "I know this is a very difficult road for you," she began. "I have also walked a rough and sometimes lonely path. You know that my man left me. Before that my father was killed fighting in a battle against the settlers. My mother died when I was only a small girl. This does not help you feel alive again, I know. My words are weak—I want to say that every time I was alone, someone was sent to help me get up again. The Great Spirit sent you to me even while your own mother's heart must have suffered a terrible pain. We are not allowed to live long here but the sun will make its journey across the dome of God's Long House, and you will be given the privilege to watch its beautiful colors again. You must decide to live, just as I have. The hunger of your heart will make delicious the feast of life."

He listened without answering—but was shaken by her next revelation. "As you have brought the stars back into my life, Joseph has brought the sunrise. I have gone with him to hear the missionaries at Gnadenhutten. They have spoken of a man named Jesus who brings peace and joy to the sad-hearted. They told of his love for us all, his forgiveness for our sins. I had heard of him before from others, but now the message has penetrated my heart. I have decided this week to become a Christian. Joseph has asked me to marry him and live with him at the Christian village. William, will you go and live there with us? Joseph would be a very loving father to you. Big Kittles, you come too!"

William glanced up and saw Big Kittles frown and shake his head. As for him, he couldn't think of anything worse than being around people who talked about God all the time. He didn't know what he would do, but moving to the Moravian town wasn't an option.

Two weeks later at the end of March the ice began to break up over the river and water was flowing again.

The men met in Council and smoked their calumets, now and then adding bits of tobacco to the sacred fire as an offering to the spirit of good fortune.

William was getting irritable from being confined to the house and village for weeks. Three small boys came by and pelted him with snow as he sat on a log outside the hut. He yelled angrily and chased them away, much to their delight. He was about to explode from inactivity when one of the Council warriors approached him.

"William, you have been with us a good while, now. You know our language and you are beginning to learn how to interpret in the Council. It is our wish along with Chief Hopacan (Pipe) that you join us on a trip to Detroit to counsel with the Five Nations concerning our role in the present conflict, and to reestablish trade with the British there. We will leave early tomorrow morning. Dress warmly!"

William explained as best he could to Moonshower about the trip. She busied herself mending and making ready his coat and leggings, winter moccasins and breeches. She even found a few pieces of jerky at a neighbor's to get him through the first hours of the trek. He was dressed and ready by the first breaking of dawn, which came in a burst of purple and pink sky over the horizon.

About fifteen warriors took William and Big Kittles and headed for the river where four large bark canoes were tethered to saplings on the bank. The boys didn't know exactly what Detroit would be like; they were only glad to be going somewhere away from Neghkaunque (Newcomerstown)—anywhere.

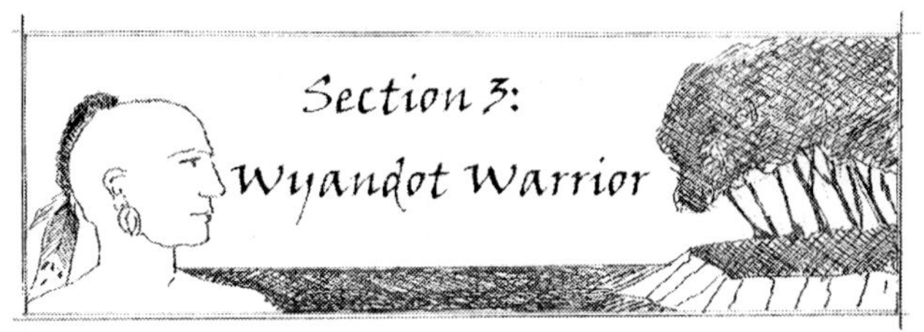
Section 3:
Wyandot Warrior

(1780-1785)

William sat near the middle of a canoe with Big Kittles and Chief Hopacan (Pipe) behind him and a warrior named Half-Scalp at the bow. Two canoes were leading them and the fourth was bringing up the rear, the better to protect the Chief. Chief Wingenund was in the boat directly in front of them.

As they started up river, Chief Hopacan explained to William: "This will be a very big and important Council. Maybe twenty, thirty chiefs—Wyandot, Seneca, Shawnee, Mohawk, Chippewa, Cayuga, Onondaga—I don't know how many will be there. Some of them were our enemies in the past but we are learning that a bundle of twigs is stronger than a lone stick. You will hear many words you do not understand but neither do I. Still I can converse with most of the warriors and chiefs. We have learned how to make our words known."

William listened without responding. He knew that such a confederacy would mean death for many settlers. Yet he had experienced enough hunger and privation, he felt empathy for the Indians.

Later he asked Half-Scalp, the warrior in front of him, "How long will this trip take us?"

The man grunted a reply, "Twice as long as it should if you and Big Kittles don't push more water with your paddles!" The others laughed and Half-Scalp flashed a grin back at William. Then he explained, "It will take us about six days on the water but since we don't have provisions we'll stop to hunt a couple of days more. We can do some fishing from the canoe but when we do we're not really moving very fast, so might as well be on the bank resting while we fish."

Chief Hopacan added, "We'll be at Wingenund's town in another two-and-a-half days—so we can rest a little there. I'm getting too old in the bones to kneel in a canoe more than a few days at a time."

"Half-Scalp," Big Kittles asked, "how'd ya git yur moniker—yer name?" It was obvious from the scar tissue above his forehead to halfway back that he had been partially scalped.

He was enthusiastic about being asked. "I got in a skirmish with some Long Knives—those settlers from Virginia and Ken-tuck-ee. We crossed paths on a hunt down there. One of them shot at me and the bullet went across the top of my skull and knocked me out. When I woke up he was holding me up between his legs and I felt the knife cut the skin over my forehead," he said, drawing his finger across the edge of the scar. "Blood was running down in my eyes but it made me madder than a mother bear. He tore my scalp halfway off but I stopped him before he could finish the job. My hand was under one of my legs and I felt my knife, grabbed it and shoved it in his thigh. When he fell and turned me loose, I pounced on him and stabbed him in the chest. I still couldn't see much until another warrior cut the loose scalp away from my head.

"I remember him saying to me, 'A lot of young men are plucking out their hair and just leaving a scalp-lock on back. You will look like you planned this.'"

William stopped paddling and Half-Scalp looked back at him and laughed. "Your mouth is open," he said.

"I know," William shot back, "I opened it." He squinted and asked, "But—didn't it hurt?"

"What—you mean having your scalp half cut off your head? Of course not!" he roared sarcastically—obviously enjoying telling the story. "Worse than that was the itching while it healed—yeeech," he said through clinched teeth. "But there wasn't much I could do but scratch and apply bear grease. Besides, I came out better than the other guy did. That's really what is important in war, you know. If you stay alive, you win. And what is it the Americans like to say—'Half a scalp is better than none'?"

Until mid-morning they moved west along the Tuscarawas River and then continued a little northwest on the Walhonding. The water was calm and the scenery peaceful. It was early springtime and after a terrible winter the plants seemed anxious to burst into different shades of green. At times the riverbed dipped between high red-stone gorges that almost threatened to swallow their small craft. They were happily surprised to see many deer feeding along the banks and on the rolling hills and fresh squirrel nests in the trees. How the wildlife managed to survive the long blizzard was almost miraculous. Captain Hopacan gave a prayerful thanks to the Mother Earth every time they saw the animals.

Half-Scalp spoke to the boys, "It will be sunset before long and the other canoes are stopping here to find a place to camp. We will go a ways farther—I know that deer will likely be drinking around the bend ahead in the little cove; I've found them there before. You young braves cease paddling and prepare your bows. Take steady aim but do not hesitate. We will have only one chance and it's either going to be a sumptuous feast or a snack on a handful of old chestnuts Moonshower gave us. Be very still and we will glide around this curve of the river."

After one more strong push with his oar, Half-Scalp slipped it out of the water and laid it down by his feet. The river seemed to stop beneath their canoe as it moved effortlessly forward. Chief Hopacan guided it, holding his paddle still in the water without even a hint of a splash. The occupants all knelt like statues, the boys with arrows aimed towards the bank.

The deer suddenly came into view—six doe and a buck with a large six-point rack that abruptly jerked into the air followed immediately by the heads of the startled doe. Whoosh, whoosh—went two arrows nearly simultaneously. William was nearest the buck which became his target but when he shot, the animal made a turning leap in midair and bounded back into the thick forest.

Big Kittles's doe fell like a stone at the water's edge, an arrow lodged perfectly in the heart. William hung his head in disappointment and shame. When they banked the canoe Half-Scalp took William by the arm and ran with him after the buck. They zigzagged following the trail of blood through the thick woods until William saw the antlers protruding up from the brush ahead. The buck had fallen dead about three-hundred steps from the spot where he had taken the arrow.

"Your shot was good, Pemsit," said the warrior, "A buck this size takes a while to make up his mind to die. You took almost perfect aim. Don't give up so quickly." Then, turning to the stag he said, "We admire you Mr. Ajapeu (buck) and your doe. Thank you for your gift of life. It is much appreciated by us all."

The two deer were gutted and the warriors pulled wild grape vines out of a tall tree, tied the buck's legs together with them, tossed the vines back over a high limb and hoisted the carcass up. They left it to swing in midair for safekeeping from wolves and bears. They butchered the smaller deer and wrapped part of the meat in a cloth saturated with bear's oil, then strung it up over a limb. Half of the venison they put over the fire to roast. When it was ready the eight of them ate like starving jackals, a welcome breaking of the forced winter fast.

"You sleep," said Half-Scalp to the boys. "I'll keep watch for awhile." They slept deeply all night (except when it was one's turn to act as sentinel). William's arm muscles trembled for a while, unaccustomed to the long hours at the paddle. He woke up feeling hot and thought he had a fever—then realized it was his first sunburn of the year.

The second day went about like the first. They made good time because the melted snow had assured high water. Only once did they have to stop and clear a logjam of brush and debris caught on a fallen tree. At midday they drifted leisurely for awhile. Wingenund had several poles and hooks he had traded from the French years before. The entrails from the deer made good bait and they landed a mess of catfish. They camped again that night and fried the fish impaled on sticks over the fire before another peaceful night's sleep with full bellies.

About noon the third day they reached the end of Black Fork River. "My house and village is only an hour's walk from here," said Chief Wingenund, "but we will have to carry the canoes. They don't paddle well over earth." Six of the men emptied the boats, turned them upside down and carried them over their heads and shoulders.

William was congratulating Big Kittles on their good luck, when he replied, "See all this stuff on the ground—we gotta carry all the supplies in to Wingenund's town. If'n ya think paddlin' is hard work try pack-mulin' it fer an hour."

Fifty or so met them as they arrived at the village. Men, women and children were shouting their greetings and ululating at the sight of the venison and supplies. The Indians at Newcomerstown had sacrificed their own goods to help Wingenund's people. William and Big Kittles were star attractions although most of the villagers had heard about them.

One little boy examined William's sunburn closely, and said to the others (who thought it hilarious), "A redskin!"

That night the town gave a feast and dance in honor of the visitors. The sound of drums and singing helped them all forget for a while the sadness and sickness they had left behind.

Early in the morning they started out again, carrying the canoes. They did not take much else with them so the boys had little to carry. "Aren't we going wrong," asked William, "this trail heads south. Detroit is that way."

Half-Scalp answered from beneath the canoe, "We go about two hours this way and find the Sandusky River. It will bend back and take us all the way to the Lake—about three more days' journey. How do you like it so far, Pemsit?"

"It's exciting," said William. "I've never seen this much of Ohio before. It is a great adventure—and there don't seem to be enemies around."

"No, it is fairly safe here. All the nations that reside in Ohio are our nephews and uncles. That is another reason for joining with the Wyandot at this time. The Lenape would be left isolated if we did not."

The next three days went by as pacifically as the first three. They visited other villages—Captive's Town, Upper Sandusky, and Half-King's Town before finally reaching the mouth of the river and gliding out into Sandusky Bay on Lake Erie—the largest expanse of water William had ever seen. He felt a sense of freedom and breathed deeply the fresh breeze coming across greenish-blue waves. Another trek in his journey was nearly over—and another about to begin.

)()()()(

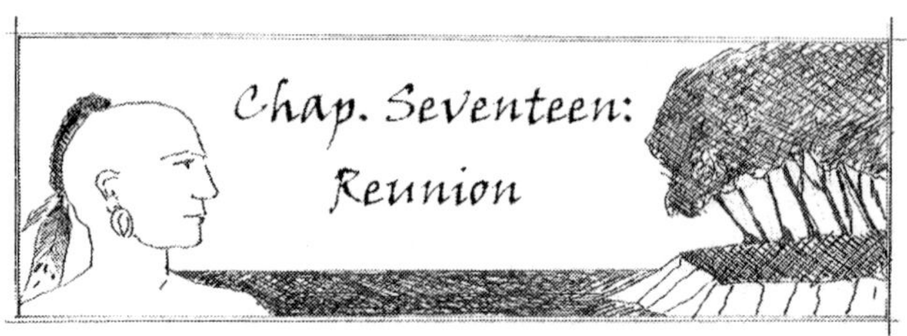
Chap. Seventeen:
Reunion

The canoes made a swing around Sandusky Bay and up the Detroit River where Wyandot villages were scattered up and down the west bank. As they glided past, women fetching water in French-made pails greeted them. Little boys and girls ran and shouted while young adolescents—arms folded over their chests to look like warriors—gazed at the sight of two more chieftains arriving at the capital site.

A group of decorated warriors met the canoes and towed them onto shore where the boats leaned to one side as if fatigued from the week's trip. There was a feeling of freedom here in the open air that was somehow different from life in the woodlands. The forests kept a respectful distance from the wide vista of the lake and river.

Half-Scalp pointed at a large log two-story structure not far from their point of arrival. "Tohunehowetu's house. Big wigwam, huh? He's an important village chief from the Deer Clan. Maybe you'll meet him. That's the Council House over there." He pointed to the largest bark-log structure William had yet seen.

"Wil-yam!" a young Wyandot brave yelled and ran towards him, tomahawk raised above his head. William instinctively put his hands over his face and ducked before he heard the brave laugh. It was Mononcue—there was no mistaking his large brown eyes and Roman nose. His face had grown longer and more handsome—the nose didn't take up as much space as before. He looked a foot taller and more a brave than the boy that helped capture him almost two years earlier. They had just begun to get acquainted before separating at the Ohio River.

William grabbed the brave's arm, still upraised holding the weapon, and tried to speak to Mononcue in Lenape.

The Indian replied in Wendat, chuckling, "I know a little of several other Indian languages, but not broken Lenape spoken with a Virginia accent."

William just stood frowning with his mouth open. The frustration of not understanding a single word hadn't struck him for over a year. Here it was, back again. He hated the helpless feeling of not being able to communicate with speech. Before, he'd always felt that "they" could be plotting some terrible evil against him and he wouldn't be able to protest against it or beg for mercy. The feeling of paranoia was worse when several conversations were going on around him.

"Halloo, young William," a deep voice boomed out from the crowd of spectators. Bigtree marched up to the lad and grabbed him in a firm handshake. William noticed he had an extra couple of rings in his earlobes but otherwise had the same friendly smile.

It was hard to realize this was the man who had murdered his uncle. It seemed like a long, long time ago.

Before William could prepare for it, the warrior had him in a bear hug and swung him halfway around. "We heard you might be coming with the Dasayane' (Delaware) representatives," he commented. Then he greeted the chiefs: "Glad you brought the young man," he said. "And, Big Kittles—good to have you back in the land of the Wendat!" They exchanged good wishes and a few small gifts and Bigtree invited them all up to his cabin for some food.

Conditions were extremely more prosperous here than at the Delaware villages. William was amazed at the healthy looking people with smiles on their faces. He noticed his own thin arms and protruding ribs.

The girls were wearing colorful clothing not tattered or faded from use. Even the dogs yapping around the camp were fat. The cabins and bark houses looked sturdier and newer than the ones he'd been used to seeing in the Ohio area.

Outside Bigtree's cabin was a totem with a Bear on top. Inside, Bigtree's wife served them a mashed corn drink out of a blue-painted porcelain pitcher. "Made in France," explained their host in his usual ebullient voice. "Traded six fox pelts for it—but it's worth it to make the wife happy."

"You never did tell me about your experiences in battle," said William, remembering the first days of his capture.

"Well, we can remedy that pretty quick," he replied. "See that sword hanging on the wall? That was given to me by a British officer—he was dead at the time—in a battle when I was only about fourteen years old. We had joined with other tribes and taken a dozen canoes full of warriors down the 'dark and bloody river'—the Ohio—to battle at Fort Duquesne—must have been about 1755 or '56. The French were our allies and called for help. There were between two thousand and three thousand British in that battle but they all stood out in the open. I've never seen anything like it before or since. Even squirrels know enough to hide in the woods. We shot them down like a flock of wingless geese, with arrows and bullets first, and then tomahawked the rest. Not many escaped.

"One of them was General Washington. My friend Red Hawk knew who he was and shot at him over and over again. Some said the Great Spirit protected him but Red Hawk later discovered his rifle was bent. I wondered when I heard that, if maybe the Great Spirit had something to do with bending the gun barrel."

The boys sat with mouths wide-open as Bigtree continued: "See that powder horn on the other wall?" He stepped over and lifted it by the strap off the nail in the log. "It's a buffalo horn carved by a Cherokee brave. That's his hunting dog's profile cut in it. That came from a warrior who captured me when we fought a bunch of them over hunting ground in Kentucky."

"How old were you then?" asked Big Kittles.

"Oh, I was a grown man but not much—maybe nineteen or twenty, not yet married. There were a couple hundred warriors in that fight on the Kentucky River. It was hand-to-hand—we all laid down our rifles and bows and arrows and fought with tomahawks. Everyone fought like wild stags butting their antlers until one gives up or dies. But nobody gave up and when night came all the warriors still living went back to their villages.

"Except me. Two Cherokee had me backed up against a tree and I was fighting with two tomahawks, swinging this way and that," he demonstrated with aggressive gestures as both boys ducked when his arms flailed around them.

"Then another one came up from behind and knocked me in the head. See this scar?" He pulled his scalp lock back and revealed a long raised mound of disfigured flesh. "They took me with them for days and finally came to one of their towns near the mouth of a river where they decided to kill me.

"When they started to paint me black for death an old woman pleaded for my life to replace her sons killed in battle. A month later I saw my chance to escape, grabbed the warrior's powder horn and gun and ran like a deer. I ran for three days with Cherokee in pursuit. I nearly starved. At the Ohio River I stopped and caught my breath, then prayed to the Great Spirit: O Homendezue, tamentare, tamentare. (Great Spirit, take pity on me, take pity on me.) Help a poor prisoner swim this river and get home to his own country. Then I tied my gun to my head and jumped in the cold water. Three moons later I walked into my village, weary and skinny but very thankful."

The boys listened with increasing awe as Bigtree reeled off one war story after another, pointing out a row of scalps hanging from a post, a silver dollar made into an ear-bob and an Iroquois wampum belt—all trophies of different conflicts.

"You notice I am always the hero of these stories. That's because I'm telling them!" he guffawed, holding his sides.

As they walked out to go to the Council House, William asked Bigtree about the large two-story log house on the hill overlooking the lake.

"That's Tohunehowetu's wigwam—he's a sub-chief of the Deer Clan. You will meet him at the Council. He was a captive boy like you, William, many years ago."

When they entered the Council House there were already about twenty chiefs sitting cross-legged on deerskin and bearskin rugs. All were very quiet, some smoking their pipes but no one speaking.

William noticed a middle-aged man wearing a single eagle feather in his headband and colorful clothing, sitting next to a Big Turtle totem. Bigtree led him and Big Kittles over to sit with the Lenape chiefs and warriors while he went over to the group near the Bear post.

After the preliminary rites, one by one the leaders of different tribes stood and gave impassioned speeches. Mostly they were proclaiming the weakness of the Long Knives (American settlers) and the sure victory of the British. Big Kittles interpreted what he could of the speeches but he only knew two languages well, Wendat and Lenape.

"They have about agreed to go to war on the side of the British," said Big Kittles after several hours of debate. "Most of the tribes already knowed what they was gonna do but they had to bring a few others along."

When the Council was over he and William walked out amid the important representatives. William felt a hand on his shoulder and looked up at the man he had seen by the Big Turtle pole.

"Hello, William," the man said, "I am Tohunehowetu—Adam Brown." The man was tall and thin, perhaps in his forties. His fine brown hair was combed across the head and his face was gaunt and leathery. "I've heard about you," he said to William. "I was a captive child, also, like you and Big Kittles. Why don't you boys come up to my yeanoughsha—my house—and have some supper. I'll introduce you to my family."

They accepted the invitation happily and soon were feasting in the beautiful two-story log house on the hillside. "See that trunk in the corner?" Big Kittles said to William. "That's where the tribe's important treaty-belts and parchments and stuff is kept. He's keeper of the tribal archive."

William noticed a crucifix on one wall and a large framed picture of the King of England on another. Tohunehowetu prayed a blessing before the food was served.

"This is my wife, Lady Scanonie (Peace)," he said. She is Irish-French-Wyandot."

They sat on the porch and ate, looking out over Lake Erie—Erige as the Wyandot called it—Lake of the Cat. The boys tried not to eat like pigs but they couldn't help devouring the sumptuous meal shared with them by the Brown's—roast boar with wild rice, fry-bread and baked winter pumpkin—all they could eat.

"You know," Chief Brown said to them after the meal, "I knew some Walker's in Virginia. I've been in touch with my birth family in recent years who are neighbors of the Walker clan that lives along Walker Creek in Rockbridge County. Is that your people, William?"

He had a strange feeling in the pit of his stomach. "Yes! My father is John Walker who lived near Broad Creek, a few miles from most of the family. But they all are my cousins and uncles. You know them?"

"I do," said Brown. "It is a fine family. My brother and I used to spend the night with your mother and father when we were quite young—before you were born. I know exactly where the house is on Broad Creek."

Scanonie continued to clean and carry the food back in from the porch, a baby bundled up on her back and couple of other children playing around them. "That is my oldest son, Tasatee—sometimes we call him Samuel," said Adam. The little girl came over and draped her arm over his knee. "And this is my daughter Seketa (Honey) who is eight. The little girl on her mother's back has no name yet—we just call her Yaweetsentho (Girl) until a name sticks to her by a happening."

A young brave walked in the doorway.

"This is my son Adam, jr., who is the same age as you." The young Adam came over and shook hands with the other boys.

His father went inside the house and came back with a book bound in leather. As the children gathered around him, the older ones seated on the floor with their mother, Chief Brown began to read a chapter from the Bible.

They sat and talked for a long while after the sun had set. When the air began to chill them, Tohunehowetu insisted they spend the rest of the night there. The next morning Chief Brown had a surprise for William. "How would you like to come and live as one of my sons?"

ӾӾӾӾӾ

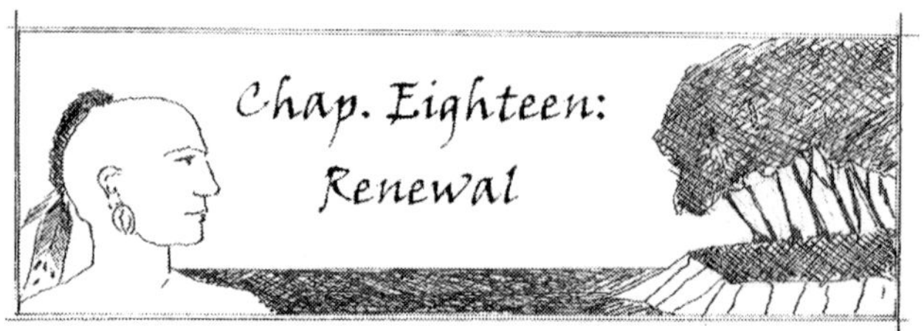

For several days William had been mulling over the thought of accepting Brown's offer. He did not have a restless spirit—something inside him wanted to find a place and put down roots. If he couldn't return to Virginia and his former life, he would just as soon stay put on the Tuscarawas. It had taken him a year and a half to learn Lenape and the Delaware ways. He had friends there and he felt fairly safe among them.

Yet he was also aware that life seemed to change whether one stayed put or not. Moonshower was talking about moving to the Moravian town and taking him along. While he was not anti-religious he wasn't interested in becoming a slave to it either. Dancing-Fire was also gone. Big Kittles was apparently going to stay with his people now, the Wyandot who had originally captured him. There was not much left for him with the Lenape.

"What has been going on in your head, William?" asked Adam Brown as they sat on his porch looking out at the water. Adam took a draw on his pipe and waited for the answer.

"Chief Brown—er, Tohunehowetu—I have been very sad at the thought of starting over in a new tribe with a language I do not know. Yet I think I would be happy here if you really want me. It is a very beautiful and peaceful place. Do you think I could learn to be a Wyandot pretty soon?"

The chief took a long drag on his pipe and exhaled the aromatic smoke. It seemed to hang in midair and ascend lazily towards the white clouds above them as if seeking its own in its own sweet time. William enjoyed the flavorful tobacco. It reminded him of the smell of his father's Virginia pipe. He wondered where his father was and if he could ever find him this far away.

Brown let him alone with his thoughts for a moment or two then gently said, "William you can adjust to anything life sends your way. The good Lord above has made you that way. I wouldn't want to pressure you to make this decision but if you choose to come be my son, I will help you. It won't be easy—the Delaware will not want to part with you. You have taken the place of one of their lost warriors and they think of you as a citizen of their own nation. If you want it—and God wills it—we can make it happen."

"I think I'd like that very much," the boy replied.

The chief put his hand on William's shoulder and looked into his eyes, remembering his own childhood. Tears welled up as he said simply, "Welcome home."

Tohunehowetu went immediately to talk with Chiefs Hopacan and Wingenund, as he knew they would be leaving soon. He had guessed correctly—they were not at all happy about his request. They argued about it for some time and finally decided to call a Council of the Wyandot and Delaware clan chiefs who were still there.

Chief Tohunehowetu (Brown) spoke first. "William Walker has been a member of your tribal family for nearly two years. Before that, he lived among the Long Knives in Virginia. I was well acquainted with his family there when I was a youth. His father and mine are close friends—like uncles and nephews.

"He is very appreciative of how he has been loved and accepted into your nation but he tells me that Moonshower his mother is planning to remarry and move to another village. One of his good friends has died of sickness and the past winter has been devastating to all of you. If you will allow me to adopt William as my son, I will be able to send trade goods and supplies that will benefit many Dasayane' (Delaware) families. The Great Spirit has brought him to us and he has been a blessing to you, so let him be to the Wyandot Nation. I am asking for this favor—that you leave William here when you return to the Muskingum."

After some moments of silent meditation on the proposal, Chief Hopacan (Pipe) stood to address the assembly. In his eloquent and forceful manner he said, in sum: "We understand your desire that William Walker become your adopted son. He is loved by our nation and in less than two years has learned our customs and language. He even plays stickball."

The delegates chuckled and murmured, "Hoh! Eh! Eh!" around the circle.

"Now we cannot think of selling someone who is a part of our family. He is an adopted son, not a slave or buffalo calf. It would be unthinkable and a breach of custom for this thing to happen. We could never explain it to his family or village."

Tohunehowetu (Brown) had known Chief Hopacan for a long time. He was aware of the chief's reputation for manipulation, politics and exploiting opportunities to get his way. He assumed that Hopacan was most interested in how much he could get for the hungry Lenape, and save face at the same time.

Again, Brown waited for some moments of silent reflection. Then he rose and passionately spoke: "Chief Hopacan speaks the truth—we do not sell a son or daughter. That would be a travesty! It would bring shame to all of us.

"Yet we know that family members sometimes are allowed to live with relatives. When a Lenape brave marries a Wyandot woman, for instance, he goes to live among her people—does he not?"

The delegates nodded and made sounds of agreement.

"And aren't we uncles and nephews—relatives? Now we have agreed to become allies. William Walker is asking to come and live with a relative and long-time family friend. What harm is there in that? I've seen him noticing some of our young maidens—he will probably marry a Wyandot woman, anyway." The men laughed and relaxed, exchanging whispered conversation—except Chief Hopacan who sat stone-faced still.

Tohunehowetu continued, "Of course it would not be right to pay wampum as if he were being purchased. However, knowing the difficulty your nation has experienced and the lack of trade from the Americans—allow us to send several canoes full of supplies to help ease your burdens, from your compassionate and sorrow-filled uncles."

After a few others spoke, Chief Hopacan resumed the floor: "Uncle, your words are good and full of understanding. Our hearts are mending from the wound of losing one of our own braves. Now we see the benefit to young William. We want only the best for him. The gift you propose would be a great kindness and save many who are weak and sick in our villages.

"You also have friends at Ft. Detroit. Speak to the British officer and tell him that many gifts at this time would assure our continued loyalty. As your nephews we would accept whatever your heart tells you to send to those who have cared for Walker these past moons. Remember how much they have sacrificed to bring him strong and healthy to this place." The deal was made, with assurances of British aid from Tohunehowetu.

Brown got the message and loaded six canoes with trade goods, food, bullets and powder and European clothing. He wondered whether any of it would actually benefit Moonshower or her old neighbors. There were a lot of needy people between here and there.

William tried to hide his excitement when he heard the news from Chief Hopacan. Hardship and poverty, sickness and death seemed far away as he began his new life—the adopted son of Adam Brown.

For several nights following, the family of Tohunehowetu gathered after sundown in the log house. They sat around the central fire on the earthen floor, or sometimes on pieces of bark that Scanonie placed around the room. The time was set apart for getting acquainted or, as Seketa put it, "Let's sit down and make friends."

The children took turns telling about themselves. Adam jr., the oldest, said, "I want to be a chief someday, like my father only not just a clan chief. I want to be head man over the whole nation! I like to hunt. I like fishing but only if they are biting pretty quickly, or I can spear them in the streams. Last year I speared the biggest pike anybody had ever seen. Do you play baggataway?" he asked William.

"No I only know stickball," he answered.

After his father translated, Adam jr. said, "It's the same thing. We will have some real fun and I can't wait to beat you. Then we can team up against the other boys."

William nodded and turned to Seketa. "How did you get your name?"

She giggled while her father explained in English, "It means honey or maple sugar."

Seketa said, "When I was just a toddler I found a big bowl of honey my mother was saving for breakfast. She had put it up on the little table. I pushed a wooden ammunition box underneath it, climbed up and pulled the bowl over on top of my head. Flies followed me around for days—father said they should have called me 'Bugs,'" she snickered. "What about you, Wil-yam, where did you get your name?"

"Well I don't think I know. Our names in Virginia were given to us at birth. Maybe I had a grandpa or uncle with that name, I don't know. But with the Lenape I was called 'Pemsit.' It means 'man who walks'; I was given it just because my name in English is also Walker. But just call me William."

Scanonie said, "And I don't know why I am named 'Peace.' It was also given to me when I was very small—I guess I slept a lot and didn't cry so much. Tohunehowetu started calling me 'Lady Scanonie' because my grandfather was a French trader and I guess he thought it sounded French."

"No," said Adam, "it is because you are a real lady—strong but gentle." She smiled and kissed his cheek and the children all clapped their hands.

Adam, sr., said, "Let me tell you my story, or at least a little bit of it. I was born in Virginia about twenty years before you, William, and captured by Wyandot warriors when I was perhaps ten or eleven. My memory is sharp about events at that time though I struggle to speak English. I had an older brother with your name. He was captured at the same time I was but soon escaped. My mother and stepfather were both killed. I never heard from my brother again until a few years ago. He located me through a British trader before the Revolutionary War began and begged me to return to Virginia. Said he'd give me half the family land for a farm. I thanked him and hoped to see him again, but told him I couldn't go back there.

"I am a Wyandot and my wife and children are Wyandot. Would they be accepted among the Long Knives? I've heard too many stories of Indians being murdered, even peaceful ones like Chief Cornstalk and Chief White Eyes. You know the Americans murdered him, don't you? He didn't die of smallpox, I'm sure of it. I'm sorry, William, I don't mean to insult your people.

"Years ago I took an oath to support the King of England and I see no reason to go back on my word. I pray for peace and hope the whites can end their warfare—it always involves us.

The land is big enough for us all." William gave a nod to show he was listening.

"Now I would like to tell you about something else—about how the Wyandot/Wendat people came to be. This is the legend that has been told by our people for hundreds of years. There was once a giant turtle that grew so old and large, moss began to gather on his back. The animals, the deer, wolf and others collected dirt and planted trees and food-bearing vegetation on his back, turning it into an island as he swam about. This was to prepare a place for Aataentsic the original woman who fell out of the sky onto the giant turtle. That is where all her descendants live, the place we call earth.

"Some are called by the clan of one animal or another. The Wyandot were the Big Turtle people. The French gave us the name Huron."

Seketa interrupted him, "Father, read us the story about you and Aataentsic. Please?" Her father laughed. "You mean Adam in the Bible? That was Adam and Eve, the first man and woman in the creation."

"Well," she replied, "some people have a lot of names. Maybe her name was Aataentsic also."

He laughed again. "Well I guess the Garden of Eden could have grown on the giant turtle's back—but I'm not quite old enough to be that Adam." He reached over to a small table and picked up the deerskin leather book.

"You see, William, the Black Robes brought us the Bible and taught us about the Creator, the Great Spirit. They lived among the Indians, loved us and suffered with us in order to bring us the message of Christ. For generations most of the Wyandot were Catholic Christians but the Black Robes have been gone a long time. Many of our people have gone back to the old ways.

"Scanonie and I are committed to our Catholic faith, however. We read the Scriptures every evening to our children—as the Moravians taught us. He opened to Genesis and read of the creation, then led in family devotions as they all brought out their prayer beads and moved them one by one on a string as they recalled the order of prayers.

Seketa let William share her beads as they prayed. Then she put her arms around his neck and said, "Yunowmoie, Wil-yam haenyeha." (I love you, my brother William.)

)()()()(

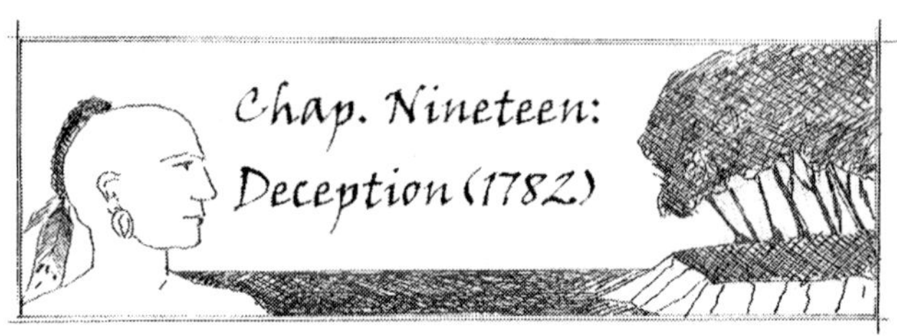
Chap. Nineteen:
Deception (1782)

By the spring of 1781, Col. Brodhead had assumed command of the garrison at Ft. Pitt. He received a secret message from Rev. John Heckewelder that Chiefs Pipe (Hopacan) and Wingenund were leading the Delaware to war against Americans.

Deciding to make a preemptive strike, he gathered an army of three hundred militia and Continental soldiers and attacked the Delaware capital at Coshocton (Goschachgunk). They captured and executed about fifteen warriors, while troops burned the cabins, destroyed chickens and forty head of cattle and plundered anything else of value. Some elderly men, women and children were taken captive.

John Gelelemend (Killbuck) —the pro-American chief run out of town by Chief Hopacan—was now Colonel William Henry, scout and interpreter under Brodhead's command. "Listen!" said Killbuck as he and Brodhead walked around the village. "Hear the sounds coming from across the Muskingum?" Chief Killbuck had a band of about twenty warriors who followed him when he left the Lenape Council in disgrace a couple of years before. He still held a grudge against Chief Hopacan for undercutting his authority and turning the Council members against him and the Americans. He cupped a hand to his ear. "Those are warriors celebrating some kind of raid on a settlement—and they're pretty drunk."

Col. Brodhead replied, "We better go finish them off before they bring more. We were fortunate to find little opposition and Coshocton nearly deserted."

"No way across the river right now," said Killbuck. Give my warriors and me some time to round up canoes. We'll wait until late tonight when they quiet down and fall into a drunken stupor. Then it will be, as you say, 'easy pickins.'"

About an hour after midnight under the eerie light of a half-moon, Killbuck and his crew boarded the half-dozen canoes they had found in the village. Their soft moccasins trod silently as they slid the boats on shore. The night seemed strangely calm except for the hoot of an owl as the revelers slept in careless rest, scattered around the remnants of a campfire. Killbuck and his men bashed one skull after another almost without resistance and left a bloodbath behind them as they paddled back across, belts laden with scalps of their Lenape kin and neighbors. Killbuck felt a sense of satisfaction. "They should have listened to me when they had the chance," he muttered to himself.

A few miles away at Gnadenhutten the Moravian Christians were still bringing in bushels of corn that had been left in the fields all winter. "This is no less than a miracle from God," said Moonshower, carrying a basket on her head.

Joseph, walking beside her, agreed. "The Book says, 'I have not seen the righteous forsaken, nor his seed begging bread,'" he quoted. "He provides for the sparrow, how much more for His children?"

They stopped to rest a moment and Moonshower put down her basket. "Joseph," she said, "I have never been happier than during the last two years. I never believed anyone could love me, even God. You have shown me His love through yours. I love you, Joseph!"

Joseph and Moonshower had married shortly after the Brown family adopted William. Rev. John Heckewelder the Moravian missionary and Rev. John Bull—Joseph's father—performed the ceremony. They were back in Gnadenhutten—Dutch for "Dwellings of Grace"—on the Tuscarawas River after spending their first two years of marriage some distance west at the settlement known as Captive's Town.

The Christian Delaware, though pacifists, had been forcefully removed by Hopacan from the Moravian towns when the tribe allied with Britain. There was some fear they might give secret intelligence to the Americans. Fifty of them had been allowed to return to Gnadenhutten in hopes of salvaging some of their corn and other supplies. They were surprised at how much of the corn was still good. They were still gathered around the village center sorting the cobs and shucking them one evening when visitors arrived.

"We have come to warn you to leave this place," Chief Buckongahelas said in a gentle tone. "Chief Hopacan told you it was too dangerous here."

Abraham, the village chieftain, stood and walked over to the dozen warriors. "You are welcome, brothers! We do not have much to offer but what we have is gladly shared with you."

"We don't need anything from you," replied Buckongahelas, "but thank you for your welcome. I want you to live to welcome me again some day. The Americans want to kill us all—have you not seen the smoke from their fires almost within sight of your towns? Should this not be sufficient warning to you that you would seek safety? Come with me, brothers.

"I will take you to a place where your fields will yield better crops, where there is abundant game, where the Long Knives will no longer molest you. You can dwell in peace and safety—I myself will live between you and them, and they will not even frighten you. There you can worship your God without fear."

Abraham replied, "It is with great respect and love that we thank you for your concern—but we know and trust the

Americans. We read the same Bible and pray to the same Christ. We are sorry you and Chief Hopacan (Pipe) have chosen the way of war and broken the commandment of God. We are happy to be back in our homes and we do not want to move anywhere again unless God leads us to do so. Do not worry about us but go your way in peace."

Buckongahelas nodded and backed away saying, "We must respect your right to choose—but I fear you have made a wrong decision that you will all regret very soon—if you live."

~~~

Across the Ohio River in Washington, Pennsylvania—about a two-day march from Gnadenhutten—several settlers were meeting in the Tenmile Tavern. "It ain't right," said a heavy-set, middle-aged man. "Them Injuns kin git a free ride jist by callin' themselves Christians."

"Yeah, and ever damned horse-thief says the same thing," chimed in another.

"Look," said the first man to a room full of eavesdroppers, "we got a bunch on the warpath what comes clean across Ohio from Sandusky. They hits us here and at Wheeling. You know how they kin ride that far, attack and git back home safely? They got a re-supply and rest stop halfway—the Moravian villages. And our gov'ment won't allow us to take 'em out!"

As the pot continued to simmer a man walked in the tavern who soon brought it to a rolling boil. He was John Carpenter—a
~~~

neighboring homesteader—known by all to have been kidnapped by Indians two weeks before. He looked like a man risen from the grave.

While excitement stirred at Tenmile Tavern, a Shawanese (Shawnee) war party arrived outside Gnadenhutten. A few days before, they had burned the cabin and outbuildings of the Wallace family on Raccoon Creek while the father was away. His wife, baby and two sons were taken captive and forced to flee in haste with the warriors heading towards the Ohio River, then to a path leading to the Muskingum. The infant cried incessantly so both mother and child were tomahawked, the woman scalped and impaled on a sharpened sapling by the trail.

Upon reaching Gnadenhutten they boasted about their bloody business and displayed the two young boy captives. Joseph spoke harshly to the leaders of the war party. "You have endangered our whole community by coming here," he scolded. "We will give you what food we have—as Christians should—but we bid you leave immediately and return to your own towns. I would further plead with you to leave the two boys with us, where they will be treated kindly and returned to their own people very quickly."

The Shawanese agreed to leave, but adamantly refused to give up their prisoners.

On the way out of the village, several of the braves showed utensils and clothing to the women. "We cannot carry so much with us," they said, "but we will be glad to sell them for very little—even some of your corn."

Moonshower was so pleased with her new calico dress she hardly noticed the small brown splatters of dried blood on the lower backside of the garment.

Later that day Joseph came home to their bark wikwames and saw her wearing the dress. "Where did you get that?" he demanded in a scolding tone of voice.

Moonshower was surprised—she'd never heard him speak that way before. She said nothing, but Joseph continued to scold: "That is not a dress for a Christian wife to wear—it is not the plain clothes of a humble believer. What will the others say? Take it off and get rid of it."

Moonshower felt her heart beating faster. "I will not! God provided it for me—it only cost a few ears of old corn."

Now it was Joseph's turn to be shocked at her tone of voice. "God? God? God will have nothing to do with a wife who speaks to her husband disrespectfully. The Bible says..."

She interrupted him, "Don't quote the Bible to me all the time. I can't read the verses like you do, but I know God makes the world full of light and color. He can't hate such a pretty cloth as this dress. Since you brought me back here, everything has been drab. Life was hard enough at Captive's Town but at least we had a little more than corn. Why did you insist on coming back here?"

Joseph's face flushed and his eyebrows tensed. "Enough, woman!" he shook his finger at her. "I will hear no more of this matter. My decisions come from much prayer and faith—it is obvious you have little of either one."

Moonshower did not have the words with which to argue against his, so she used the ability she had relied on in the past. She reached for an iron kettle, raised it over her head with both hands and threw it at him.

Joseph dodged to the side but it struck him on one shoulder and he let out a yell—"Yeeow!" He flew out the door, yanking the bearskin down as he went. Confused by his own rage he spent the night in the horse shelter. He couldn't get the scripture out of his head: "Be ye angry, and sin not: let not the sun go down upon your wrath."

"Forgive me, Lord," he prayed, "but I will not go back and talk to that woman until I've been mad longer than this!"

~~~

About the same time, a band of Delaware warriors was arriving to a boisterous welcome at the Upper Sandusky village of Wingenund's Town. As the local women and children crowded around them, the triumphant warriors rode in, waving pieces of clothing and shouting the war cry. The women scrambled to catch dresses and hats, the booty of attacks made on settlers. Women and children alike paraded around in
~~~

whatever garments they were able to acquire as the warriors continued to toss them into the crowd.

Later the braves shared their exaggerated exploits with the elders around the Council fires. They were especially proud of one bit of deceptive strategy.

The chiefs were all ears as a brave named Damaskus (Muskrat) explained it, “You all know the problem we’ve had with the Christian Lenape called Moravians.”

Chief Hopacan (Pipe) grunted a hearty assent. Damaskus continued, “Our chiefs convinced them to leave their towns near the Ohio and start a new village at Captive’s Town. We left them in peace to pray to their God and till the rich soil while we lost many brave men attacking the Long Knives where they live, keeping them away from our land.

“Now, you know that some asked to return to Gnadenhutten and salvage what’s left of their corn, and then more of them slipped away and went back.” The men shook their heads and made exclamations of disgust.

“We know that the missionaries are warning the Americans before we attack. The Moravian Lenape are also feeding the horses and giving food to the enemy. It is a big problem!”

The elders said, “Eh, eh!” and nodded in agreement.

“Here is our plan,” said Damaskus. “We are sowing seeds of distrust between the Long Knives and the Moravians. Some days ago we captured a man named Carpenter and two of our braves made sure he heard them talking about being Christians. They wore crosses around their necks, slapped him around and beat him severely. They even spoke sounds like the Dutch—as if the missionaries had taught them. Ja, ja," he mimicked, to the group's delight.

"We talked about killing him when we got back to the village. We all acted tired the next morning and sent him to fetch the hobbled horses—knowing he would run. If the settlers attack the Moravian towns, it will unite all Lenape and the Five Nations in a strong desire for vengeance."

Chief Hopacan (Pipe) stood and gave an eloquent accolade to the warriors, concluding, "I stand tall with pride—you have out-Piped Pipe!"

)()()()()(

The settlers at Tenmile Tavern were amazed at John Carpenter's story of escape. He was tall and thin—emaciated by his recent ordeal and still somewhat in shock. Energy seemed to flow into him, however, while he recounted the events.

The others sat in wide-eyed silence as he spun the tale. "I was out digging for ginseng roots in the woods when all of a sudden I heard a war whoop and looked up.

"I found myself surrounded by a dozen Delaware warriors with spears and rifles aimed directly at my chest. I raised my hands in surrender and they put a garrote 'round my neck and dragged me choking along with them down a path that led to the Ohio River. We swum it with two horses they stole, me gagging for air the whole time. That night I heard 'em talkin' about how they would burn me when they got home.

"Two of 'em what wore crosses around their necks beat me pretty bad. They said, 'Why wait to get back to Sandusky? Our home is closer, just yonder at Gnadenhutten. We can burn him there.' They said I wasn't a good Christian and deserved to die. I heard 'em talk pretty good Dutch a time 'er two."

The men began cursing and shouting, angry at the "soft-hearted and fool-headed government" that was protecting these Moravian savages. "Men, what are we waiting for?" said one of the leaders. "If we wait any longer they'll burn all our homes and carry our children off to become warriors against us."

"Form a militia immediately!" another demanded. Expressing their sympathy to Carpenter, they all headed to Fort Pitt insisting that action be taken without delay.

The commandant at Ft. Pitt, Col. Gibson, had just recently assumed command from Col. Brodhead who was under charges for malfeasance of office. Gibson was also concerned about the Moravian Delaware in the nearby villages.

He met with the militiamen as soon as they arrived from Washington, Pennsylvania. "I can see you are up-in-arms about this situation," he remarked, noticing John Carpenter in the group. "As I told John a few days ago, we are going to need a force of about one-hundred men to enforce compliance with our orders. I intend to put the whole village under command to vacate the area. They will be compelled to either remove farther west to Sandusky or come back to Ft. Pitt for relocation. We cannot take the risk of leaving safe refuge for the hostiles to use.

"At the same time, we do not want to harm peaceful and friendly Indians."

A murmur went through the group of settlers.

One of the men spoke out loud, "Better wipe them out—you know they can't be trusted. Once an Indian, always an Indian!"

The others concurred with shouts of "Yeah!" and "Burn 'em out like they done Carpenter!"

Gibson motioned for the men to calm down and spoke once they were silent. "You men form a militia and report back to me within two days."

He nodded towards an officer standing nearby, "I believe you all know Col. David Williamson from your own county. I'm giving him command of the operation. Col. Williamson you will have full authority over a force of militia—at least a hundred, probably one-fifty. I trust you to assess matters once you are in the location and act with your best training and judgment. You do understand my wishes?"

"Yes, sir," saluted Williamson. The settlers returned to the countryside to spread the word. Soon, a force of one-hundred and sixty men was marching towards Gnadenhutten.

~~~

Joseph awoke early from an almost sleepless night in the horse pen. As he staggered to the entrance he realized he'd left a log loose that served as a gate to the shelter. Several horses had wandered out and were nowhere to be seen. He brushed
~~~

the loose hay from his shirt and trousers and headed towards his bark house, knowing he might as well try to patch things up with his wife before it got worse. He didn't like the angry feelings that had shared his bed that night. A scripture verse also haunted him—something about "giving honor to your wife...that your prayers be not hindered."

Moonshower was outside sweeping around the wikwames, wearing the same calico dress. "Moonshower," he said, "I am sorry—truly, truly sorry." I have not been a husband long and I am not used to it. I don't know how to make you respect me. The dress is not my choice—but you are. You mean more to me than clothing, which is of no importance, anyway. Please, from now on, stop throwing kettles and talk with me instead." Then he added, "If you have to throw something let it be a blanket or a moccasin."

She turned her back so he couldn't see her smile. She thought to herself, "After today, I'll give this dress away."

She turned to Joseph and said, "I would embrace you—but you smell like a horse." He grabbed her in a bear hug as she tried to push him away, both laughing like children teasing. Then he was off to find the stray ponies—feeling right with God.

Joseph trailed the horses through the woods and stepped out onto a warrior's trail. He was surprised to see a group of mounted men—part of Williamson's militia—just a few feet away. He was glad for the surprise visitors, especially

Americans. As he decided how best to greet them, a rifle blast spun him around and knocked his leg out from under him. Baffled by the unexpected attack and knowing these were Americans, he stammered for words. Surely, he thought, they have mistaken me for a hostile.

"Don't shoot!" he yelled, "I'm Joseph Sabosh—my father is John Bull, a minister. I am a Christian!" Several men gathered around him. One rested the muzzle of his rifle on Joseph's chest, stared into his eyes and squeezed the trigger.

The gunshots alerted the villagers, some working the cornfield on one side of the river, the others doing sundry tasks on the other. Unaware of any possible danger, they greeted the militiamen with their usual hospitality to strangers. The Indians were informed that the Americans had come only for their safety and comfort.

Charles Bilderback, who had just killed Joseph, assured them, "If you will turn in your weapons we will escort you out of harms way to Ft. Pitt, and see that your needs are met from then on."

A little boy tugged on his father's shirt. "What are they saying?" he asked with some anxiety.

"It's nothing to fear," replied the father, "They are offering us a chance to be free from Chief Pipe and the British. He says we will be allowed to go live at the fort in peace and security."

The armed men accompanied the group back to the village where they invited the others to join them.

As soon as the Indians were disarmed, they were divided into two groups, the men herded into a shed and the women and children into the chapel. When another group arrived from the nearby village of Salem, they joined the others, making a total of twenty-seven men, twenty-nine women, and thirty-four children of various ages.

While they waited in the buildings Williamson's men turned the town upside down searching for evidence of treachery. "Look at this!" hollered a private named Luke, leading a couple of ponies. "All these animals have brands on 'em. The Injuns don't use brands—these was taken from settlers." They brought two of the Moravian leaders outside and confronted them vehemently with the accusation.

An old man named Joshua spoke very softly and humbly: "We have adopted many customs from the missionaries—I will be glad to show you our branding irons in the blacksmith's shed."

"Liar!" Luke said, "You stole the irons, too."

Other men brought cloth sacks they had filled with kitchen utensils and dumped them on the ground in front of Joshua.

"See them tea kettles and pewter pitchers," said a rough-looking, pudgy militiaman the others called Slim. "Where'd you git them if it warn't by lootin' settlers?"

Again, Joshua answered calmly, "Those and the silver ladles were bought by Rev. Heckewelder from the traders."

Slim and his companions scoffed at the Indians. "Good thing you got them missionaries to blame," said Luke.

Robert Wallace was with the raiding party. Because he'd been riding up front on the trail leading to Gnadenhutten, he was one of the first to see his wife's body impaled on the sharp tree. When a volunteer opened up another sack, Wallace grabbed Joshua by the shirt collar and spit in his face. "That sack of stuff came right out of my cabin! See that kettle with the broke handle? My boys dropped that on a rock just days ago, the boys your friends kidnapped. Don't tell me the missionary bought that for you!"

Joshua stammered, realizing it was one of the pieces the Delaware warriors had tossed out or sold for corn when they were leaving.

While they were confronting the men with the articles, Wallace saw Moonshower at the chapel door, comforting a little girl. "My wife's dress!" he shouted. "By God, she's wearing my wife's calico dress!" Moonshower, startled by Wallace's yell but not understanding him, caught the girl's hand and quickly closed the door, further infuriating the man.

Col. Williamson, being regular army, had little authority over the men. He called them all to stand in formation. A vote was the democratic way of deciding the thing. "All of you who want to return these captives to Ft. Pitt to be kept under watch of the government forces, move foreword three steps." Eighteen of the men stepped out in front. Over a hundred stood still, voting for execution. Nearly all of them had lost close relatives, friends and neighbors—some of them tortured and mutilated—by raiding Indians. The eighteen were dismissed to reconnoiter the next village.

Slim was chosen to inform the Indians of their fate. Inside the men's shed he motioned for quiet and simply said, "You are all gonna pay for what you've done. The evidence points to guilt and you have been sentenced by military court to die tonight." The Moravian Delaware stood totally silent for a long time. "Did you understand me?" shouted Slim.

Joshua stepped forward. "We heard but we do not understand. If there is no way out, we would ask for time to pray and prepare our hearts for death. We are Christians and not afraid to die."

Slim started to curse but Col. Williamson arrived and stopped him. "The sentence will be carried out at dawn—you will have this night to prepare."

Some of them began singing a death song. Others sang the Psalm, "Though I walk through the valley of the shadow of death, I will fear no evil, for Thou art with me." The militiamen left and bolted the door.

The singing alerted the women and children in the chapel. Soldiers bound their hands behind them to prevent escape and they spent the night in prayers and singing hymns until, one by one, they fell into an exhausted sleep.

The next morning several men found a cooper's wooden mallet and took turns smashing the kneeling men in the back of the head and scalping them. The first man killed fourteen, then announced his arm was "wore out" and handed off the mallet to another who continued the bloody work.

When they finished the slaughter there, they turned to the chapel and began murdering the women and children. Beginning with the oldest wrinkled grandmother they systematically worked their way down the line until all twenty-nine women—representing the elderly, some widows, the young (a few of them pregnant)—as well as boys and girls under twelve, all of them were murdered.

Luke took special enjoyment over killing two boys about twelve years old. "This is for Wallace's missing boy," he said, swinging the hammer in a wide arc that ended at the boy's small head. "And this is for the other one," he added, repeating the swing.

Private Johnston had felt guilty since he'd failed to vote to save the Indians. As he stood at the back of the crowded chapel, all eyes on the blood-splattered mallet, an eight-year old boy got free and ran wildly into him grasping him around the legs for dear life.

The boy looked up and said in broken English, "Pleeze! Hay-elp me!" Johnston began to weep as he looked down into the little boy's big frightened, pleading brown eyes. He scooped the boy into his arms, bolted out the door, mounted his horse and left at a fast gallop for home.

All the scalps were laid out in a row on the church benches pushed along the back wall: long gray hair, a girl's jet-black braids, a boy's single scalp lock, an infant's tiny tussled strands. All of them were worth a nice bounty from the government of Pennsylvania—adult trophies a bit more valuable than a child's.

When the executions were finished and the other buildings looted, every edifice was set afire. The militia moved on to Salem and Schoenbrun, the two nearby Moravian Christian towns and burned them also. Smoke rose into the sky along the Tuscarawas, the fires turning the evening clouds a light orange—like a lantern reflecting off a plastered painted wall.

A young boy and girl had wriggled out of the ropes and slipped into the cellar, escaping through a small window.

A ten-year old named Thomas was hit in the head with the blunt end of a tomahawk and fell to the floor. The man underestimated how hardheaded Thomas was, or else his arm was tired from being overworked. Blood poured from the gash but Thomas was not even knocked unconscious though he pretended to be dead. Even when the scalper's knife cut around the top of his head and the hair and skin was yanked off with a popping sound he was silent. While attention was drawn to the other victims Thomas managed to work his hands loose and dash for the door. The men let him go, no doubt thinking he wouldn't last long.

~~~

When word reached the new Moravian settlement at Captive's Town, a Mr. Weiss wrote a letter to the Bishop in Pennsylvania describing briefly the massacre. The Bishop was asked to make a statement to Congress, which he did—concluding with Weiss's letter. Weiss had penned, "The tragic scenes...and killing in cold blood 95 browne or tawny sheep of Jesus Christ, one by one, is certainly taken notice of by the Shepherd, their Creator and Redeemer."

~~~

A week or so later at the Detroit village, Adam Brown welcomed visitors—one of them a boy named Thomas. He wore a white cloth lightly over the top of his head to cover the exposed rounded bone. William sat in unbelieving awe as he listened to Thomas' story. As the boy spoke Lenape, William understood him well. He ended by saying, "I just kept walking and praying even though my head ached so bad. Why did they do it? We have always loved the Americans. Why would they want to hurt us? Don't they know Jesus?"

Thomas kept fiddling with the gold cross on a strap about his neck. Adam went over and put his arms around the boy. "Not all white men are Christians and not all are good. There are evil men and women in every nation. Remember—there were people who tortured and killed the Son of God and laughed as He suffered. But He rose from the grave and conquered death. 'Blessed are the dead who die in the Lord.'

"God has helped you live to tell this story, to honor your people. We are here to help you heal and be strong again in your heart as well as your body."

William watched and listened. He felt sick and went out to the porch thinking of Moonshower—wishing he weren't white. Then he remembered his uncle's murder.

)()()()(

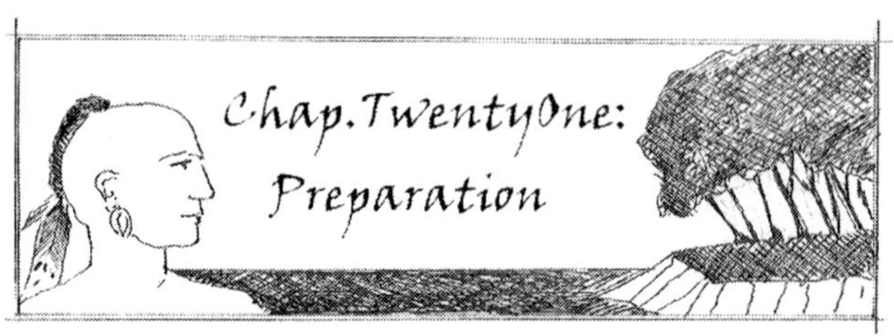

Chap. Twenty One: Preparation

Alex hobbled out behind the barn where his father was splitting green oak logs to season for next winter. "Look, Paw," he hollered, "I'm walkin' without a cane!" John Walker hailed his son's effort with a nod and a clicking sound from the side of his mouth.

"Pretty good job. How long's it been since you was shot? Three years?"

"Almost exactly," said Alex, now nineteen years old. I thought I'd never be able to put my weight down on it—somethin' just told me to go ahead and do it today."

His father put his hand on Alex's shoulder. "Let's talk a minute." They each turned a log up on end and sat down. "Son, I've been thinkin' lately I should go and make another search for William. Since the news of Cornwallis' surrender it's been fairly peaceful so far as the Revolution is concerned—just a matter of time before they make it official, I reckon. The battle at King's Mountain and then at Guilford's Courthouse took me away from home a good bit. I didn't want to leave again until you were able to help your mother."

"Paw, I don't want you to leave again—but I can handle anything that needs to be done here. Who knows what's happened to William—that's the worst part—not knowing. Do you have a plan?"

John took off his cap and wiped his brow with his sleeve. "Neighbor Cunningham rode by yesterday and told me there's a call for volunteers to gather at Mingo Bottom at the Ohio River in the next few days. The raids on Kentucky and other frontier settlements have got to be stopped once and for all. With the Brits out of the way there's a march planned all the way to the Wyandot villages on the Sandusky. Alex, I've got to go. I'd never forgive myself if there's even a chance William could be set free and I wasn't there to accomplish it."

The next day, having kissed Mary goodbye for the umpteenth time to head for battle, John Walker rode north towards his meeting in Kentucky.

~~~

The chiefs of the Wyandot clans who had taken their seats around the Council room at Sandusky town, were discussing recent events and future warfare when word came that a runner had arrived with urgent news.

He was breathing heavily as he related the situation: "I came....from Mingo....Bottom," he began—and was interrupted
~~~

by Chief Tedyata (Roundhead) the elder war-chief of the Detroit area around the British fort.

"Please stop and catch your breath so we can understand you," the chief demanded.

The runner took several deep breaths and continued. "Many settlers are gathering....there with the soldier.... Williamson, who slaughtered the Dasayane' at village Gnadenhutten."

The chief was excited. "This is a gift from the sky-spirit! It is the time to get vengeance for our massacred nephews!" He pointed to the runner: "Get some other braves and go in pairs. Spy out the trails and possible route of this army, from here to the Ohio. Send us reports every day—more often if necessary. This time they will not find us on our knees shucking corn."

Bigtree, who had become a war captain, spoke next. "You have anticipated this for many days," he said, raising his fist for emphasis and shaking his long silver-bobbed earlobes. The Long Knives will no doubt reach first the old village of Half-King's Town—which they will be surprised to find abandoned. Good planning, to move the people across the Sandusky River."

The chiefs and war captains responded a self-congratulatory "Eh! Eh!"

"Their puzzlement will delay them for a few hours—a day at most—and they will no doubt continue marching north. We must send messengers to our allies and seek urgent help."

Chief Pomoacan (Half-King) rose to speak. "Messengers have already left to alert the Delaware since their villages near the Sandusky are vulnerable. Several other braves will soon be on their way—our nephews the Miami's and the Shawanese. Others of the Five Nations will no doubt send a war party. I am also notifying the British commandant at Fort Detroit—Col. de Peyster—to send mounted troops and artillery if possible. Our spies are already along the trails from Mingo Bottom. The Long Knives have no doubt advanced some miles since the last report we received. I expect messengers to arrive twice a day or more, keeping us very well advised as to the location of the enemy and any changes in their strategies.

"You all know that I myself am like an angry mother bear, in the way of vengeance. My two sons that fell in the skirmish last year at Harmon's Creek are watching us. My blood relatives in the Dasayane' (Delaware) tribe are waiting. We must not fail them or our little ones!"

Captain Bigtree outlined some of the battle plans: "You are aware of the deep ravine along the trail south from Leith's Trading Post between it and the swamps. It is deep and wide enough to hide a hundred warriors on horseback. We will take a detachment of Wendat braves and join forces with Chief Wingenund and Chief Hopacan (Pipe) and the Dasayane' (Delaware) fighters there. If the enemy comes close enough in that direction—and they almost certainly will—a few warriors can try to decoy them into the hornets' nest. We shall swarm the Long Knives, avenge our brothers who were massacred, and teach them to stay south of the Ohio!"

~~~

About twelve miles north of Sandusky, across the bay, William and Big Kittles had just returned from a successful trip spear fishing on the Detroit River. William stepped up on the porch of the Brown cabin and greeted his new father: "Look at these catfish!" he exclaimed, holding up a string of half a dozen two-pounders. "Their bellies are all bloated with eggs."

Big Kittles had a similar mess on a string and Adam congratulated them both. "It's a good time of year to catch them when they're hungry. Looks like you made good use of your time. I can hardly wait to ask Scanonie to fry up those egg sacks for a crunchy treat at supper."

As the boys started to show off their catch to little Seketa and two other girls who were playing with her, a drumbeat sounded. The leading women and men of the village were being summoned to gather around the outside of the Council House. William and Big Kittles left their fish with the girls and followed Adam. Others, running from every direction towards the meeting, joined them.

The assembled leaders stood with their arms folded as Chief Myeerah (Walk-in-the-Water) stepped up on an oak stump to address them: "A runner has just arrived with an urgent
~~~

message from Chief Pomoacan (Half-King). Spies have discovered an army of settlers—with some soldiers—setting out from Mingo Bottom towards our villages at Sandusky. It is believed that Col. Williamson—who scalped, mutilated and burned the peaceful Moravians a few months ago—leads them. Our intelligence is they have around five-hundred mounted men and may arrive within the week. We need every able warrior to prepare his horse and equipment and be ready to ride south. We will go when the soldiers come from Fort Detroit to lead us. Return to your homes and prepare for war! We will meet tonight for the war-dance."

As they ran back to the cabin, Big Kittles asked William, "What're ya gonna do? Yur old enough to be a brave. Do ya think yur ready to fight?"

William shot back, "I've already been in battle against the Cherokee."

"That weren't no battle—it were jist a skirmish. This is gonna be big. It's gonna be agin yur own people, 'member. You ready fer that?"

William stopped walking and was silent, putting his hands over his face to think. Finally, he looked up. "Those settlers are as much your people as they are mine. Are you going to join the fight even against your own?"

"You bet! Ain't none of 'em done a thang fer me lately. If I ain't Wyandot now I ain't got nobody. Yur in the same fix whether ya knowd it er not."

Adam looked serious as the boys arrived at the cabin. "William," he said, "I just spoke with Chief Pomoacan about you. We need you to help us. We are your family now—your people. But we are not sure how you feel about fighting with the Indians and British against the Americans. You have been raised as a Dasayane' brave and now adopted as a potential Wendat warrior. But it must come out of your own heart and the Chief doesn't know your heart on this matter—whether you've been with us long enough to be loyal to the nation."

William again put his hands to his face and thought deeply. "My blood-kin are in Virginia," he said. "They are not these settlers or soldiers—these cowards who slaughtered women and children at their prayers and burned them alive." He looked over and saw the boy Thomas walk in, his head still raw and covered with scabs. "The Lenape accepted me, raised me and taught me for nearly three years. Moonshower loved me as her own son. Now you have adopted me as your own." Seketa put her arms around his neck and squeezed him.

"It is true my birth-father is a soldier against the British but he is a man of honor. There is no honor among these men who are riding to destroy our villages. If I did not fight against them I would also be without honor and without gratitude for the life I have been given. I am ready to join you in defending our honor, our families, and our nation."

"I am proud of you," said Adam. "Someday you will have your own wife and children here and then you will be very thankful you have shown courage this day and your sons and daughters will glow with pride in their father!"

Brown went with William and Big Kittles to speak with Chief Pomoacan. "I know," said Adam, "that the young man William Walker has only been with us a number of weeks. He has been a Dasayane' (Delaware) citizen longer and he wishes to be a part of their defense and of the Wendat Nation. I trust him and recommend him as a warrior."

The chief looked William over. "He is strong and agile—I've seen him play stickball! When his face has war-paint he will not be distinguished from any other brave."

Big Kittles commented, "I've never had no trouble fightin' fer us. Ain't no chance he'd git clost enough to go over to the enemy nohow. They'd shoot him dead afore he could say his name. Besides, them settlers is plumb gun-shy about bein' decoyed. They won't trust anything an Injun says. When I was twelve years old I used to let the braves tie me to a tree on a hill, then I'd shout down ta the whites passin' by in canoes or on horses, askin' 'em ta rescue me. When they'd come ta help, the warriors'd swoop down on 'em like a dawg on a bone. Weren't long, they got wise ta that ruse. Cain't fool 'em that way no more."

The two young men and Adam headed back to the cabin to prepare for departure as soon as the signal was given.

~~~

Col. Crawford had wanted to move out earlier but the recruits were slow arriving at Mingo Bottom. Finally, on May 25th—four days later than planned—he felt they were at full strength. Four hundred and sixty-six men with some still trickling in—hunters and trappers, farmers and their sons, and some soldiers—were ready. The troops were in a rowdy mood, greeting one another with tall tales and pranks—mostly dressed in buckskin and riding their own horses—carrying provisions from home to last a month, even counting a few guests.

They were divided into four groups of about one-hundred and twenty men each with an elected major in charge, and then crossed the Ohio River at a low point, winding their way north through the forests. It was a clear spring day, about two hours after sunrise.

One of the last to arrive had ridden hard to get there. He was a crack shot like most of the frontiersmen and a welcome addition to the troops. "If I hadn't gotten poor directions to the Bottom I'd been here two days ago," he said to one of the group of men drinking camp coffee around a fire before orders had come to move out. "Where should I sign up?"
~~~

One of them motioned with his tin cup, “See that tent up ahead? We just elected Col. Crawford to lead this expedition—I reckon he be the one to report to.” Col. Williamson had lost the vote by only five ballots.

“The colonel’s pretty busy at the moment but you can sign up right here,” said a heavy-set man sitting at the wobbly wooden table in front of the command tent. Can you write your name?”

The man nodded.

“Then sign on this paper with your current rank if you have one, and place of residence and I’ll give you a form for your last will and testament. It’s required. Fill it out in a hurry—we’re pullin’ out right soon.”

The volunteer wrote down “John Walker, ranger—Virginia.”

)()()()(

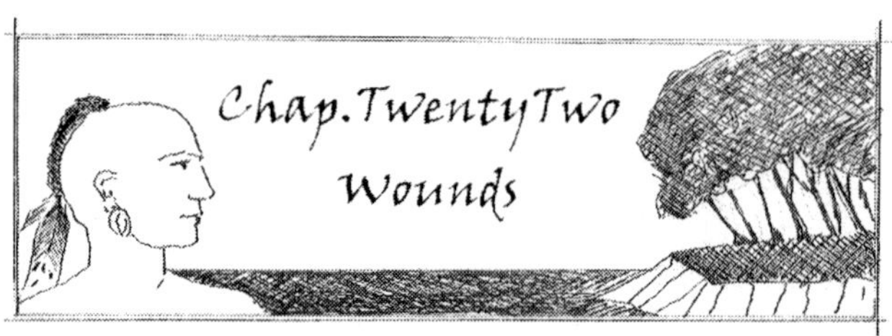

Chief Pomoacan (Half-King) met the messenger as he raced his pony into the village, stopping sharply in front of the chief's house. The two Delaware war chiefs—Pipe and Wingenund—were at his headquarters to plan the defense of their villages.

"The sarayumigh (Big Knives) have started their journey, like a huge snake twisting their way through the forests, avoiding the trails. They think they are invisible to us," the young messenger said with a smirk.

Pomoacan did not smile. "Do not underestimate them," he cautioned, "if your eyes are not like the eagle's, the soldiers may vanish in one place and suddenly reappear in another. Eat something for strength and return as fast as you came!"

"How long do you calculate it will take them to reach Sandusky Plains?" asked Pipe of the other chiefs.

"If they move swiftly," said Wingenund, "I would guess six days. But the frontiersmen are not disciplined warriors. Add about two days more to reach the abandoned villages."

Pomoacan rubbed his chin. "We can wait two days to learn the exact line of their march and still arrive at the big ravine several days ahead of them. Even if they move as rapidly as possible through the forests, that will give us a few days to rest and be prepared for confrontation. By that time our reinforcements should be arriving. We'll plan the war dance for two nights from now."

~~~

"Hey, Virginian!" yelled a man riding an appaloosa twenty feet behind John Walker. His loud shrill voice echoed through the forest as the long column of riders ducked low-hanging branches and coiled through the trees. "I was born in Virginia," hollered the man.

Walker turned and tried to see who was making the racket. "What's your name?" John called back.

"Ken-tuck!" the man shouted, "That's 'cause I don't wanna be called 'Virgin.'" Raucous laughter rolled through the woods, adding to the noise of clomping and whinnying horses. The trip was starting out more like a parade than a military march and the majors seemed unable to change it.

Most of the men were placed in companies with others not from their own regions but the march was so disorderly that many of them were soon riding beside friends and neighbors. Some had even grown up together so they were full of stories
~~~

and filled the forest with boisterous conversation and occasional pranks as the columns moved along.

A man in front of Walker was knocked off his horse because a close boyhood friend was riding in front and purposely bent a limb that, when he turned it loose, clobbered the man behind him square in the face.

He got up swearing and vowing revenge. "Better watch your back!" For fifty yards the line of march stopped to observe and then took time to join in some moments of unrestrained laughter.

At the front, Col. Crawford was not happy at all. He and Col. Williamson were conferring together in the command tent that night. "We've only traveled ten miles today. Ten miles! My plans were to average at least twenty-five," said Crawford, frustration evident in his voice.

Williamson shook his head, "These volunteer militias are a pain in the ass. I know most of the men in my squadron. The young ones think of this as a great adventure—they have no sense of military method. You have to remind them over and over again about the mission and strategy and the risks of ignoring either."

Crawford glanced at a letter he'd received earlier from Gen. Irvine at Fort Pitt which said, in part, "Your best chance of success will be, if possible, to affect a surprise." In the morning the commander gave a hand-written notice in large letters to one of his assistants. "Nail this to a tree in plain sight of the passing columns," he said, "I want every man to see it whether he can read or not." The flyer read: "Our success depends upon a RAPID and SECRET march!"

Four days later they came within sight of the Muskingum River. One of the three men riding four-abreast with Walker commented, "Up yonder is the Moravian town of Gnadenhutten. I rode with Williamson when we destroyed it and killed every one of those filthy redskins. Too bad we didn't get their white missionaries too. Any white man or woman that has lived with them very long should be tomahawked and cremated—it don't take long to get contaminated."

Walker gritted his teeth and slowed a pace or two so he could maneuver his horse in next to the man. He was continuing to spew out his hatred for Indians when Walker reached into his own pocket and wrapped his fingers around three silver shillings he carried. He swung his fist vigorously backwards into the man's open mouth, knocking him off his horse. He lay on his back spitting blood and teeth while the horses following reared up and tried to avoid trampling him.

At that moment a shout from the front of the column signaled that two Indians had been sighted on the flank. The militia was distracted long enough that Walker moved on ahead without as much as a reprimand from anyone. "That was for William," he muttered as the coins clanked inside his pocket.

They had only covered sixty miles when they reached the ruins of Gnadenhutten. Col. Crawford gathered his officers. "I am now convinced we have lost all hope of having the element of surprise. We must now push the troops to move more rapidly towards their goal to engage the Indians before they can make preparations for defense or receive reinforcements. Tell your men to gather what corn is still in the fields tonight because we must not delay departure at dawn." Six days later, traveling west-northwest, the front of the militia finally came in view of the Sandusky Plains, only twenty miles from their target village.

~~~

As the volunteers advanced towards what they thought was the main Wyandot village, they were too far away to hear the ominous sound of drums coming from several miles north. The sky over the newly built Half-King's Town was lit by torches as nearly five-hundred Wyandot and Delaware warriors stomp-danced and chanted in a circular line, moving around the central sacred fire-pit for hours. Screams echoed into the night, sending dogs scurrying under cabins and pigs squealing in fear.

Seventeen-year-old William Walker sweated under the red-painted marks lining his cheeks, forehead and chest, preparing to join courageously in the anticipated battle to come.

When the moon was high above them the last sounds of the war dance faded into the stillness of the night.
~~~

The forest around them was deadly silent for an hour or two, until gradually the creatures began to reclaim their natural habitat. Timidly at first the owls began their guttural calls, followed by nightingales and finally the wolves as they slipped back into the surrounding forest.

The warriors, who were fasting before the battle, slept an exhausted but restless sleep. William wrapped himself in a blanket under the stars and lay a long time trying to slow down from the frenetic activity of the evening and the excited fears about the morrow. At some point he slipped into a deep slumber—and dreamed....

An eagle flew from its nest at a high mountain cliff, and sailed carelessly across the sky. It viewed two camps in the plain below, one a village of permanent log cabins near tilled cornfields. The other camp consisted of many wigwams that were ever moving closer to the other camp. The eagle swooped down into the valley between the two and caught a white fawn in its enormous talons. It carried the small deer high up to the cliff and deposited it in its nest.

The deer suddenly began to grow into a strong antlered stag and leapt out of the nest, falling towards the valley below. Men in both camps began to shoot rifles and arrows at the white stag as it fell towards the earth. The missiles whizzed by without hitting the stag but it continued to fall. Then a single bullet struck it in the left side. As it felt the burning sensation and saw its own blood sprinkle down, the stag thought: "Only someone who loves me can wound me."

Just before it hit the ground, the man-painted-black spread a thick mountain-sheep skin below the stag and it landed like a feather on the soft bloodstained fleece. Immediately the injury was healed. The man-painted-black began to sing, and men from both camps came and knelt beside the fleece and prayed to the Great Spirit.

The stag returned safely to its place in the valley where a doe with fawns jumped and played around it....

William awoke with the dream etched in his consciousness. He wanted to meditate on it and try to discover some insight but the warriors were assembling and getting ready to move.

Big Kittles came with a message. "Captain Bigtree wants you and me to scout out the militia and try to decoy 'em towards the ravine once we arrive. Our Wendat warriors will be there—the Dasayane' (Delaware) will secure the forest on the enemy's flank. You ready?"

~~~

"What's going on?" asked John Walker of the man riding beside him.

"There's nothing here but deserted huts. Don't look like there's been an Indian around for weeks. Looks pretty ominous to me," the hunter-soldier replied. They all had ridden in with
~~~

rifles loaded and pistols drawn, ready for the onslaught, hearts beating with anticipation. Now—nothing.

Col. Crawford called another meeting of the militia. "It's obvious," he said, "the enemy has had plenty of advance notice of our march."

"I don't understand this at all," said John Slover, one of the guides. "When I was a prisoner here in February there was Wyandots everywhere. They must have moved the whole town—maybe gathering an army somewhere down river where they can hit us full force."

The decision was finally made to go forward at least for one more day—against the advice of the three main guides who wanted to retreat to the Ohio.

The men filled their canteens, ate jerky and munched on the raw corn they'd found the week before. Fires were not allowed for the first time.

"It's too damn quiet," said Walker to the other men seated around him, leaning against trees and stumps. "I don't like the looks of it—no-sir, not at all."

"They's a haze over the moon," replied one of the volunteers. "That's a sign o' trouble. Don't know 'bout you boys, but I'm jist 'bout ready ta go back home—and I ain't no coward, neither. I jist don't cotton to ridin' into where I caint see."

The others agreed, Walker commenting, "I've fought in a lot of battles and chased a wounded panther through the woods along the Clinch. But I let him go when he disappeared into a cave. Don't like crawling around in the dark lookin' for a fight. I'd say wait awhile and see if they'll come looking for us."

The next morning they mounted and moved out. A dense fog had surrounded them. "Just like I said," repeated Walker, "I don't like crawling around in the dark looking for a fight."

About noon the whole force was energized with news that was repeated all the way down the line: "One of our scouts says there's a large body of Indians just two miles away!"

~~~

William and Big Kittles were instructed by none other than the Captain William Caldwell who had assumed command of the entire force of Wyandot and Delaware warriors. He was still waiting for his own British troops and artillery to arrive.

"You scouts," he said, "are to go stealthily south of here towards the abandoned village where the settlers have spent the night. You know the terrain—stay hidden in the tall grass and groves of trees until you spot them riding this way.

"While still at a safe distance we want you to get out in the open plain and even fire a shot or two at the enemy. Then ride like the wind back to the ravine, leading them into the ambush. Do you understand?" They both nodded, a little awed to be this close to a British officer in full uniform. "Oh, yes," he added, "there is a third scout joining you who doesn't speak English. Explain the plan to him."
~~~

William turned to see a familiar-looking brave walking towards him but he couldn't quite recognize him through the war-paint. "This is Mononcue," said Caldwell, "he will lead the way."

The three had little time to renew their friendships. Mononcue said something that Big Kittles translated: "He says he's here ta keep ya from tryin' ta escape. Says he'll shoot ya if'n ya do." Mononcue flashed a sly smile at William.

They rode out immediately and within fifteen minutes spotted the militia, spread out across the Sandusky Plain, the horses' legs hidden by tall prairie grass. The three of them broke out of the trees and made a long swing towards the troops, Mononcue firing a shot toward the lead horses. They delayed only long enough to see the four-hundred-and-some militiamen break out in a race towards them.

John Walker was now part of the advance since the columns had spread out to cover more ground. He urged his horse into full gallop while aiming his buffalo gun towards one of the fleeing Indians. The distance was too great for most rifles but he had once killed a running elk over a mile away. He held onto the horse with his knees and hugged the weapon's stock tightly against his chest, steadying the barrel with his firm left forearm, biceps clinched. With the Indian in his sights he squeezed gently on the trigger and the ball of lead exploded from the muzzle as he heard the command, "Company—Halt!" A split-second later he watched the distant target tumble from his horse, and snapped his fingers. “Got him!”

♓♓♓♓♓

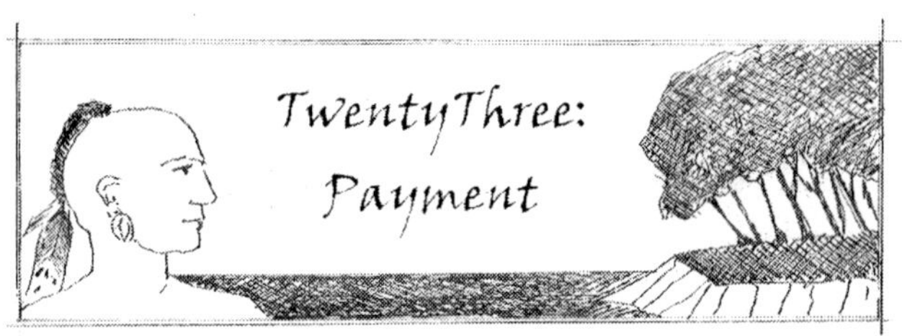

"Halt!" Crawford shouted again. Most of the men were galloping at top speed and couldn't hear the command. However, they did hear the bugle sounding retreat and whirled around, gathering at the edge of the grassy field. "I didn't like the looks of it," explained the colonel, "too few Indians for us to be chasing like that. Probably leading into an ambush."

At least a hundred Delaware warriors swarmed out into the field just west of the militia. "They're heading for the grove of trees!" shouted Williamson. "Don't let them take it or we'll never dislodge them!" The men commenced firing and headed for the trees, arriving before the Indians could, and successfully drove them back into the tall grass.

Mononcue and Big Kittles quickly dismounted and ran back to where William lay bleeding. They both grabbed him and carried him down into the ravine, barely getting there before the hundred warriors left their hiding place and rode forward out of the ditch with fierce war-whoops. The dust rose behind them from the ravine and settled like brown snow on William's prone body. Big Kittles picked up a handful of dry leaves that had collected there and stuffed them in the bullet-hole in William's lower left side.

"I am sorry we can't do more," said Big Kittles, "but we must join the other warriors. We will be back soon."

Mononcue said, "Hume'dat (Sorry) Will-yam," knowing it was a Wendat word he would understand, and dashed away to catch up with Big Kittles.

Like the others, John Walker had taken cover and was firing and reloading behind a large oak.

"I can't hit them," complained a man named Daniel Canon who was shooting from behind the same tree. "The band we drove out of the woods is just as well hidden in the prairie-grass. Why do you figure the ones from the ravine are keeping such a safe distance?"

"My guess is they're waiting for more warriors to arrive. The odds seem to be about fifty-fifty right now," he said, holding wadding between his teeth and pouring powder into the barrel.

"I shore can't get a bead on 'em," said Canon, "they duck down in the grass as fast as they fire."

"What's the alternative?" asked John, dropping his lead ball on the ground and kneeling to search for it.

He hadn't expected an answer. Canon said, "Watch me," and started climbing the tree, rifle in hand. "Come on up, John," he called as he fired at the raised head of a Delaware brave. "This is the place to be!"

Walker followed, each taking a position on opposite sides, their feet firmly planted in limbs forking from the huge trunk. For nearly three hours they fired at warrior's heads, then ducked and reloaded and fired again.

"I don't know if I'm hittin' any but they ain't raisin' back up in the same place," said Canon.

"Same here," answered Walker, "like turtles in a creek."

At dusk the Indians pulled back and gathered at the ravine.

~~~

William was unconscious until he heard someone say the British force was only an hour away, bivouacked for the night. It was Bigtree speaking English, leaning over him examining his injury. "You've lost some blood young William," he said, cleaning out the soaked leaves. "You have 'oki' though."

"What's that?" moaned the boy.

"Oki is power—supernatural power. It may come through the sky or the thunder or a dream. You have it—I can feel it. The bullet went through your back at the side and came out just a few inches away."

"I—it hurts to breathe," said William.
~~~

"Maybe broke a rib or two. Your lungs look like they're both working. The Spirit gave you oki for sure!" Someone brought Bigtree a piece of torn cloth and he poured spring water over the wound and wrapped a bandage around William's body. The boy drank the rest of the water and blacked out.

~~~

The next day was a long one for the militia. Most of the shooting was sparse, long-range firing. "The Indians are waiting for reinforcements," said Crawford. "We'll wait until evening and attack in force. If we wait longer it may be too late."

A scout arrived with a message: "There are more warriors moving down from the north—perhaps another hundred. They are followed by at least fifty redcoats, probably from Ft. Detroit."

Crawford turned to his officers. "Inform your men to prepare to retreat at first dawn. Meanwhile see that the wounded are treated and stretchers improvised for those who cannot ride."

In spite of the Delaware and Shawanese attacking them at the front, and Wyandot and British at the rear, the troops moved on. Canon rode beside Walker most of the entire way to the Ohio River low-water crossing.

When they passed the abandoned village, John Vance spotted a brass kettle, dropped by the former inhabitants. He jumped from his horse, grabbed a large boulder and began smashing the pot flat, to the disbelief of his companions.
~~~

"Let's git outta here," Canon said, "the racket will bring those braves right down on us!"

Vance took his flattened brass kettle and began tying it on his saddle. "My kids'll love this," he shouted. "Best war souvenir I've found yet."

"What's the word?" Walker asked another group of men that caught up with them later.

"The word is Crawford is missing, along with Dr. Knight and John Slover, and a few others. They went back looking for the commander's son, nephew and son-in-law. About half the rest of us are sick as dogs from drinking the stagnant water at the battlefield. I feel like up-chuckin' now." He leaned over the side of his horse and vomited.

Canon said, "I'm just tired of this heat and humidity. I'm sweating like a horse and I've been rode hard and put away wet—except I ain't been put away yet."

Walker noticed the sky. "There's a black wall-cloud coming at a distance. If that hits it'll more'n cool you off, but we better be lookin' for some shelter by the end of the day."

The next day's thunderstorm rendered useless most of the gunpowder. The Indian forces experienced the same thing, ending the attacks against the rear guard of the militia. The latter reached Mingo Bottom in a little over eight days and disbanded for home.

Daniel Canon rode a ways with John Walker, then split off to head towards his own destination. "I know you're sad you didn't find your son," said Canon.

"It always was a long-shot," John answered.

"Well," said Canon, "I'll never forget that long shot you made, racing on horseback. Watching the Indian scout plummet off his horse was a sight for sore eyes!"

"Lucky shot," said Walker. "Guess God was smilin' on me," he grinned.

~~~

William half remembered riding behind Mononcue on a horse. He wasn't sure if it had happened within the last three days, or if he was remembering the day of his capture. At any rate, he knew he hadn't fallen off so it must have been recent. When he fully regained consciousness he was in Brown's cabin. A pretty young girl was dressing his wounds with a poultice of boiled roots.

"Who won?" William asked.

Big Kittles seemed anxious to fill him in on the battle. "There was an awful lot of runnin' around and shootin' but not many killt on either side. In the end ever one of 'em turned tail and run like a sceered tanyonyeha' (rabbit) when our reinforcements arrived. Yup, when six hundert warriors came up over the hill—and a couple handfuls of them Britishers with a cannon 'er two—them settlers was gone!"
~~~

Mononcue had come in and sat down while Big Kittles was talking. He said something in Wendat.

"What did he say?" asked William.

Big Kittles translated, "Oh, he's jist wantin' me ta be sure and tell ya 'bout the prisoners. While some of the Delaware were trailing scattered Long Knives through the woods, who ya think they come upon? Colonel Crawford, no less! Danged if'n he hadn't got lost and his army done went home without him, a doc and one of the guides."

Mononcue made a remark and sneered.

"Blind guide, he says," translated Big Kittles. "Well sir, I reckon Chief Pipe wanted ta burn 'im but the Wyandot is agin it—they don't do that no more. So Pipe tells Chief Tedyata (Roundhead) the Delaware want permission from him—as their uncle—ta conduct some war council like they thinks best. Now, Tedyata thinks he's jist talkin' about a skirmish 'er something, see. So he says 'yes'—not knowin' they's wantin' ta burn Crawford at the stake."

"Why Crawford?" asked William. "He hardly did any damage at all, did he?"

"Naw. But that's the thing—they was mad at Williamson who led the Gnadenhutten massacre. They thinked Crawford was him at first. Then they was jist so mad they burnt him anyway. Mononcue went down and saw it."

Mononcue began talking with great gestures and expression. William could guess at a lot of what he was saying: "They tied his hands behind him—like this—and then put a long tether from his hands to a big stake. They built a fire around him—close but not too close, so he could wind the tether around the pole, then walk back and unwind it. At first the sun was in the center of the sky, but the torture continued most of the day."

Big Kittles resumed translating. "He was stripped and painted black. Girty was there and Crawford begged him to intervene fer him. He says Girty tried twiced, but Pipe tole him to shut up 'er he'd burn him too. The women and children spit at him and shot gunpowder at him. It seared his skin with many spots. He cringed and ran around the pole. They kept the fire hot around him and he roasted like a pig until the sun was about here"—he indicated four o'clock—"then they threw coals around his feet and he walked on them until he fell face down. The relatives of the Moravian Delaware ran and scalped him and cut him. He got up again and tried to walk and finally he died."

Big Kittles added, "Maybe it was a good revenge for 'em. I know that Chief Tedyata (Roundhead) was pretty angry when he heard 'bout it. He says it'll jist bring more Long Knives to kill more of us. Wish I'd been there to see it!"

"What does Mononcue think about it?" William asked.

Big Kittles relayed the question, then the answer: "He says that Bigtree says the Long Knives never pay fer their crimes.

Indians will punish bad Indians. The settlers let their criminals go free—if the crime's against us. The good whites don't do nuthin'. So—revenge is up to us. Chief Tedyata (Roundhead) says it's wrong to burn prisoners no matter what they did. Mononcue don't know what to think. He says it was good at the time but he cain't git it outta his head."

The pretty girl came and shooed the boys away from William so she could check his bandages. "Who are you?" he asked.

She smiled and said, "I'm Catherine—my family is from Detroit up the river."

William was surprised she spoke English but with an accent he hadn't heard before. "But—you're Wyandot aren't you?" She smiled again. "Of course—but my papa is Irish and mama's French-Wyandot. We're visiting the Brown's while papa is at the council meeting. Mama asked me to watch you while she and Scanonie went to see some other women in the village."

William winced from pain and she apologized, "I didn't mean to hurt you but the cloth is sticking to your skin. I'll warm some water to help loosen it."

William watched her and thought, "She's not very old—or is she?" He watched her walk gracefully across the clean earth floor and pick up a bucket to get water at the spring. "I wish I could go with you," he said, "but I don't think I can get up."

"It's all right," she replied, "you will be running around again soon—if you rest." She walked through the door, pushing the bearskin covering to one side. Then she stuck her head back in and added, "If you don't rest you'll get fever and the medicine woman will come. She'll put hot coals on you and blow ashes over you and sing mournful songs." She giggled as she left, swinging the bucket.

For the moments William lay alone on the bark platform he remembered his dream. With the memories of the vision came some bits of understanding. He was the fawn taken away to a far place. He was growing into a man—the stag. Suddenly he remembered about falling from the nest and his heart beat faster—he had left Moonshower's little house. A bullet had hit him on the left side. How did the dream know all those details and what would happen?

Maybe it did come from the Great Spirit to teach him something. He recalled the words the stag thought to itself, "Only someone who loves me can wound me." Doesn't seem to make any sense, he thought.

And who is the man-painted-black who was singing? Too many "loose-ends" as his mother would say. That reminded him of his Aunt Ann's words to him: "The Bible says, 'All things work together for good to those who love God.'" Even the "loose ends"? Even mistakes and evil things? His mind began reeling from so many thoughts, questions and so few answers.

He awoke to the aroma of fish being cooked in deer fat over Scanonie's fire. His little sister Seketa was whispering in his ear, "I think Catherine likes you. The girls like boys with scars, especially warrior's scars." William understood some of what she said. "Catherine—likes you—boys—warrior." His chest swelled a little. Then he flinched from the sharp pain and was quickly humbled.

ꞲꞲꞲꞲꞲ

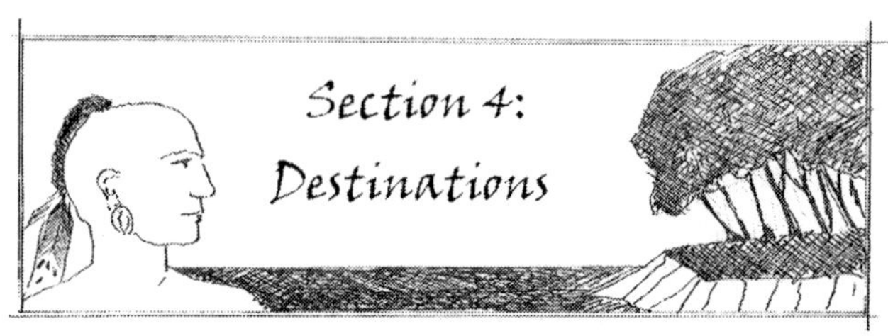
Section 4:
Destinations

(1785)

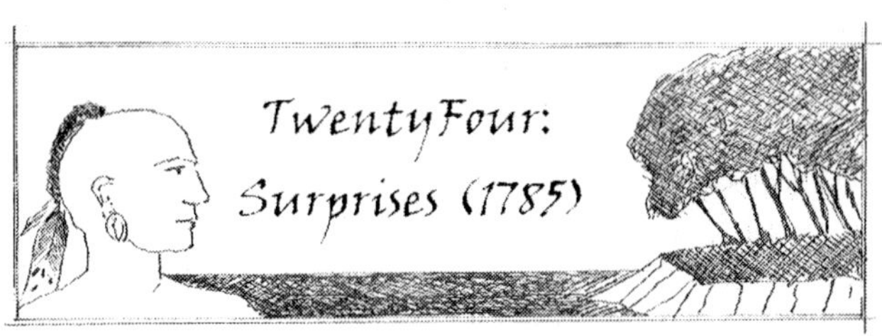
TwentyFour:
Surprises (1785)

The summer of '85 was a peaceful one, giving time for hunting and long lazy evenings fishing at the shore of Erige--Lake Of the Cat (Lake Erie). William's wound healed quickly without infection leaving only a round puckered red spot in front and back.

Bigtree reminded him, "Those scars are your birthmarks as a Wendat warrior." William wore them as proudly as he would have worn an eagle feather or medal.

He spent much of his time playing stickball, or trapping and fishing with the young men and exploring the wilderness by canoe. Still he found a lot of time to be around Catherine and her friends. Catherine decided to spend the summer at the Brown's village even though her family was up the river in Detroit. She was a good tutor in Wendat and William a quick student. He even picked up a few Irish and French words here and there.

One night that summer they were getting better acquainted, relaxing on the sandy beach while other young Wyandot were swimming in the warm waters.

"The moon looks funny on the lake when it shimmers," said Catherine, "like the shivering heat you can see sometimes above the fire, but luminous."

William liked the way she used unusual words. "I was going to say," he commented, "it looks like a big dog shaking when it comes out of the river."

They both laid back and looked up at the clear night stars and the full moon. "Do you know," she said, "there are people all over the world tonight who can see that same moon?"

"Never thought about it," he answered. "Wonder if they see it on the Clinch River in Virginia. I used to see it there, but it didn't wiggle as much as it does on the lake."

"When were you last there?" she asked.

"Don't know. I think when I was about thirteen."

"How old are you now," she asked.

"Don't know. Maybe eighteen or nineteen. How about you?"

"I'll be sixteen in three months. My family writes the dates down in a big Bible that belonged to my grandfather."

William was surprised she was so young. He thought, "She's only fifteen! She has a woman's body, and she's more mature than most girls her age."

Catherine read his thoughts. "Do you think I'm too young to be friends with an old warrior like you?" she laughed.

"No," he said. "I wasn't thinking about that at all."

"Well, you know that most of the Indian girls are asked to marry by the time they're fourteen. If you wait too long, there won't be anybody left but old toothless widows!"

William answered, "Oh, I won't wait too long—if I ever find anybody I like that will take orders and obey my commands, chop all the firewood and clean the venison..."

She interrupted him, "Oh, there are lots of Indian girls like that—if you want a companion who is a plow-horse."

"Is Catherine your only name?" he asked, changing the subject abruptly.

"I have an Indian name but I'm not going to tell it to you yet. You have to earn the right to guess what it is—but not for a long time. It is a secret until the time is right. I was named Catherine after my mother who was named after a great-aunt of mine in France who was named after a queen I think. How about you—do you have an Indian name?"

"Not really. The Lenape called me Pemsit because it means man-who-walks. I've had the name William since I was a very little boy, I reckon. Walker is a Scotch-Irish name, grandpa said, and there are lots of 'em around Virginia."

"What do Scotch-Irish do?" she asked.

"Mostly fight Indians—guess they don't like us much."

"Do you like Indians?" she asked, scooting over closer to his side.

"Of course—certain people I like, some I don't like." He ran his fingers over the smooth skin on her cheek.

"Am I one of the certain people you like?" she asked.

She put her hand on his side and said, "I like your scars, too—they make you look brave."

"They would be lots bigger if you hadn't taken such good care of me."

She leaned over to kiss him—then they heard their friends coming from the river.

As William, Catherine and other Wyandot youth returned that evening, Captain Bigtree was talking with Adam Brown. "Sit down here with us, William," said Adam, "you ought to hear this."

Bigtree brought him up to date on their conversation: "You know that last January we renegotiated a treaty with the United States at Ft. McIntosh which surrendered much of the eastern and southern areas of Ohio territory to white settlement. We have enjoyed several years of peace and hope for many years more. One of the terms of the McIntosh treaty concerns you and what will happen to you now."

"I think I know what it is," he said. "Does it have to do with the freeing of prisoners and captives?"

Bigtree looked at Brown. They both nodded.

William looked out at his friends who were enjoying each other in the yard. Several boys including Mononcue and Big Kittles were wrestling with each other. The young girls were in a circle around them, cheering them on. He looked out across the lake and listened to the ducks chattering along the shoreline. He put his hands over his face and thought for a few moments.

"I'm not a prisoner," he said. "I'm not a captive. This is my home—the only home I've known for years. I hardly remember any other place. My first family may not even exist anymore. I'm not going anywhere."

"It may not be your decision," said Adam. "It is clear that I am a member of the tribe. I have a wife and family and am a local clan chieftain. My father died before I was captured and then my stepfather and mother were killed. There is no question that this is my nation and people now. But even Big Kittles may have to go back and see if he has family that will take him. There is always the possibility that the Long Knives will discover you boys among us and use you for a pretense to invade and take more land. They will just say we violated the terms of the treaty as they kill us."

William sat in stony silence. Bigtree spoke: "It doesn't mean you can't voluntarily come back here. If you go and see your childhood family, then return to the Wendat, it will prove once and for all that you belong with us."

"I don't even know where they are residing if they are still alive. My father was always moving around and talked about going back to Rockbridge County from the Clinch River."

Bigtree looked down at the ground. "I guess it was wrong to take you captive William. I owe you an apology. It was the only way we knew to build up the tribe when we were losing so many warriors. We also believe it set free the soul of a dead brave, when a captive took his place."

William waited to speak until he caught Bigtree's eye. "You once told me that a real warrior would never say he was sorry. You don't have to be. This has been an exciting journey for me—I would not have missed it! Why would I have chosen to stay on the frontier—chopping wood and plowing cornfields—when I could live free and be a warrior at age thirteen?"

Big Kittles had come up, overheard the conversation and added with a laugh, "And get shot in the back running away."

Bigtree reached over, grabbed him by his scalp lock and pulled him close, so the Captain's nose-jewel dangled in Big Kittles's face. "You may want to listen to the rest of this talk before you start joking around. It concerns you too. We've signed a treaty that requires all captives and prisoners to be returned. What do you think about that?"

Big Kittles wiggled loose and vehemently shook his head declaring, "A-a! (No!) Icar trizue egh stahar taken ome enumah!"

Bigtree and Brown both burst out laughing so hard they turned over the bench they were sitting on.

"What?" said William. "What did he say?"

Bigtree interpreted, "He said, 'I don't like white men!'"

~~~

Catherine and William sat outside later that evening. "I may have to go away for awhile," he said. "The new treaty requires all captives to be set free. If I don't go and try to visit my Virginia family it might bring problems to the tribe."

"I don't understand." Catherine said. "If you don't want to leave why would anybody make you? Aren't we a free people?"

"If the American government officials thought the Wyandot Nation was keeping captives against their will, they might say the treaty had been broken. Settlers might try to take our land. If I make the effort to go and then come back, it will be proof that I am free—I guess. Sounds kind of confusing doesn't it?"

"If you are going to Virginia," she said, "I'm going with you. It would be interesting to meet some of your other family, especially if we....I mean....someday you may want me to....know them because....they might want to know me if...."

William was too deep in his own anxieties to understand what Catherine was saying. "No! You can't go with me—it would be extremely dangerous. It would mean going through Cherokee country as well as frontier places that have been at war against all Indians. Kentucky is probably more hazardous now than
~~~

ever. No, I couldn't take the risk of anything happening to you. I can travel faster and stay hidden easier if I'm alone."

"William I couldn't stand it if anything happened to you. What will I do if you decide to stay in Virginia? Would I ever see you again? How could I live without knowing?"

He put his arms around her and kissed her lips and she held him tightly and began to cry. "Don't worry," he said.

"At least take Big Kittles with you," she begged, "I'd feel a little better if I knew you had someone to help you."

"And make sure I come back," he added, laughing. "But maybe that's a good idea. I'll talk to him."

~~~

William looked for Big Kittles all week. No one seemed to know where he was. Early one morning he stuck his head in the Brown's house hollering, "Will'am! Come here quick! I got some news you ain't gonna wanna miss out on!"

William crawled out of his bed and staggered to the door. "Whatdaya want and whereya been?" he asked in an irritated voice, rubbing his eyes.

Big Kittles smiled broadly and put his arm around the waist of a shy young Indian girl. "This here's 'Blowing-Leaves,' a Mohawk gal. In the old days we might have said she was 'Mrs. Big Kittles.' We done got married Will'am. Ain't no goin' back now—I'm a full-fledged Mohawk Injun!"

)()()()(
~~~

The trip to the Clinch River country was not something that he could accomplish without some careful planning. Since Big Kittles was living at the Mohawk village William turned to others for advice including Mononcue—who was his own age but was experienced in traversing the wilderness—along with Half-Scalp and Bigtree.

He had learned enough of the Wendat language for conversation with Mononcue—if the words were simple enough.

Mononcue offered to accompany him on the first leg of the trip. "My advice," said his friend, "is to appear like an Indian as long as you're this side of the Ohezuh (Ohio) River. Once you are in Virginia you can dress like the Long Knives. The biggest danger will likely be In Kentucky. You will be traveling on the eastern side which has many settlements of whites but also marauding—eh—raiding bands of Watayuruno (Cherokee) who are angry that the whites are encroaching—eh, you don't know that word—living on their land. The route that will get you there and back quickly is by river to the Ohezuh and overland by horse from there. But that means taking a horse with you in the stern of the canoe."

"Wait," said William, "what did you just say? It sounded like 'take a horse in a canoe!'"

Mononcue laughed. "That is what I said—I was testing you to see if you were listening. You are getting much better in understanding Wendat. The real question is: where will you find a horse once you cross the Ohio?"

William said, "Now let me see if I really did follow you. I should dress normally—like an Indian—in Ohio. Then I should try to look like a white man in Virginia. But in Kentucky I can't look like either or they'll both want to kill me."

Mononcue laughed again but quickly looked serious. "The way I see it, those are the problems you will face just getting there safely."

William ran his hand over his head—plucked bald except where the scalp lock grew in the center. "This will be all right until I leave the Ohio country. How am I going to disguise myself as a white man?"

"Maybe some kind of hat?" suggested Mononcue. "You know those fur hats they wear?"

"Yeah, maybe that would work," he replied, "but my bald head would still be obvious on the sides. I guess I'll just have to stay out of sight as long as possible."

"You'll be safe once you're close enough to talk English with the frontiersmen," said Mononcue. "You can explain your looks by telling them you are a freed captive. It's those at a distance that will be dangerous. They'll shoot if they think you resemble an Indian."

In a few days the two young men had stocked a small canoe with enough venison jerky to last a few days, gunpowder and bullets, and started down the river towards Sandusky Bay and points south. They expected to be on the river at least a week. Wild game was plentiful and the weather was perfect for fishing.

~~~

"We've made good time," said Mononcue. "We've only been on the river three days and I think tomorrow will bring us to the Ohezuh (Ohio) border. What do you say let's bank the canoe and try to kill some meat for supper?"

"Sounds like a good idea," said William. "It may be my last cooked meal for awhile—no fires once I'm going through Kentucky for sure."

When they had walked a short ways into the brush Mononcue said, "Let me show you how great I am at calling up game." He began clucking his tongue in a turkey-call, which ended in a series of short, high-pitched screeching sounds. They both crouched in frozen silence waiting for an answering gobble.
~~~

William whispered, "I'm still waiting. I'm even listening for a...bird (he didn't know the word for "turkey") running through the leaves."

"Shhh," said Mononcue. Again he made the cluck and screeching sounds. They waited.

After half an hour of this, William said, "It's going to be dark before long. I don't think there's going to be any of those big birds around. Don't you know any other sounds?"

"I know a lot of sounds," he replied, "But you have to have patience. It may take some time. Animals don't give themselves up to unworthy hunters and they have to determine how sincere you are—that probably takes time."

William wasn't sure what "unworthy" meant so he just kept quiet. "Listen to this," said Mononcue. "This is the sound a wounded tanyonyeha' makes. It attracts all kinds of meat-eating predators—panthers, wolves, even bears."

"What's a tanyonyeha'?"

"Oh, what do you call it in English? Do you know tschimamus in Lenape?"

"Yeah," said William, "I knew a boy named that—it means 'rabbit.'"

"Listen," said Mononcue. He gave several sharp screams that sounded somewhat like a baby's loud cries. William flinched and put his hands over his ears. "Don't move!" ordered

Mononcue, "you'll scare them away before they come anywhere close to us."

William smiled and muttered, "I don't know who 'they' are but I'm not sure I want them to get close."

"That's part of the fun," said Mononcue. "You never know what will come looking for the wounded rabbit. Maybe a fox, maybe coyote—maybe a wolf or even a bear. If we had built a fire we could hide in the brush and see the light reflect from their eyes as they approached. Be quiet! I think something is coming." Again he screamed the loud cry that shattered the night and caused a chill to run up William's spine.

"Once I saw a..." Mononcue's words were cut off in mid-sentence as a tree's small limbs cracked over their heads and an object came hurtling out towards them. William watched as his friend pitched face-forward out of the brush—a snarling, scratching animal wrapped around his head. Mononcue was yelling, "Yaiiii, get off, get off!" and fighting to knock it away while it was biting him on the scalp and digging its claws deeper into the sides of his head.

William yanked the tomahawk from his waistband and tried to swing it at the growling, shrieking ball of fur—but Mononcue was falling and rolling around on the riverbank.

"Knock it off me," cried Mononcue.

"I'm trying," shouted William, "but you won't hold still long enough!" He got hold of one of the beast's legs and it turned loose of the young warrior and leaped onto William, sinking its teeth into his arm while its hind claws lashed out at his stomach.

While William yelled in pain, Mononcue clenched both of his fists together and swung, hollering, "Take that!" as he smacked the animal's mid-section and sent it flying into the brush.

"What was that?" William said between heavy breaths, as the beast clattered away in the distance. Both he and Mononcue plunged into the river and washed the blood from their many scratches and puncture wounds.

"That," said Mononcue, "is a skainkquahah. I don't know the word for it in English."

William nodded, "From its size and scream it must be a wildcat—a huge, angry wildcat!"

"I think that's what it was," agreed Mononcue.

Later by the fire they ate the last of their venison jerky. "Mononcue," said William, "I'm not really very hungry. Don't call up anything else tonight."

"Well," said his friend, "at least we might have eaten the meat of a brave wildcat instead of a running-scared turkey. I don't like eating something with a cowardly spirit that might enter into my spirit and contaminate it."

William tried to swallow the meat he had been chewing for awhile. "I don't think we have to worry too much about the jerky—it's so tough it can only make us stronger."

~~~
~~~

As their canoe approached the Ohio River, a band of warriors calling from the other side surprised them. "Hallooo!" They motioned for them to bring the canoe to the southeast bank where they stood with their horses. "Don't worry," one of them shouted in English. "We are friends of Bigtree—he sent us word to meet you here."

Mononcue looked back at William, frowned and said, "I don't trust them. They look like Watayuruno (Cherokee) to me."

"Why aren't they shooting instead of yelling at us?" asked William—"I don't think we have much choice but to go over and meet them. We can't paddle fast enough around the bend to avoid their bullets."

"You're right," Mononcue replied, "but keep your eyes open and your weapons ready."

"Welcome, welcome!" said an Indian dressed in his finest, wearing two eagle feathers in his hair. He spoke to them in English. For once, William had to translate for Mononcue. The boys warily stepped out of the canoe and were given bear hugs by the four warriors.

"How do you know Bigtree?" William asked.

"He's an old friend of mine from many wars ago," said the obvious leader of the band, "and I am Chief Dragging Canoe. We are Chickamauga Cherokee and have been Wendat enemies for many years—but no longer. Our braves have joined in alliance with the Shawnee on the Scioto River.

"A band of our warriors are also moving their families to the northwest villages of your Chief Tedyata (Roundhead), even as we talk. Our people have fought each other for enough seasons. It is time to come together to defend our land against the settlers and militia."

The man continued, "Bigtree sent a rider with a message that you were coming. Welcome, Walker and Mononcue, brave warriors. We have brought food for both of you and a horse and blanket for William.

"We will accompany you along the trail that follows the Kentucky River to the Virginia border. There is little chance of attack as long as we keep out of sight of the frontier settlements. We've been invading them for years but like mosquitoes they keep coming back to sting us."

William studied the chief. He had a prominent sharp nose and his scalp lock was turning white. In spite of his age he looked lean and muscular. His moccasins were laced up his calves to just below his knees and he wore a short, embroidered green vest above his breechclout, with red "V"s along the bottom. A purple wampum belt decorated with small shells and beads was slung from his shoulder. He had old scars on both legs that looked like the bullet-marks on William's side.

"You are looking me over thoroughly," laughed the chief. "Don't worry—I'm not interested in fighting any more Indians. We are melting like snowballs as the white's advance."

Later as they sat around the campfire and finished a mouth-watering meal of fresh trout, William asked the chief, "Where did you get your name?"

"When I was a boy of twelve my father was a chief. He and the other warriors were getting ready to travel up river to attack the French and I wanted to go with them. He pointed to a canoe hewed from a huge tree trunk and loaded with supplies for the trip, and teased me: 'When you can get that canoe from the shore down into the water you will be old enough to fight.' I immediately grabbed the bow and began tugging at it. Then I ran around and pushed on the stern with all my strength. It began to barely move. Inch by inch I worked from one end and then the other. All the warriors gathered around and cheered me on—until I had conquered the task. From then on Dragging Canoe was a warrior.

"It was about that time that we captured Bigtree. I taught him to speak some Cherokee during the months before he escaped." He shook his head. "Damn good Indian. Wish we could've kept him and made him part of the Ani Yviwiya—the Real People.

"Now William—what about you? Are you going back to become a Long Knife and kill more of us?"

William cleared his throat and put his hands over his face. He shook his head. "No. I don't even want to go back—it's been so long. I have no friends there and maybe no family. I'm only going because of the treaty that requires the release of all captives, both whites and Indians."

"I understand," said the chief. "We are negotiating just such a treaty with the government. We have to—they have burned all our villages and cornfields and winter is approaching. My own inclination is to keep fighting to the end, but I'm getting old and the young men need to think about wives and children. How do you feel about returning—you can tell me the truth. Aren't you a little curious and maybe excited about it?"

"Of course," William admitted, "I wonder what has happened to my father and mother and my brother Alex. There is a hollow place in my spirit. I don't think it can be filled until I finish this trip. At the same time, I miss my family and friends in Ohio."

Mononcue, who had been listening quite awhile, spoke in English: "Pretty Indian friend—Catherine."

"Ohhh!" said the chief, "I don't have to worry about you leaving us after all! That empty place in your spirit has a cord tied around it—the rope tightens and it gets smaller every day."

The next morning they started out on horses, traveling the trail close to the Big Sandy and Tug Fork Rivers.

By early afternoon the next day they were at the foot of the Allegheny Mountains. "This is where we will leave you," said Dragging Canoe. "Good luck, my young friend. May the Great Spirit protect and guide you safely through your search for your childhood. I brought some settlers' clothing and boots for you to wear, and I suggest you wrap your head in this bandage," he said, handing William a yellowed cloth with brown stains on it. "Don't worry—it's deer blood. You can say you were scalped. Cover your whole head with it. We"ll watch for your return and escort you back."

Mononcue put his hand on William's shoulder and spoke to him in Wendat: "I too must return. No use trying to disguise this face as a Long Knife," he grinned. "May the hawk guide you on the last part of your trip to find your first people—and may you not forget your 'Ani Yviwiya' (Real People)," he said half-joking but somber.

William grasped Mononcue's arm and looked him in the eye. He spoke to him in broken Wendat, "You....me since....beginning my 'dark river' passage—since my head smashed your chin with my skull to you get from my back. We began—enemies—but parting awhile as friends. I look forward....hunting and long talks with my brother—you. Watch you...until I be there to watch you."

Mononcue replied, "Your grasp of the language is still fragile so I'm not sure about long conversations—but I'll be looking over my shoulder hoping every day to see you climb out of a canoe at Sandusky again!"

)()()()(

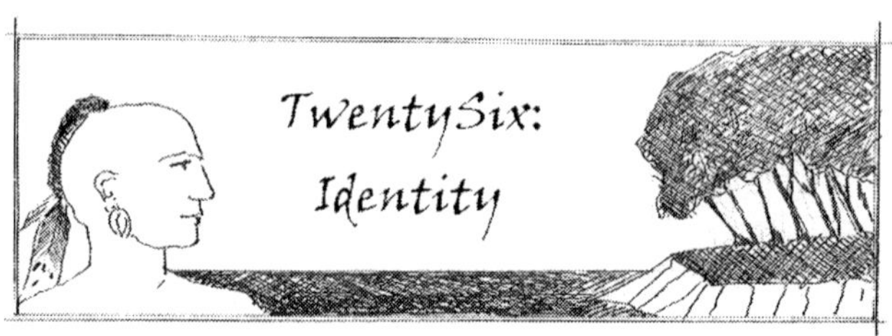

William changed into the breeches and deerskin fringed shirt and boots. He wrapped the bloodstained bandages around his head. Better to disguise the scalp lock than try to explain about being a captive, he thought. The chief had urged him to keep the horse, in order to travel faster and easier. He led it to a low-water site on the river and rode slowly across.

A strange feeling of aloneness crept over him as he waved goodbye to his companions and rode parallel to the Big Sandy. A hawk screeched in the cotton-boll sky, pointing the way.

His journey to the Clinch River settlement was almost straight south "as the crow flies." The countryside was gradually getting more mountainous, though he was still crossing mostly small hills. In the distance he could see the Allegheny Mountains taking a long jagged slice out of the horizon.

Before he parted from the chief, Dragging Canoe had taken a stick and drawn a dirt-map for him. "Go south and follow the mountain ridge over the smaller hills. The riverbanks are thick with greenbriers and brush. You will arrive at the long valley. The Clinch runs through it and you do not have to cross any really large mountain ranges. Follow the Clinch until you come to the area where your family lives. Do you remember the location or the scenery?"

"No," William replied, "I remember almost nothing about it—but maybe it will begin to come back to me while I'm riding the trail."

As soon as he was alone the memories began flashing in his brain. They came slowly and only remained very briefly in his inner vision, as if he saw images by bursts of lightning. As he rode, he recalled once as a very small child, chasing a horse in the rain. He was riding a horse with his father, a belt strapping him to his father's waist. Another moment he saw himself swimming with Alex in the river and being carried home on his brother's shoulders. Oh, yes—they had found crawdads under rocks in a shallow part of the stream. They found an old dented kettle and built a fire to boil them. "I can't remember eating them. Why didn't we eat them?" he asked himself.

There was a collage of memories—none in any kind of order—just random pictures that kept emerging for an instant or two, then disappearing to make room for another.

It had been a long time since he'd prayed. That night after he secured the horse to a tree and wrapped himself in a blanket against the mountain chill, he talked with the Lord. "God—Great

Spirit—it is William here. I don't think I know who I am anymore. I'm not sure I know who You are. I'm not the boy I remember who seems so distant and dim. That boy had never killed anyone or wanted to. He disappeared and an Indian brave took his place, a brave who has shed blood in battle—his own blood and the blood of a stranger. Ho mayendezui etterang! (God forgive me!)

"See—I think and pray in Wendat and in English. My heart is pulled back to my Catherine and my bark home. Yet something is pulling me towards the Clinch and the white boy memories. I am both, I am neither. Help me!"

Suddenly a man appeared—a vision at once real and ethereal. He said, "I have always helped you and I never left you. You will know who you are when you find yourself in me." As the vision seemed to evaporate, the man spoke once more: "Even when you cannot see me I am with you. Trust me."

William knew the man. He had seen him on other occasions when he was desperate and alone. Though the face was never very clear, some kind of intuition assured him he knew the man. He did not know his name or where they had first met but he felt it was a long, long time ago.

With the dawn he knelt at the stream and splashed the cool water on his face and upper body, led the horse to water and soon was on his way south.

It was late afternoon the next day when he saw the store—a trading post snuggled against the side of a small mountain leading into a valley. "This must be the entrance to the valley," he thought. "Wonder if I could stop and trade for food and test out my ability to pass for a settler." He rode up to the hitching post—a small sapling fastened low across two stakes. There were no other horses around.

He dismounted and walked nervously through the door, his borrowed boots squeaking on the plank floor.

"Howdy, friend!" said the bearded, lanky man behind the counter. "Welcome to Smith's Store, last stop on the way to Hell." William avoided the man's eyes. "Where's Hell?" he asked. "Oh, that's just what we call Clinch River since the Injuns have done their burnin' and pillagin' the last some years. Most of the settlers has left and gone back whar they came from. Whar ya comin' from? I take it you ain't from around h'yar, least wise I don't recall seein' ya before."

"I'm on my way to visit relatives," said William, hoping the questions would not go much further. His hopes were not fulfilled as the proprietor continued to pump him for information.

"Relatives, huh. Who be your kin here?"

William picked up a red silk scarf and pretended to be examining it. "Walker. John and Mary Walker down along the Clinch. Know if they're still around?"

The man rubbed his chin and shook his head. "Don't know—that's still a ways south. Most likely they'd trade across in North Carolina territory, or what's bein' called the State of Franklin. Wish't I could help ya."

Both men looked towards the front window as they heard the noise of horses and loud voices. A moment later three men came through the door, stomping the dirt off their boots as they entered. "Howdy, friends," said the owner, glad you stopped in. What can I do fer you'nses today?"

The men were all dressed like trappers, wearing similar outfits to the one William had on. They looked to be in their thirties, with shaggy moustaches and three-day old scraggly growths of whiskers. The storeowner walked over and extended his hand, "Name's Simon Smith."

The one who was the obvious leader stepped forward. He was not the tallest, standing only about five foot seven inches. He shook Smith's hand and answered, "Hughes. Jesse Hughes from Wheeling." He motioned with his head and added, "These here's my friends and huntin' companions, John and Giles." His face was pockmarked from an apparent bout with smallpox in earlier years and he now looked to be in his forties.

Smith's mouth dropped open. "You're not the Jesse Hughes known all over the frontier?" he said with a broad smile. "Not the famous Indian-fighter?"

Hughes nodded but stared at William with penetrating steel-grey eyes and walked over by his side.

William continued to seem interested in the scarf and calmed himself by picturing Catherine wearing it.

"That's some head-bandage you got," said Hughes. "What the hell happened to you?"

William put the scarf down and turned towards the man. "An Indian shot me and tried to scalp me," he replied, lifting his shirt to show the bullet scar on his side, "but I fought him off and killed him with his own tomahawk."

Hughes took a step back. "Hear that, boys? We got us a real Injun-killer!" He looked back at William. "Must've been a youngun to have botched up the job and cut all the way down to your ears. That your horse outside?"

"Yes, that's mine."

"Where'd you get him? I knowed a man had a horse a lot like that one. And boots like those you're wearin', come to think of it. You sure that's your pony?"

"Mister," William said firmly, looking him in the eye, "there's horses like that all over this country and boots like these, too. Every third settler you meet has a mount and boots like these."

"Maybe so," nodded Hughes. "Maybe so." He turned and walked toward the door, then stopped and whirled around. "But not every settler talks English with an Injun accent. See ya around," he said as all three shoved their way through the door.

"Son," said Smith, "give ya some advice. Don't know who ya are or whar ya come from—but keep clear o' them. Hughes has a reputation all over the frontier as an Injun killer. Hates all of 'em, good and bad, grown-ups and chill'in. Lives to kill 'em, since they cut up his daddy in a raid years back. They say he's killt over sixty Injuns hisself. He's a hero to the settlers who've been harassed by the savages—er, Indians—all over this whole damn region."

William thanked him for the advice. "I don't intend to be anywhere around him or Indians. I just want to find my relatives. I would like to buy this scarf if the price is right and not too much trouble for you. What you askin'?"

"Time was," said Smith, "I could sell it fer a good beaver hide 'er a couple a' deerskins. But with all the fightin' that's goin' on, it's harder to come by this kind of material." He rubbed the scarf between thumb and fingers. "Whatd'ya give me fer it?"

"What about an Indian tomahawk?" he asked. "It has engraving on the blade and a hickory handle." He was taking a chance that he could continue to avoid any need for the weapon until he could get back to Ohio. It was the only thing of value he had with him.

"Fetch it," said Smith, "but carry it in here with two fingers."

William obliged. He knew the trader suspected him of being an Indian sympathizer, but Smith was no fool and knew the value of a beautifully decorated weapon. William stuffed the scarf up his sleeve, thanked him, got on the horse and headed south. He thought to himself, "I stopped to trade for food—but love lasts longer. I'll just have to watch for some small game on the trail."

He had traveled only about an hour when he thought he heard noises in the brush beside the trail. Before he could take precautions, Hughes and one of his friends rode out behind him and pulled their horses up on either side of his.

"Well, lookee here!" said Hughes, putting his hand on William's shoulder. "We done run into our friend the Injun-killer! Whatdya think John, should we invite him to go fishin' with us?"

The man named John laughed a hearty yellow-toothed guffaw. "What Jesse means," he explained, "is like the time he made friends with a Indian at a trading post. He invited him...."

Hughes butted in, "Well let me tell the story John, since it's mine. There was this Cherokee that got real friendly with me and so I asked him if he liked to fish. He got so excited when I told him how big the fish were at a stream I knew about. Told him I'd meet him when the sun got finger high above the trees near Hacker Creek.... Oh you don't want to hear this do you boy?" He reached over and squeezed William's shoulder, who immediately jerked away.

"Now don't get mad," said Hughes, "I'll finish the story if you're gonna be so jumpy about it. Well that Cherokee came out of the woods just as the sun was above the tree-line but I was already hidin' in the brush by the creek. He was lookin' around but he didn't see me anywhere. I'd rubbed that brown chestnut oak ooze all over my shirt—just like now. I looked like part of the scenery. That is until my rifle smoked and a lead ball was tearin' through his chest. He never knowed different than that we was just good buddies. Shame—to die in ignorance, ain't it?"

William's mind was racing as he watched the trail ahead for a possible route of escape. "Don't panic," he told himself, "think." It was advice he'd once learned from his father.

Hughes continued to chatter. "You know I've been wonderin' about that bandage. Sure looks too big for a scalpin'. Know what I think? I think you'd be dead if you got cut that low. Besides, looks like it's bulky in the back—kinda like maybe it's coverin' up something. Wonder what that might be?"

Hughes reached up and grabbed the cloth at the back and William's hand instinctively shot up to hold the bandage in place. John, the other man, seized the reins from William's free hand and pulled the horses to a stop as Hughes lunged across, pulling him to the ground and landing on top of him.

William struggled to get free but the older man hit him two solid licks to the jaw. He was addled but felt the bandage yanked off his head and heard Hughes yell, "Yeehaw! We got us a Injun or a Injun-lover, don't we John? Look at that pretty scalp lock! Now why would a white man wear one of them? He could get shot in this country for just lookin' like a Injun!"

John nodded his head enthusiastically and kicked William in the top of his skull.

"Don't kick him too hard," shouted Hughes. "We want him around awhile to enjoy the fishin'."

John roared an evil-sounding laugh. "What do ya wanna do with 'im? Make a rug out'n 'is skin?"

William wanted to resist but the man was kneeling on his arms. "You don't understand," he said, "my name is Walker and I'm looking for my family." He tried to say, "I'm not an Indian," but the words wouldn't come out of his mouth. He felt it would be a betrayal to those he loved and hoped to rejoin, particularly Catherine. Head throbbing, he imagined her face and relaxed.

"No self-respecting white man would wear a scalp-lock even if he'd been a captive. He wouldn't be gone ten minutes before he'd shave it off and go bald. No, boy, there's somethin' not quite right about you. I can smell an Injun a hundred feet away downwind. And you know what? You smell just like one to me!"

A rifle shot echoed off the mountain and Hughes' hat flew off his head.

John's hands went up over his head as he said pleadingly, "Don't shoot! Don't shoot! I ain't done nothin' to 'im!"

Hughes' hand reached for his pistol but another rifle shot grazed his leg. "What the...! What do you want here?" he yelled. "Who are ye?"

"Jesse this is Patrick Porter and we've got another rifle aimed at your heart," said a voice from behind the thicket.

"Hell, Pat! You almost shot me!" Jesse hollered. "I was just getting ready to turn this boy loose. I don't think he's Injun after all. If you'll just hold your fire, me and John will slowly walk back to our horses and be gone."

"Toss your weapons in front of you and don't move an inch.," commanded Porter. Hughes hesitated, trying to kill time.

A young boy's voice yelled from somewhere in the thicket: "Look out, Papa; I see another horse behind those big trees!"

Porter's eyes quickly spotted the animal and instinctively followed the tree trunk up to the top. He caught sight of a few inches of gun barrel among the branches, aimed at his head, and dove for cover a split second before the blast.

Hughes and his accomplice used the diversion to quickly rein their horses around and disappeared at breakneck speed into a clump of trees.

Porter fired at the man descending the tree but wasn't sure his aim was true. The man landed on his horse and also vanished into the woods.

A few minutes later William felt a hand in his, drawing him to his feet. He squinted through bruised and swelling eyes at the man with a short red beard standing over him. "Who are you, son?" the man asked.

William rubbed his eyes and got up close to his face. “If you’re named Porter, I think I’m your nephew,” he said.

)()()()()(

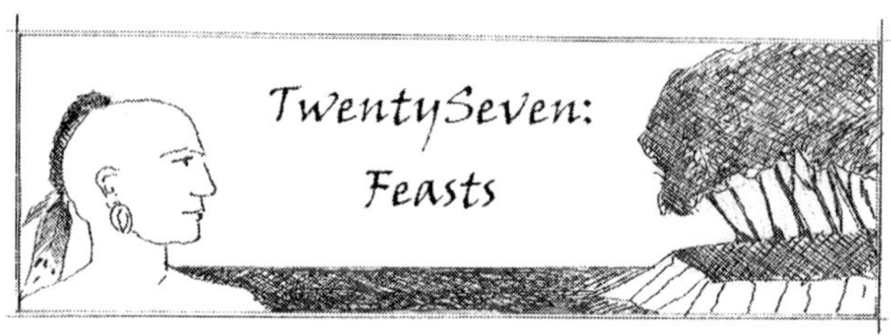

"William!" Porter yelled in his gruff and gravelly voice. "We've been prayin' for you every day for—what's it been now—seven, eight years? Nephew, we've got lots of catchin' up to do!"

William was startled to see a young Indian boy emerge from the briar thicket behind his uncle. The man motioned and he slowly approached. William got to his feet as the boy reached out his hand to him.

"This is Arthur," said Porter pronouncing it "Arter." "He's been with me for about five years. We figure he's eleven years old or so. Arthur, this is my nephew William."

"But you look like an Indian!" Arthur exclaimed.

"So do you!" said William.

Porter smiled, "Guess there's gonna be lots of questions from all of us. Let's go ahead and start back down the trail for home and we can talk when we get there. We don't want to stay here long in case Hughes decides to follow us."

The three moved quickly down the trail for about fifteen minutes. "Come with us," said Arthur, "our boat is hidden by the river, in the leaves."

"I'm glad to hear that," said William, "I've walked a long ways and I'm kinda sore from the scuffle."

Porter pulled the flat-bottomed boat from under a pile of brush. Once they started down river, it was easier to converse.

"So tell me where you've been all this time, nephew," growled Porter, slapping him on the back.

"Well I don't know where to start," William replied. "I was adopted by the Delaware for the first several years. Just recently I've lived with the family of Adam Brown near Fort Detroit. He was a captive who is now a local chief in the Wyandot tribe. They've been good to me—almost all the Indians have.

"I've had lots of experiences I could tell you but—what I'd really like to know is where my family is. Are they still alive? Do they live near here? Where is my brother Alex?"

"Whoa!" said Porter. "Let's just grab one possum-tail at a time. Alex married and went with his bride's family to Kentucky. I think they had a couple of kids last we heard. Your ma and pa are living on south of here in the mountains. Your pa is working with Preacher Houston and others to try and establish the State of Franklin in what used to be North Carolina territory."

William looked despondent. "How far away is that?"

"Well it's not too far. The boat'll take us right past the old place. You'll probably remember the scenery but the cabin and outbuildings were all burned down by the Inj....eh, by enemies. Then it's just a couple of bends of the river to the Porter homestead near Copper Creek. Only about a days ride from there down to Franklin but it's a darned rough and mountainous trip. Don't think I'd advise your goin' it alone either. Lots of outlaws like the ones you already tangled with plus Cherokees."

"I'm not worried about Cherokees," William replied, "but I'm getting tired and don't know if I want to add another two days—down there and back. I was really hoping to get to see my parents and my brother."

"Brothers, you mean. You've got three more of them and a couple of sisters. Trouble is there's no tellin' where your pa will be from one day to the next. You know how he has to be on the move all the time—and generally takes the family somewhere new every so often. Hope you can find him—but of course you're sure welcome to stay with us as long as you want."

More brothers and sisters. That information hit William like a blacksmith's hammer. It seemed like a black crow was perched on his shoulder, whispering in his ear: "Nobody misses you. There are five more to take your place. They didn't even leave you word where they could be found in case you showed up." He fought off these thoughts but still couldn't shake the discomfort he felt at having to meet strangers and greet them like family.

Besides, he disliked answering lots of questions. No doubt there would be many. He didn't reveal to Porter his plans to return to Ohio before many days. He wanted to avoid having to defend his decisions.

They pulled the boat out of the river and concealed it in brush. "We'll go the rest of the way on foot. It's a pretty steep climb," said Porter, "but it's a beaut. The creek spills over a cliff in several places. Makes a right nice place to live, it really do." His voice growled out the words and brought a smile to William's anxious face.

Susannah Porter met them at the cabin door. She was a large portly woman who never hesitated to display her emotions intensely. She hugged her husband enthusiastically and then Arthur almost as much. "And who is this young man," she asked, observing William's scalp lock. "Arthur, is this one of your kin?"

The boys both laughed. They'd had little conversation up to now and the thought of being kin struck them as funny.

Patrick threw his head back and gave three throaty guffaws. "Naw he ain't kin, Susie. Except to you—this here's your brother's boy William!"

Susannah put her hand to her chest and drew a gasping breath through her wide-open mouth. "Lord have mercy!" she shouted. "Lord have mercy!" She grabbed him around his shoulders and began kissing him and shouting over and over, "Lord have mercy! It's William come back from the dead!"

William didn't know what to do with his hands so he placed them on her waist. He was sweaty and felt embarrassed that his face was so dirty. It didn't bother Susannah one bit. She continued to make over him and burst into tears of joy, pulling him into the cabin door.

"You've got to sit down and tell me all about what you've been through. Oh William, you don't know how many years we all prayed every day for this day. Oh Lord it's a miracle—a real live miracle! You are a sight for sore eyes."

Patrick tried to calm her down: "Now Susannah don't smother him. He's had a long trip and a hard one and needs some time to simmer down. Let's don't go hog-wild over him tonight. There'll be time later if he feels like talkin'. How 'bout we all get some vittles down us first."

She'd already gone to the breezeway adjoining the double log cabin, put her fingers to her lips and whistled a wavering call to the children's room. "Come on over here, children!" she hollered. "Your paw's home and we've got some visitors joinin' us for supper."

The children came in single-file and Susannah introduced them to William: "Now this is John—he's nineteen, about your age I expect; and Catrine, who's seventeen."

William's eyes widened and he commented, "I like that name—sounds like Catherine."

Susannah continued, "Mary is fourteen; and Patrick jr.—we call him Jun, is nine. Children, this is William Walker, your long-lost cousin who has escaped from captivity among the savages!" William winced at the words but bit his lip.

They all shook hands and nodded politely but said nothing—except Jun. Wide-eyed and curious, he began firing questions at his new cousin. "Wow! You've been a captive of the Indians? How long did they hold you? Did you have to run the gauntlet? Did they shoot arrows at you?"

"Hold on!" his father barked. "That's no way to treat a guest. Give him time to get to know you first. It's easier to talk if you've got a heap of food in front of you."

In a short time the rough-hewn plank benches, which had been turned upside down on top of the pine table, were right-side up around it and the surface covered with steaming dishes—warm bread with a jar of peach-jam from the cellar, heaps of fresh green beans boiled with the butt of a smoked ham, two fried chickens and sweet yams, potatoes baked in the fire and a pan of red-eye gravy. Three green-apple pies sat on the windowsill acquiring the right temperature for dessert. It was more food at one time than William had ever remembered. The only thing he recognized at first was an iron kettle of hominy grits. "I'm sorry there's no kernel corn," apologized Susannah, "we just didn't have a very good crop this year."

William started to reach for a chicken leg but noticed Jun—who crowded in beside him on the bench—pick up a pewter fork by his plate. He watched to see how he used it, but Patrick startled him by gruffly calling to the boy. "Jun! Put down that fork until we've said a proper grace. We may live in the backwoods but we're not heathens."

Jun placed the fork beside the tin plate, reached over and took hold of William's hand as others around the table followed suit. When they bowed their heads William imitated them but kept his eyes open anticipating danger—a habit he'd learned from his Delaware family.

Porter prayed loudly, "Father God almighty whether we abound or are in want we have learned therewith to be content but we most heartily enjoy abounding. Thank Thee for these mercies and may we always share what has been given from Thy hand. And tonight we say a special hallelujah for our nephew William's release from bondage and captivity, O Thou Who didst give exodus to the Hebrews from the Egyptians. A-man and aaa-man!"

He looked at his guest. "William, you look plenty strong but you're nearly skin-and-bones. Must be from the years of meager rations and long days in the forests and on the rivers.

Eat all you care to but better go slow—your belly's probably not accustomed to this fare."

William had already puzzled over how to not eat without insulting his hosts. Not being accustomed to the variety and quantity of the meal, he was afraid he wouldn't be able to eat much. As he began to taste the food his fears lessened and he was soon partaking with exuberance, especially the chicken. Glances were exchanged when he reached into the serving bowls with his hands and put globs of food to his mouth.

Mary and Catrine tried to stifle giggles as their father frowned at them and shook his head.

While the food was disappearing, Jun finally could wait no longer for answers to his questions. "William," he said, pulling on the visitor's deerskin shirtsleeve, "how'd you get away? Did you have to kill any of them?"

Porter pointed at his son, "Boy, I told you…"

But William interrupted him. "It's alright, uncle, I don't mind his questions. No, Jun, they let me go. In fact they had to talk me into leaving."

Jun squinted at him in disbelief. "What? They wanted to get rid of you? You must've been awful bad!"

William grinned but the rest of the group looked confused. He tried to explain, "The Indians have been my family for almost as long as I can remember. They have treated me like one of their braves. I have laughed with them and suffered with them. I've fought in battle with them. They are my friends and my family now and I love them. They wanted me to come and visit you and my first parents because the treaty said I should. I wanted to come but I was also afraid that I would not be accepted anymore because I am a proud Wyandot warrior."

While the others tried to sort this out in their minds, Jun broke the silence quickly. "Wow! You've really been in battle as a warrior! A real Indian soldier? Ever kill anybody? Ever get shot? Got any scars?"

William raised his shirt and showed him the marks on his side. "Just this one—here's where the bullet went in and here's where it came out."

"Wow!" said Jun as he examined the scars.

Susannah said, "Jun, this is not a proper subject for supper."

Patrick added, "I don't think it's a good idea for you to tell this around here, William. Some folks might not understand. There's been a lot of killing and burning around the settlements. You children had best keep this to yourselves, understand?"

Arthur, who had been very quiet, entered into the conversation. "I was only five when some white men came into our village. Some of us Mingo were living with the Shawnee. Many of us were killed. My parents…"

Susannah again interrupted: "Could we please talk about this later. It's not the kind of thing we want at supper."

)()()()(

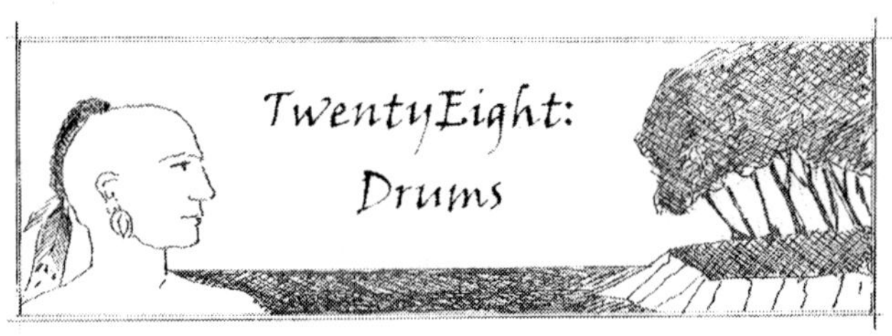

A cool welcome breeze was coming off Sandusky Bay early in the evening that day in late August. Drums and chants filled the air as travelers from as far away as Wingenund's Town walked the trails up the Detroit River, leading to the village becoming known as Brownstown.

There was a high degree of energy and excitement as Indian women made preparations for the annual Green Corn Festival. Relatives and friends of the Wendat representing several different nations were arriving every minute. The sound of many voices shouting greetings grew louder as the Festival time approached and old friends gathered around the clan totems.

Tohunehowetu (Adam Brown) was sitting in his usual place on the porch, leaning back against the log-wall of the house, smoking his favorite clay pipe. "Kweh! Kweh! (Hi!)," he exclaimed as Bigtree came up the walk, his long earlobes dangling with chains of silver coins.

"Kweh!" answered Bigtree as he climbed up the steps. They both waved a welcome to Big Kittles and his young bride

Blowing-Leaves as they also approached the house. "It is good to see all of you!" said Adam. "Bigtree you have a new and expensive looking nose-jewel I see."

"This is my special ruby I got in trade for a raccoon and three muskrat skins. I save it especially for the Green Corn Festival. The cheap ones I wear in battle. Most warriors wouldn't wear any jewelry to a fight. I say, if you may die you might as well look pretty good, huh?"

Big Kittles shook hands with them both. "Whatcha hear from our travelin' man, Will'am?"

"Nothing," Adam replied, "but he's been gone less than a couple of weeks. Mononcue returned and said he'd waved goodbye at the Virginia border. If he made it through Kentucky he'll be alright I'm sure."

"My friend Dragging Canoe will watch for him," said Bigtree. "He owes me a favor or two."

Blowing-Leaves lifted the door covering and met Lady Scanonie coming out carrying a large kettle of sagamite (boiled corn) flavored with flakes of trout and blue berries. "You look beautiful," said the younger woman, "I haven't seen you in that dress before."

Scanonie smiled appreciatively—she seldom got a compliment anymore. The men were too busy to notice, discussing politics or war or the latest hunt. "Tizameh (Thank you)," she said, "this is my special festival dress." She wore a deerskin skirt fringed in pointed red cloth. Across it were draped seven strings of shells, each looped larger than the one above it and each strand alternating red and blue. Similar stings decorated her wrists, arms and neck. "I have some more necklaces inside," she said, "would you like to wear them?"

Blowing-Leaves nodded in excitement and the two women went inside chattering something about embroidered moccasins.

An hour before dusk people began moving towards the Sacred Fire area of the village, the Brown entourage included. As the drums increased in volume, painted warriors led by several shamans circled the fire and began dancing. Each carried stalks of corn freshly gathered from the fields. These they tied to various totems as offerings to the spirits of harvest and the Great Spirit. The other participants sat on woven mats around the dancers. After the religious ceremony, they also joined in the dancing, followed by a great joyful banquet of many different corn concoctions—boiled, roasted, baked—even a corn cake mixed with berries.

Scanonie noticed one girl who did not seem to be enjoying herself. Catherine Rankin was arrayed in a woven blue dress covered with flower designs in beads. "You don't seem to be having much fun tonight," said Scanonie. Catherine looked down as tears came to her eyes. "You miss him, don't you?"

She nodded and asked, "Do you think he'll come back?"

The older woman smiled and brushed Catherine's braided hair with her hand. "I'm sure he will," she replied. "He left his heart here to wait for him."

The celebration ended in the early hours of morning, when everyone was too exhausted to dance, chant or drink any more.

~~~

Patrick Porter looked at his guests and remarked, "It's a miracle, it is! Just like Jesus turning water into wine—we've gone and turned two whole chickens into a pile of bones. Well, the hounds will work their magic on the rest. Now who's gonna help me milk and put up the horses for the night?"

The boys—John, Jun and Arthur—all jumped up and followed their father out the door while Catrine and Mary stayed to help their mother.

"Oh go on out and help your Paw," said Susannah, "I'll clear off the table. Get the chores done fast and we can have some fun together afterwards." Mary grabbed William's arm and pulled him along with them.

At dark the boys put the benches upside down on the table while their father reached up on the mantel and got a worn oblong wooden box. Out of it he brought a fiddle and as each one found a seat on the floor around him, he began to play. As the strings whistled a marching tune, William raised his head in surprise. He thought he heard a Wendat turtle-shell rattle accompanying the music.
~~~

Jun punched him and asked, “Can you hear the snake rattles? Paw always keeps them inside the fiddle for a special sound.” Then the boy turned over a kettle and kept time on it with a wooden spoon.

Soon everyone but William was singing with gusto, stomping and clapping:

We led fair freedom hither, and lo the desert smiled,
A paradise of pleasure new opened in the wild;
...Lift up your hearts my heroes
And swear with proud disdain,
The wretch that would ensnare you
Shall spread his net in vain;
Should Europe empty all her force,
We’d meet them in array,
And shout and fight and fight and shout
For brave Ameri-cay!

“Hooray!” barked Patrick. “Hooray! Hooray!” shouted the others. William laughed and clapped with them, caught up in the enthusiasm.

“Sing my favorite,” said Mary, normally a quiet girl. Her father put the fiddle to his chin and began to play and sing a lilting patriotic tune:

Young ladies in town and those that live ‘round,
Wear none but your own country linen;
Of economy boast, let your pride be the most
To show clothes of your own make and spinnin’.
...Though the times remain darkish,
Young men will be sparkish,

And love you much stronger than ever.

They all clapped and hoorayed again, and Patrick played a few more songs. Catrine was the next to make request. "Papa let's sing mine now."

"Oh, daughter—you'll make us all cry, you will. What do the rest o' ye say? Shall we sing Catrine's love song?"

"Yes! Yes!" rang out around the room. A mournful wail poured out from the fiddle:

Here I sit on Buttermilk Hill,
Who can blame me, cryin' my fill
And every tear would turn a mill,
Johnny has gone for a soldier.
... I'll dye my dress, I'll die it red,
And through the streets I'll beg for bread,
For the lad that I love from me has fled--
Johnny has gone for a soldier.

The boys saluted and shouted but the girls wiped their eyes with handkerchiefs.

The music had brought back some forgotten memories to William. He thought to himself, "What are my songs?"

Arthur, sitting across the room from him, asked in a quiet voice, "Is it time for my song now, Papa?" Porter nodded and began to play and sing a melody he'd learned at an outdoor brush-arbor meeting:

In the dark wood, no other Indian nigh,
I look to heaven and send my cry,
Upon my knees so low;
Then God on high in shining place
Sees me in night with teary face,
The priest he tells me so.

He sends an angel to take my care
He comes Himself to hear my prayer
As Indian's heart does pray;
He sees me now, he knows me here
He says, poor Indian, never fear!
I'm with you night and day.

So I love God with inside heart,
He fights for me, He takes my part,
He's saved my life before.
God loves poor Indian in the wood,
Then I love God, and that is good!
I'll pray—and pray some more!

Arthur laughed and clapped with abandon, as he had not for any other song that night.

Patrick put the fiddle in the box and placed it on the mantel. "It's time for readin' the Bible and family prayers," he said. "But first—maybe it's a good time to tell William about Arthur's story. Do you want to tell him how you came to live with us Arthur?"

"You tell it Papa. You use words better than I do."

"Well your words are just fine son but I'll have a go at it if you like. You correct me if I get it wrong will you?"

"Arthur came to us about five years ago and it was like this. I was camping in the woods after a hunt on my way back home. There hadn't been any fighting around these parts for a while so I wasn't much on my guard—just sitting around smoking my pipe and enjoying the fire.

"All of a sudden from outa nowhere steps this big Indian in warpaint and feathers! I started to grab for my rifle but he raised his hands over his head and spoke to me in perfect English.

"He said, 'Patrick Porter—I know who you are! I am Chief John Logan.'"

William stuttered, "You mean Talgayeeta? Chief Logan of the Mingo confederation?"

"That's right. Well sir he says to me that he'd been watchin' me for a while. Right then I recalled that Catrine had gone down to the spring to get water and found several painted war clubs with a note under them. She brings 'em in her apron to me and when I see what they are I says, 'Well Kate you must have had a powerful fight with the Indians and took their war clubs from them!' The note was a letter from Chief Logan saying mysteriously, 'Patrick Porter, I want to speak with you soon. Do not be afraid when I arrive. I intend no mischief. Logan.'

"The chief sat down beside me and told me he had a favor to ask. 'I've watched you and you are a good man—good to the children,' he said. Then he began to weep and said, 'I try to be a good man but when my family was slaughtered I was filled with rage. All I wanted to do was kill, kill, kill. I had always been a friend to the white man but when some of them murdered my wife and children, an evil spirit entered my heart.' He sobbed again, 'Not a drop of my blood runs in any living creature. Who is there to mourn for Logan? Not one.'

"I told him I was sorry for what the murderers had done. 'I have also murdered,' he said, 'when the bad spirit controlled me. But now I want you to help me do something kind and good. I want you to meet Dale.' As he waved his hand in the air an Indian boy stepped out from the trees. He looked about five years old. 'This is Dale,' said the chief. 'A short time ago the soldiers came and killed everyone in his village including his mother and father. Only Dale escaped because he was swimming and heard the screaming, so he hid. His family all were Christians, as my father and I have been. He tells me he has had a dream that he was preaching love and forgiveness to the whites. Are you a Christian, Patrick Porter?'

"Yes, I said, but not always a good one. Sometimes I fight with Susannah and when I drink too much I curse at the horses.

"'You must fight against the bad spirit too,' he said. 'I want you to take Dale and teach him more English and about Christ and the Bible. Maybe the Great Spirit has called him to do this thing, to be a preacher and missionary to your people.'

"I refused every way I could. Chief, I said, the Mingo warriors would hunt me down and kill me. 'No they won't. I'll just tell them the boy drowned in the river. You must take him Patrick.'

"I never saw Logan again. When Dale—Arthur Dale I named him later—held out his hands and looked me in the eye, I had to say yes. So here he is—a great boy and part of this family. Did I tell that about right, Arthur? "

Arthur smiled and nodded as the other children gathered around to hug him. He turned to William and said, "You see—I am an Indian in a white family as you are a white man in an Indian home. But God sees us both and gives us two families to show us His love. We are both where we are for a reason. Though I am only a boy, I know this because His Spirit has shown me. Do you also know it William?"

It was all an unexpected and emotional surprise for William and he sat stunned and wordless. He put his hands over his eyes to think, knowing that it would take a lot more thought before he could put it all together in his mind.

)()()()(

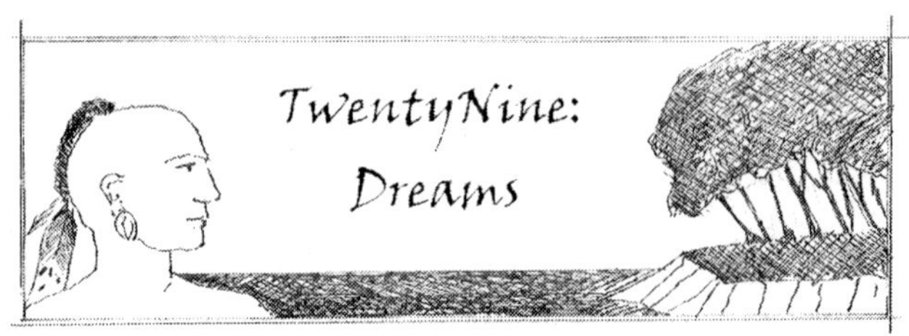

William watched with interest as his uncle opened the glass door of an old enclosed burled-oak bookcase. Porter retrieved his Bible with the spotted fawn-hide cover he'd made himself. As the smaller children stretched out on the floor and leaned their chins on their elbows, and the others sat cross-legged, he began the family devotions.

"You remember that last night we read another portion of the story of Jacob son of Isaac and grandson of Abraham. In that part of the account, Jacob had to leave home and go to a distant land because his brother Esau threatened to kill him. Why was Esau angry with him?"

Several hands shot up and Porter pointed to Jun. "Because Jacob cheated Esau out of his father's blessing," he answered.

Mary added, "Yes, but you forget that he had also tricked him into selling his birthright."

Porter asked, "And would someone tell us all what a birthright was?"

Mary said, "It was the biggest share of the stuff whenever their papa died."

"I get the biggest share," said John, the oldest.

"Nuh-huh," said Catrine, "you're just the oldest one at home."

Porter explained to William, "Susannah and I have three more grown children you haven't met."

"Oh," said William, "I remember them—one is named Samuel isn't he?"

"That's right!"

"Anyway," said John, "it's a good thing it's Samuel because a girl couldn't get a birthright."

"That's just back in Hebrew times," said Mary. "Girls can inherit anything now. I've got a friend in the valley that..."

Her father said firmly, "That's enough! You all talk about that later. Now we're reading from where Jacob is spending a night in the wilderness between home and his destination at the region of Paddanaram.

Arthur whispered to William, "Sounds like an Indian name."

"This is from Genesis 28," said Porter:

> And he lighted upon a certain place and tarried there all night, because the sun was set; and he took of the stones and put them for his pillows, and lay down in that place to sleep. And he dreamed, and behold a ladder ...and the top of it reached to heaven; and behold the angels of God ascending and descending on it. And behold the Lord stood above it and said, I am the Lord God of Abraham thy father

> and the God of Isaac...thy seed shall be as the dust of the earth and thou shalt spread abroad to the west ...and in thee and in thy seed shall all the families of the earth be blessed. And behold I am with thee, and will keep thee in all places whither thou goest and will bring thee again into this land; for I will not leave thee until I have done that ..."

After prayers, William went with the other children across to the adjoining cabin where John showed him a feather tick in the loft next to Arthur's. The boys had poked several holes in the chinking between two logs under the eaves of the roof, so they could lay on their backs and look out at the moon and stars over the mountain range.

"What's it like to be adopted?" John wondered aloud.

"I think," said Arthur, "it's kinda like Paw said about that rose bush by the front door. He dug it up by the roots when they left North Carolina and replanted it in the Virginia sunshine. It just kept growing and making blooms."

John said, "Sometimes when I've been griped at by Paw I've wished I could've had some other father—ya' know what I mean? 'Course, I'd want to choose which one."

"It's a strange feeling for me," said William, "when you know you have a mother and father someplace but after awhile you can hardly see their faces anymore. Sometimes you'll be busy hunting or playing stickball and you suddenly wonder what they are doing at the same time. After awhile it's like they are dead but you keep wishing you could talk with them one more time, just to tell them you're all right or ask a question. Sometimes I won't even think about it for months—then something will remind me. It's as if part of me is missing—like a muskrat that chewed off its foot and left it in the trap. He's free but part of him is gonna always be gone."

"I've felt that way about my parents," said ten-year old Arthur. "I know they're dead but I keep thinking I should go talk to them. Sometimes I do. I just go out into the woods and look up at the sky and tell them things I want them to know. Most of the time I'm just glad to be with the Porter family. Your real family is the one you have. I can read now and someday I will preach to people about God's love for everybody—red, white, black—everybody. That's what God wants me to do, I'm sure of it."

"What makes you so sure?" asked William. "You're just a kid."

"I've always known, even since I was very young, back in the Indian village."

"But don't you miss the Indian way of life?" asked John. "I've always thought that would be a real adventure—to just live in the forests and hunt and fish and fight wild animals and enemies with nobody tellin' you what to do."

"Yeah," said Arthur, "but we do all those things here. Except the not gettin' told part."

"Yes," said William, "and sometimes there's no food—sometimes there's danger. Just like here I guess. I think the main thing is to appreciate who you've been given—and anytime you can put your feet under your momma's table you'd better do it—no matter which momma she is."

The three of them lay in silence looking at the stars and thinking their own private thoughts, dreaming their own dreams—John trying to picture himself as an Indian chasing buffalo; Arthur, preaching in a brush-arbor to settlers and Indians together; and William, looking at the night sky on Sandusky Bay with an Irish-French-Wyandot lass by the name of Catherine.

He heard Arthur talking under his breath. William carefully leaned his head closer to hear what he was saying and to whom he was talking. He heard, "...Thanks for sending William here. You know Lord, I thought for a long time I was the only kid that ever felt this way. But since I've met William, I don't feel so strange. I hope he knows you and can take you with him if he goes back to Ohio. Wouldn't that be great, Lord—you would have a brown Indian boy here and a white Indian boy there. I hope we catch some fish tomorrow. G'Night."

~~~

Thinking about his momma's table made him want to go on looking for the Walker's but the thought of going farther away from Brownstown was like taking a spoonful of kerosene for a cold—the taste was awful and there was no guarantee it would do any good. He knew where his home was—and where
~~~

Catherine was. After a week at Porter's he decided it was time to go back home.

It was Saturday night when he told them. "Uncle Patrick and Aunt Susannah," he said, "it has been good to find you and spend time getting to know you—but I think it's time I start back home. The weather can get pretty bad sometimes, even in September. Thank you for everything you've done for me."

Susannah was almost in shock. "What did you just say? You are going back? To what? We want you to stay and make this your home, at least until you find your parents. Don't even think about leaving us! Has somebody told you to leave or hurt you in any way? Don't you want to stay and find your real family?" She began to cry and so did the girls.

William put his hands to his face to think. Then he looked at the floor and said, "I think 'real' is what you know you have."

Patrick stroked his beard and growled, "That's about the dumbest idea I've heard since the Jones boys tried to corral a family of bears. I won't hear of it. William you are my responsibility as long as you are under my roof. Just what do ya think your father would say to me if I let you leave? I can just hear it now, 'Oh brother-in-law the boy wanted to go starve with the Indians until the cavalry burned down their homes. So I just let him go—just like that, I let him go.' Is that what you'd want me to say, son?"

"There's no lettin' me go about it," said William. "I'm sorry if you don't understand but I've been makin' my own decisions for a long time now. I know what I have there. It may not be what you want but it's mine. I have a Wyandot family that loves me. I have a warm fire at night. I have the same moon you have but it shimmers on the blue waters of Sandusky. Best of all, the wars are over and we are far enough away from the frontier that settlers will no longer bother my people. That is what I have, that is why I must return. I'm very sorry if you don't understand."

John walked over and stood beside William. "I understand. I wish we'd had time to hunt and fish together while you were here. I want you to remember your Cousin John Porter. If I can someday, I'd like to come and see what life is like in the Indian country of the northwest!"

The boys shook hands and after some time all the Porter's wished him Godspeed and embraced him. Patrick spoke in a kinder voice, "Tomorrow is the Lord's Day, William. Would you just stay and go with us to our little church for mornin' worship? Then we'll see you off and John can ride with you through the mountains if he'd like."

The "preacher-boy"—as they had begun calling Arthur—took William by the arm, looked up with big brown eyes and said, "The Lord will be pleased with that—and so will Arthur."

~~~
~~~

William sat on the bench next to his Aunt Susannah with the rest of the family arranged on either side of them. He had worn one of his uncle's straw hats but was told he had to remove it as they came in the door of the log chapel. He could feel the stares at his scalp lock as Patrick introduced him to his friends and neighbors as his nephew.

A woman commented in a loud whisper, "Looks like Porter took an Indian for a son and the savages retaliated by makin' his nephew an Indian."

Patrick whispered as loud to William, "Don't mind her, nephew. That's just Mrs. McMahan exercisin' her gift of tongue."

A man in a long black coat with split tails in back strode to the front, prayed loudly and read from the Bible. He led the congregation in three long hymns, waving his hands in the air as they sang.

William thought, "There is no fiddle and no drum—how can they sing without them?"

The man began to talk. Then he talked and talked and talked.

William whispered to his aunt, "Does he have the gift of tongue also?" Susannah just put her finger to her lips and said something that sounded to William like wind blowing gently through trees.

The black-coat man was talking about faith—you live by it, you have to have it, you can't be saved without it.

William's mind was in a swirl. It wasn't the language that was confusing him. He had no idea how to get this thing called "faith." Surely, he thought, the man will tell me how to obtain this if it is so important.

The bench was hard and he wondered if they would soon sit on the floor around the walls. "Maybe the dancing will begin soon," he reasoned, trying to stop squirming because the bench squeaked and a crack in the wood kept pinching his leg.

At the end of a long time, the man in the black coat passed around a basket and read a final scripture.

William, who had been struggling to stay awake, suddenly listened. He had heard the same words years before, from his Aunt Ann the night they were captured: "We know that all things work together for good to them that love the Lord..." For some reason they were like a cool brook to a dry tongue. He had not felt the Great Spirit the whole time, but his heart came alive at that verse.

On the way out of the chapel, a man walked up to his uncle. "Porter have ye heard the news? McPheeters says that Ann Cowan has been freed from captivity! Mrs. Scott seen her on the Crab Orchard Road jist this week, she did. Says it was on account of a new treaty the gov'ment signed with the Injuns. Guess them things do some good once't in awhiles after all."

"Did ya hear that, William?" Patrick asked. "Another miracle in the family! Your Aunt Susannah has got you back and now she and your mom have their sister back too. What a time we'll have when we have a Walker family reunion again!" He put his hand on William's shoulder with a firm squeeze. "We'll be expecting you to join us, hear? Even if ya have ta cross three rivers and two mountains ta do it!"

William smiled, "Someday it'll happen—and if you get me the word I promise I'll be there!"

~~~

When Arthur learned that William and John were about to ride off towards Kentucky he determined he would go with them. "It's just not safe for man or boy out there but especially for a small boy," Porter advised, but to no avail.

"I stayed in the river while soldiers burned our village," Arthur said, "and I was a lot smaller then than I am now."

In the end Porter gave up in admiration of Arthur's courage but told John, "You remember—both these boys look like Indians in spite of the hunter's clothing. Keep off the main trails and don't go near trading posts and for sure not taverns, hear? If it weren't for your mother and the little ones I'd go with you—but I can't take that risk."

"Don't worry," John replied, "we'll be careful like always."

"It's the 'like always' that worries me," said his father.

After saying their goodbyes, the boys were off on their adventure, exuberant at the sense of freedom they enjoyed. Throughout the valley they felt the mountains were funneling
~~~

them towards their goal. When they crossed the mountain they were engulfed in pine trees that seemed to point like Indian spears towards the roof of the sky.

The sense of smallness was not lost on William. Riding his horse beside Arthur, he took the opportunity to quiz the "preacher boy." "Arthur I've heard you pray on your bed at night. You seem to have a different kind of friendship with the Great Spirit that I don't have. I mean you can just talk with God like he was your big brother or something. How do you do that?"

"I don't know," he replied, "it just seems natural."

"Has it always been that way?" William asked.

Arthur thought about it and said, "'Bout as long a I can remember. My Mingo father told me that I put my trust in Christ when I was very small. I guess that's when I first experienced my own real faith."

"There's that word again," said William. "How do I get faith for myself—like you have?"

"I don't know. I think the Lord has to give it to you," he answered—then added, "I'll talk to Him about it."

ӾӾӾӾӾ

All three of the travelers overslept. A heavy dark cloud had rolled in from the west and it looked more like night than day. Arthur was the first awake and had to shake the others. "The sky looks dangerous," he announced. "We better get to shelter somewhere."

John rubbed his eyes and poured water from the goat-bladder canteen on William's face, who sprang up immediately ready for battle. "It's just me," said John, "tryin' to get you up so we can get outta here."

"What are we gonna do?" asked Arthur. John looked around to get his bearings. "There's an old log shack less than an hour from here. It's kinda hidden in a gulch between two mountains. Only problem is we gotta cross the Clinch River to get there. If we get ridin' quick we can maybe beat the storm."

They had just mounted up when a thunderclap exploded and a five-fingered lightning bolt split the sky. Torrents of heavy rain began beating against the three riders and their horses. The animals obediently ducked their heads and trotted forward at their masters' signals. The boys could barely see ahead and were forced to follow the trail because of thickets of briars. The wind was so ferocious they could not hear each other yell and the trees around them bent like taut arrow-bows.

They arrived at the Clinch within the hour but the river was already rising. "Let's go!" shouted John. "There's no shelter here and the water will only get deeper if we wait." He urged his horse into the stream. Arthur followed with William bringing up the rear.

The horses swam with their riders with great effort. John was about to reach the far shore when a wall of water from a flash flood came smashing through the channel, sweeping the legs out from under Arthur's horse and pitching both beast and rider into the current.

Neither of the other boys saw Arthur being carried downstream—William had turned his horse to try to regain the near shore and John had pushed his onto the far bank. The noise of the storm muted the boy's cry for help as well as the horse's frantic whinnies.

John turned just in time to catch sight of the horse's head vanishing downstream. Yelling across at William was futile, but by exaggerated waving and pointing, he finally got the message to him and each of them headed downstream on opposite sides of the river.

William found it tremendously difficult to walk. The bank was slick from the rain, and between the river and forest was thick brush and briars. More than once he was nearly blown off his feet by the strong winds. He guessed that John was having as much trouble on the far side but they both focused on trying to spot Arthur. The rain was like a curtain, preventing sight for more than a few steps in front of them.

A memory flashed in William's brain, something he hadn't thought about for years. He recalled falling into the river the week of his capture and the tremendous fear that gripped him as the powerful water pushed him under and threw him violently against submerged rocks and debris.

William stopped suddenly and cupped his hands behind his ears. He thought he heard a sound like a human voice but not like a cry or scream. He listened again—nothing. He moved slowly in the direction from which he thought it came. Nothing. Wait—there it is again. Sounds like—music—singing?

Close to the river a tree had fallen with trash collected in the branches. As he approached the pile he again heard a voice. "It is singing!" he said to himself, still listening intently.

Now he heard the words in a high-pitched child's singsong: "...He sees me now, he knows me here, he says poor Indian never fear, I'm with you night and day..."

"Arthur! Arthur—where are you?" he shouted. "I'm right here," said the voice, as yet unseen. William squinted and searched the debris. He was as close to the edge of the river as he could get without slipping in.

"Keep singing!" he yelled, and the voice began, "He sends his angel, take my care..." At last William saw a small brown foot wedged between a branch and the tree trunk.

"I can't walk or crawl across the fallen tree without being washed into the river," he told himself. He looked around to see if there was anything he could use to rescue the boy. He thought about the times he had gone swimming in the Tuscarawas with the Lenape youth and the long grape vines they used to swing on. "Hold on, Arthur, hold on," he yelled. I'll reach you soon!"

Arthur stopped singing for a moment and then began, "I'll pray and pray again..."

At the base of the fallen tree there were tangles of strong grape vines as William expected. Some of them were still rooted in the ground and he tugged until he got one loose from the top of the tree. He tied it around his waist with a strong knot and began crawling along the slick bark towards the branch where he'd spotted Arthur's foot. A few moments later he wrapped his arms under Arthur's arms and over his chest. William locked his fingers together and with Arthur in front of him, he pulled the boy as he inched backwards, straddling the log with his legs, hanging on with his knees.

As soon as he had the boy safe under a thick bush that kept out some of the rain, William went out looking for John. "I've got to mark this spot so I don't loose Arthur again," he thought. When he got his bearings by a walnut tree, he walked down the riverbank and saw John searching on the other side.

He was only able to get John's attention by climbing part way up a tree and waving his arms. He walked back to the bush and crawled underneath with the shivering boy. He hoped John had figured out that he'd found Arthur.

"This isn't the driest place to be but it's a little better than being out in the downpour," William said as he lay down on the ground next to his young friend. "I wish I could get you dry but I'm afraid we'll just have to wait here 'til morning."

Arthur was shivering but said, teeth chattering, "This is better than underwater."

"Were you scared?" William asked.

"A lot. So I started singing. I'm not afraid when I sing. I knew God was with me."

"How'd you know that?"

"He said he would be—and I don't think he ever lies, does he? Not that I know of, anyway."

The storm ended sometime before dawn. The river dropped rapidly and John was able to come back across. They agreed he should take Arthur with him on his horse and head back home. "I'll be fine the rest of the way," said William, "there's no use risking Arthur getting really sick and two on a horse will wear it out soon."

"Goodbye William," said Arthur. "You saved my life. That means we're something like brothers, doesn't it?"

"You bet," said William, "I'll always remember you—and you, Cousin John. Hope all your dreams come true. The good ones, anyway—and may they all be good ones."

William rode on alone up the Clinch River and across the rolling countryside until, somewhere along the way he crossed over into the hunting grounds of Kentucky. The sun warmed him and dried out his clothes by midmorning.

That evening he was afraid to build a campfire so he lay under the stars and thought about many things. He remembered the fight with Cherokee warriors when he was a captive. He recalled the blurred face of the stranger who several times had come to his aid—the first time when he ran the gauntlet and thought he couldn't get up to finish the run. The man had lifted him to his feet and kept him going.

He thought about the scripture his uncle had read about Jacob running from home. "Here I am," he thought, "alone under the stars just like Jacob. I don't know whether I'm running away from my home or going towards it. Yes I do! I'm going home, home to Catherine and home to a future and a destiny. I was meant to be with the Wyandot—at least I think I have a purpose there. What if I miss it? What if I'm supposed to do something great and I miss it?

"But what was that other scripture? 'All things work together for good.' That's for 'those who love the Lord.' Arthur loves God, in his growing boy kind of way. I'd like to love God but I don't know how. I want to believe, to have faith, but I don't know how. Why can't the Creator show me the way?"

William looked up at the stars again. "Lord God—the Great Spirit of all—I want to love you but I don't feel worthy. I've tried and tried to find the way. Now I give up trying."

Suddenly there came an image to his mind—a face. He knew it to be the face of the rescuing stranger and he realized where he had seen it before. It was the face of the man on the cross he'd seen on the wall of Tohunehowetu's (Adam Brown's) home. In that moment there came such a sense of a divine Presence that William's heart felt overwhelmed. He began breathing with fast, shallow breaths and he had a perception of being part of the whole creation—as if the stars were smiling and the trees whispering their affirmations that he, too, had a place in the purpose and plan of the Great Spirit of all.

He knew. At last, he knew. The pull he felt in his heart towards Sandusky was not only his love for Catherine. It was the Spirit calling his name and beckoning him to find his life by losing it in Him—for the sake of his people.

As "The Man Who Walks" rode north in the morning to face the next adventure of his life he possessed the greatest gift of all and the one thing he really needed. Faith—his very own—establishing his place in the Creator's world. It was the assurance of his hopes fulfilled, the evidence of a destiny not yet seen with the eyes but now firmly held within his heart.

~~~

And somewhere—in Detroit or Ohio—a lonesome young girl prayed: "Oh, Great Spirit! Our Father! Protect William today, and bring him home safely, soon, into my arms."

And somewhere—perhaps beyond the mysterious, wooded boundary that separated Virginia from the territory of Tennessee—a mother began her morning prayers (as she had for years): "Dear Lord, watch over and guard William today, wherever he walks. Keep him safe, and if it please Thee, grant me the joy of holding him once more on this earth. If not here, then in Heaven. Amen."

Epilogue

When William Walker was dying in 1823 (after years of service to the United States and the Wyandot Nation), he rose up on his bed, lifted his hands to heaven and said, "Oh! Did I ever think I should love Jesus in this manner...I love Him! I love Him!" An hour later, he was with the Creator- Redeemer.
~~~

Endnotes

For complete information on sources cited here, see the Bibliography.

<u>Page</u>

10. The date of William Walker's capture is given as "about 1774" (White, GDJWF, pp. 12) and then as 1781 (White, ibid. p.13; Draper, LWW). His birth is also listed as 1770 and 1765 (White, ibid.) The place of capture is disputed as either Greenbrier Co. or Rockbridge County, VA. Public records show his uncle, Samuel Cowan (or Cowen, husband to Ann) died in Washington Co. (later Russell) VA, along the Clinch River in 1778/9. I believe he was the uncle with whom William was plowing when captured. Ann Cowan was taken captive at the same time, so the locale would have been along the Clinch Valley. For that reason, I believe William was born about 1765, since he was old enough when captured to have learned to read and write. See also testimonies in Draper by Chas. Bickle and Mrs. Samuel Scott, confirming the Clinch Valley as place of capture.

12. Mononcue and Bigtree are historical persons who resided at Sandusky village near Walker in later years. (Finley, AJBF, pp.436f) Though there is no evidence that any Wyandot warriors were involved in the Delaware raiding party that captured him, it was not unusual for various tribes to travel together, especially those living near one another in the Ohio area. (See JSW, "captured in 1789" by "a mixed band of marauding Cherokee, Delaware, Shawnee, and Wyandotte Indians." And, "In 1780 the greater number of Delaware...took up their residence with the Senecas, Shawnees and Wyandots on the Sandusky..." (HSC)

12. Mononcue's features as a child are "age-regressed" from a portrait of him as an adult. (Marsh, MTC p.39)

13. Bigtree's physical description. (Finley, AJBF, pp.447f).

15. Events surrounding the capture see Draper, 11U & 13ZZ, as told by William Walker, jr.

17. The word Wendat is sometimes Wandat, used interchangeably for the language/people of the Wyandot (also spelled Wyandotte.)
18. Walker's thoughts when first captured I surmised from similar thoughts of one of his later captured cousins, James Moore (Brown, CAV, p.24).
24. "Watayurunoh" is the Wyandot word for Cherokee. When the speaker is Delaware, Lenape vocabulary is used. (Doyle, L/ED)
26. "The settlers...were entirely off their guard; nothing calculated to excite their alarm had occurred for a very long time." (White, ibid. p. 13)
27. Ann Cowan's capture. (Draper, ibid. 11U)
32. Ann discourages escape. The hunts are unsuccessful. (Draper, ibid.)
48. Walker's son says they took his father to the Delaware towns "on the Whetstone" after first taking him to villages on the Muskingum. (Draper, LPDC.)
53. Big Kittles (William Spicer). John Johnston, Indian Agent, says Spicer was a large land owner and farmer in his adult years. (Draper, LCJJ) But it is also said that "Spicer's cabin, like himself, is said to have been the filthiest west of the Alleghenies." (Stenoien, WBKS)
53. Running the gauntlet. (White, ibid. p. 14)
56. Delaware homes (Weslager, DI p.51-52)
56. Moonshower is a fictitious name—no record exists of Walker's Delaware mother's name.
61. Dancing-Fire is a fictitious character.
61. Lenni Lenape. (Weslager, ibid. p.31f)
62. John Killbuck. This was actually John III. (Weslager, ibid. p. 309-11)
63. Stickball—also called baggataway or lacrosse (see B; SR;& Vennum, HNAL.)
64. Chief White Eyes (Wicocalind) and Killbuck (Gelelemend) and the political dilemma, see Weslager, ibid. p. 298f and "Message to the Chiefs" in the Miami Collection of history.
71. Council House (Weslager, ibid. p.293)

75. There is no record of William Walker's Indian name.
82. John Walker, ranger. (Gilbert, WM p. 37f)
82. Scotch-Irish (Leyburn, TSI)
85. Tomahawk markings. (Buser, WC)
89. Indian boys (Gilbert, WM p. 42-43)
89. "Wigwam" is an English derivation of the word for an Indian-style house. The Lenape wikwames and wigawan are slight variations.
98. Buffalo hunting (Standing Bear, TB) "These big animals are not afraid of wolves and some of the hunters could dress up in wolfskin and sneak in to the middle of a herd." (See also Catlin's famous painting at the Smithsonian, "Buffalo Hunt under the Wolfskin Mask.")
104. Rumors about Killbuck (Weslager, pp.312-313)
104. Princeton. (Weslager, ibid. pp. 310-311)
105. White Eyes' death. (Indiana Docket 317)
105. Cornstalk (Morton HRCV, p.78)
107. Killbuck and Pipe conflict. (Weslager, ibid. p.309f)
109. The sweat lodge. (Windwalker, NASL; also, "Hist. of the SL")
114. Col. Morgan (Weslager, ibid. p. 308)
116. Jump Mountain legend. (Morton, HRCV p. 10)
117f. Col Bowman's expedition. (HMCO, p.222f; Eckert TDABR p.202f; also RR) The cousins' enlistment is fiction, but may have some basis in fact. It is known that their Porter relatives were involved. (Willis, PPFB)
125. Simon Girty was one of the most hated men on the frontier because of his adoption by the Shawnee and his enthusiastic leadership of attacks on the Americans and his later alliance with the British. Some of the Indians, of course, admired him. William Walker, jr., for instance, wrote that Girty did try to help Col. Crawford but was threatened with death himself if he persisted. (Eckert, TDABR, numerous references; OHC,SG; Pitz, DMCSG; Draper, LWW)
130. Story of Boone and the Chief's son. (Eckert, TDABR p.21)
134. Joseph Sabosh (Crumrine, HWC pp.105 & 107; also GMCI) His relationship with "Moonshower" is fictional.

142. Indian stories. (SIL)
146. Story of Joseph is found in the Holy Bible, Genesis 37-50.
153. Indian burials. (Bonvillain, TH p.36-39)
159. The character Half-Scalp is fictional.
166. Tohunehowetu (Adam Brown) was considered by some to be a local chief—he could not be a War Chief because he was white. (Clarke, OTHW; Draper, 6C "Letter from William Walker"; WNO, "Adam Brown.")
168. When William Walker arrived in Detroit, he was described as a "poor sickly-looking white boy" by Clarke (Draper, LPDC)
169f. Bigtree's battles—he was very young when he fought against the British at Braddock's defeat, 1755. Finley (ARJBF pp.247f) gives a lengthy biography of Bigtree and says, "When but a boy he was in 'Braddock's defeat…also in the war with the southern Indians, where he was taken captive by the Cherokees…", and includes the chief's own testimony of his escape and prayer for safety, etc.
169. "The Wyandots were prominent in the defeat of Braddock in 1755." (see WNK.)
169. Washington and Red Hawk's rifle. (Eckert, ibid. lxi)
170f. Bigtee's capture and escape. (De Voe, LTK, chap.6)
172. One souce says this Detroit meeting was after the McIntosh Treaty of 1785 but that would have required his return to his original family. I believe it was probably at an earlier council in Detroit that Walker and Brown met. (Draper, ibid.)
173. The Brown's were devout Christians, probably Catholic, Adam possibly influenced by the French heritage of his Wyandot wife. He was, however, respectful of ancient Indian rituals and later of the Protestant missions. (Walker, SBNOW.)
173. Lady Scanonie is a made-up name since, unfortunately, no record seems to exist of her given name. I'm sure she was a "lady of peace" like her husband (Clarke, OTHW p.67; De Voe, ibid.)
173. William Walker was a descendant of the original Scotch-Irish settlers along Walker's Creek, the son of one John Walker. (White, GDJWWS pp. 6,12f.)

174. When the first property taxes were assessed in 1782 (Rockbridge Co.) there were 5 John Walker's listed. White's record seems to rule out all of them as William's father except the one who settled at Broad Creek, south of Walker's Creek. If he is the father, he married a "Miss Long" and was in Washington Co, VA, in 1778 when his father (also John) died. He then left the area and his destination afterwards has been disputed by various family historians. (White, ibid.; RCV, PPTL)
174. Several sources say that Adam Brown had been acquainted with William's family in Virginia. (Draper, LWW 11U)
174. Seketa is a fictitious name. Brown's daughters' names are unknown. (WNO, AB)
183. Adam Brown's capture. One source says he was captured in 1776 but another says 1756. The latter seems more realistic since he was old enough to have been an adopted father to William. (Arbuckle, CAB; WNO, AB)
184. Wendat Creation myth. (WNK)
185. The "Black Robes" were French Jesuit priests who lived and labored among the Huron (Wyandot) from 1634 until the late 1700's.
186. Broadhead and the Heckewelder message. The Moranvian missionary's warning to the American military was intended to help protect the Christian Indians at the Moravian towns, including Gnadenhutten. It backfired, infuriating Pipe and Wingenund, who were British allies. (Weslager, ibid., p. 314)
189. Chief Buckongahelas warning at Gnadenhutten. (Weslager, ibid., pp. 315-316)
190. John Carpenter (Crumrine, WCH p. 103)
200. Joseph Sabosh's murder. (Crumrine, ibid., pp.105-107)
204. The killings may have taken place in storage sheds. Clarke says it was in the chapel and the mutilated bodies were burned there. (Draper, LPDC)
204. Private Johnston is a fictitious name for an unnamed militiaman. The legend is that the boy grew up in the soldier's family and then returned to his Delaware people. If it's not true, it should be. (Crumrine, ibid., footnote p.108)

205. The scalp bounty in Pennsylvania. The state that led the way in peaceful coexistence under the Quakers had succumbed to the outrage of settlers and passed a bounty price-list for Indian scalps.
205. Escape of three children. (Crumrine, ibid., p.108)
206. Weiss' letter to the Bishop. (Crumrine, ibid. footnote p.107)
210. The Indian's advance warning of a march towards Upper Ohio. (Eckert, ibid. p.341)
210. Col. Williamson who attacked the Gnadenhutten village was not, in fact, the leader of the militia that left from Mingo Bottoms.
211. The details of the Indian's counterattack plans. (Eckert, ibid. pp. 341f; Crumrine, ibid. p.114f)
214. Did William Walker fight at the Crawford battle in 1782? There is no evidence he did, but given the emphasis on young Indian men needing to prove their bravery, and his later influence in the tribe, it seems probable.
215. Big Kittles (Spicer) acting as a decoy. (Stenoin. ibid.)
217. There was, in fact, a John Walker on Crawford's march. I've found no proof of his origin.
225. John Slover's surprise at the abandoned town. (Eckert, ibid. p.343)
231. Daniel Canon's shooting from trees. (Crumrine, ibid. p.118)
231. "Oki" power. (Bonvillain, ibid. p.32)
235. Pipe's request to take the prisoner, Crawford. (Crumrine, ibid. pp.125-126.
243. William Walker, jr., said his mother, Catherine, was the daughter of an Irish trader (James Rankin) and a French-Wyandot (Mary Montour). (Draper, LWW, 11U)
247. Did William Walker ever see any of his birth family again? The only record I've found is a note from Col. John Johnston, Indian Agent: "His relations (relatives) were respectable, and desired his return to reside with them. This he firmly declined." (Draper, LCJJ, 1847.)
248. Big Kittles's wife was Mohawk, but, like so many Indian women, her actual name is sadly unrecorded. (Stenoein, ibid.)

255. Chief Dragging Canoe was a famous Chickamauga Cherokee. His meeting with Walker, however, is fiction—but they were allied with the Wyandot by this time. (CC)
263. Smith's Store was a trading post in Abb's Valley. (Brown & Woodworth, CAV, p. viii)
264. John & Mary Walker and the State of Franklin. The failed attempt to establish a state named Franklin across the VA border into present-day TN was promoted in Rockbridge County by Rev. Samuel Houston, who performed many weddings for the Walker family. (His wife was a Walker.) After several years he returned to Rockbridge—sometime around 1789. I've always thought it possible that John Walker left Washington County to join the effort and also returned to Rockbridge.
264. Jesse Hughes was a hero to many frontier settlers. His hatred for the Indian was well known—revenge, they said, for his father's murder. (McWhorter, BSNWV pp. 34f)
270. Patrick Porter was married to Susannah Walker, the sister of both Ann Cowan and John Walker, William's father. His home was at Falling Creek, now Falls Creek, Scott Co., VA. His physical description is imaginary. (Martin, PUP p. 143)
276. Porter's children and ages are from an old book that was known as the "Patrick Porter Sermon Book." (Willis, PPFB)
280. William's bullet wound is fiction. Arter (Arthur) Dale's parents' deaths are part of the story Chief Logan supposedly told about him. There were Mingo who were Christians—Moravian missionaries baptized Logan himself—and some of the tribe lived among the Shawnee. It is possible they were in the attack that destroyed Chillicothe (Chalahgawtha) either 1780 or 1782. Chief Logan said earlier that not one drop of his blood flowed in any living person's veins. (Eckert, ibid. pp.237 & 429.)
281. The Green Corn Festival. (GCF & IGCF/C)
284. Porter's violin had been "played so much that it is worn thin in the chin area…the violin had rattlesnake rattles inside…" (Martin, PUP p. 222)
285f. Patriotic songs of the Revolution. (FA; JHGS)
287. Camp-meeting song. While this comes from an 1831 songbook, it was sung no doubt for some years previous to

being printed. The original lyrics are in heavy dialect. (Scott, "Indian Hymn" no.66)

287. Arter (Arthur) Dale's story comes originally from a letter written by T.W. Carter, the grandson of Patrick Porter. Carter's mother was Porter's daughter "Catrin" (Catherine.) Arthur Dale became a Methodist preacher. He is listed as a "Methodist exhorter" in two U.S. censuses' which means he was probably a lay preacher who assisted the regularly appointed ministers. He died in Wise Co., VA, probably in the 1860's. (U.S. Census, 1850 & 1860; Draper, LTWC; Addington, TIM)

288. Chief Logan. (Hupp, LFWM)

299. Mrs. Samuel Scott reported seeing Ann Cowan on her way back from captivity. (Draper, 11CC, 224-225.)

309. Letter from Rev. James Finley, Feb. 8, 1823 (Bland, YWIQ, 129.)

Bibliography: Books, Manuscripts

Addington, Luther. "The Indian Missionary" (from booklet, Historical Sketches) VA: Historical Soc.of SW Virginia, pub.3, pp.38-41.

Bland, Bill. Yourowquains, A Wyandot Indian Queen. Elk Creek, VA: Historical Pub., 1992.

Bonvillain, Nancy. Indians of North America—The Huron. New York: Chelsea House Pub., 1989.

Brown, Dee. Wondrous Times on the Frontier. New York: Harper Collins Pub., Inc., (reprint) 1991.

Brown, James Moore & Woodworth, Robert Bell. The Captives of Abb's Valley. Staunton, VA: The McClure Co., Inc., 1942.

Clarke, Peter Dooyentate. Origin and Traditional History of the Wyandotts. Toronto: Hunter, Rose, 1870.

Connelley, William E. "Wyandot Folk-Lore." 1899

Crumrine, Boyd. History of Washington County, Pennsylvania. Philadelphia: L.H. Everts and Co., 1882.

Draper, Lyman C. *Draper Mss.* (microfilm) Western Heritage Lib.University of Oklahoma.

__________. "Letter from Col. John Johnston," 11U, 1847.

__________. "Letter from Peter D. Clarke.

__________. "Letter from T.W. Carter." 6C49f, 1883.

__________. "Letter from William Walker (jr.)" 13ZZ

Drimmer, Frederick. Captured By The Indians, 15 Firsthand Accounts, 1750—1870. New York: Dover Pub., Inc., 1961.

Gilbert, Bil. Westering Man: The Life of Joseph Walker. Norman and London: The University of Oklahoma Press, (reprint) 1985.

Eckert, Allan W. That Dark and Bloody River. New York: Bantam Books, 1995.

Eckert, Allan W. The Frontiersmen. New York: Bantam Books, (reprint) 1970.

Felkner, Myrtle E. In The Wigwams of the Wyandots. Ohio: K.Q. Associates, Inc., 1984.

Finley, James B. Sketches of Western Methodism. Cincinnati: The Methodist Book Concern, 1854.

__________. Life Among the Indians. Cincinnati: Jennings & Pye; New York: Eaton & Mains, 1853.

__________. Autobiography of Rev. James B. Finley. Cincinnati: The Methodist Book Concern, 1872.

Heckewelder, John. History, Manners, and Customs of the Indian Nations, Arno Press & The New York Times:1971 (reprint of 1876).

Hen-Toh (B.N. Walker). Tales of the Bark Lodges. Jackson, Mississippi: Harlow Pub. Co.,1920.

Holden, Robert John. The Hunting Pioneers, 1720—1840. Bowie,Maryland: Heritage Books, Inc., 2000.

Johnston, John. A Vocabulary of Wyandot. Bristol, PA: Evolution Pub., (reprint) 2003.

Leyburn, James G. The Scotch-Irish. Chapel Hill, NC: The University of North Carolina Press, 1962.

McClung, James W. Historical Significance of Rockbridge County, Virginia. Staunton, VA: Mcclure Co., Inc., 1939.

McWhorter, Lucullus Virgil. Border Settlers of Northwest Virginia. Hamilton, Ohio: The Republican Pub. Co., 1915.

Marsh, Thelma R. Moccasin Trails to the Cross. Upper Sandusky, OH: United Methodist Hist. Soc. of Ohio, 1974.

Martin, Henry G., Pickin Up the Porters. (Private Printing) 1983.

Morgan, Ted. Wilderness At Dawn. New York: Touchstone, 1993.

Morton, Oren F. A History of Rockbridge County, Virginia. Baltimore, Maryland: Genealogical Pub. Co., Inc., (reprint) 1994.

Raphael, Ray. A People's History of the American Revolution. New York: The New York Press, 2001.

Rockbridge County, VA. "Personal Property Tax List, 1782." (microfilm)

Scott, Orange. The New and Improved Camp Meeting Song Book. E. & G. Merriam, printers, Brookfield: 1831.

Vanderwerth, W.C. Indian Oratory: Famous Speeches By Noted Indian Chieftains. Norman, OK: University of Oklahoma Press, 1971.

Walker, B.N.O. "Sketch of B.N.O. Walker," Oklahoma City:Chronicles of Oklahoma, OHS, v.6, pp.89-90, 1928.

Weslager, C.A., The Delaware Indians. New Jersey: Rutgers Univ. Press, 1972.

White, Emma Siggins. Genealogy of the Descendants of John Walker of Wigton, Scotland. Kansas City, MO: Tiernan-Dart Pub.Co., 1902.

Electronic Sources (Websites)

"A Bashful Courtship." <http://www.earthbow.com/native/sioux/bashful.htm> 2/13/2005

"Arbuckle Family." (Capture of Adam Brown,sr.) <www.rootsweb.com/~wvkvgs/ newspaper/farbuckle.html> 12/15/2004

"Baggataway—The History of Lacrosse." <http://www.shakerlacrosse.com/id34.html> 2/25/2005

"Buffalo Hunt,1846." EyeWitness to History, <http://www.eyewitnesstohistory.com> (2002) 1/29/2005

Buser, C.A. "Tarhe Grand Sachem."
<http://www. wyandot.org/sachem.htm> 12/28/2004

________. "Wyandot Clothing." ibid.

"Cherokee Treaty, November 28, 1785." <http://lcweb2.loc.gov/learn/features/timeline/newnatn/nativeam/chereokee.html>4/1/2005

"Chickamauga Cherokee, The." <http://members.tripod.com/thssite/stt2/chic.html> 4/16/2005

"Colonial and Revolutionary Songs."
<http://www. mcneilmusic.com/rev.html> 4/30/2005

De Voe, Carrie. Legends of the Kaw. <www.kancoll.org/books/kaw/cdchap6.htm> 12/29/2004

Doyle, Kevin. "The Lenape/English Dictionary." <http://www.gilwell.com/lenape/> 9/16/2005

"Dragging Canoe"<http://cita.chattanooga.org/slcmdc/timeline.html> 4/16/2005

"Dunmore's War." <http://newsarch.rootsweb.com/th/read/VATAZEWE/199810/0909803653> 7/29/2005

"Free America." <http://www.contemplator.com/ america./freeamer.html> 4/30/2005

"Gnadenhutten Massacre of Christian Indians, The."<http://www.whiskeyrebellion.org/chapt5. htm> 3/6/2005

Gorin, Sandi. "Some Old Trails, Traces and Paths…"<http://www.rootsquest.com/ ~jmurphy/ lessons/tip_03.htm> 1/10/2005

"Green Corn Festival,The." <http://www.geocities. com/SouthBeach/Cove/8286/culture2. html?200530> 4/30/2005

Hamilton, Emory L. "Samuel Walker Slain, Anne Cowan and William Walker Captured" (from the unpublished manuscript, Indian Atrocities Along the Clinch, Powell and Holston Rivers, pp.69-71) <http://www.rootsweb.com/~varussel/indian/35.html> 5/13/2005

History of Montgomery Co.,OH. Chicago: W.H.Beers&Co.,1882.<http://www.heritagepursuit.com/ MontgomeryChap.II.htm> 2/4/2005

History of Pan-Handle (WV), "Simon Girty." <http://www.theroundup.com/sixnations/Girty.html> 2/12/2005

History of Seneca Co., OH. Chicago: Warner, Beers&Co.,1886. <http://www.heritagepursuit. com/ Seneca/SenChapII.htm> 12/30/2004

"History of the Sweat Lodge." <http://www. crystalinks.com/sweatlodge.html> 2/8/2005

Hupp, James. "Logan, A Friend to the White Man." (1965) <http://www.wvculture.org/history/notewv/ logan1.html> 4/27/2005

Indiana "Consolidated Docket No. 317" (concerning John Kilbuck at Princeton). <http://www.gbl. indiana.edu/archives/dockett317/31741.html> 2/5/2005

"Iroquoian Green Corn Festival/Ceremony." <http://www.1704.deerfield.history.museam/list/ glossary/all.do> 4/30/2005

"Jenny Selards Wiley." <http://www.libby-genealogy .com/misc_but_interesting.htm> 12/14/2004

"Johnny Has Gone For A Soldier" & "The World Turned Upside Down." <http://www.fssd.org/ PGS/PGS_ Digital_Museum/music%20Folder/> 4/30/2005

"Links to Ancient Footpaths." <http://www.over-land.com/trindian.html> 1/10/2005

"Loveless Family, Martin's Fort, June 26, 1780." <http://www.shawhan.com/loveless.html> 2/4/2005

"Mary Moore of Tazewell County." <http://www. housechurch.org/miscellaneous/foote_ mary.html> 5/31/2005

"Moravian Massacre."<http://www.rootsweb.com/ ~indian/morvma.htm> 3/6/2005

"Native American Courtship and Marriage." <http://www.augustana.edu/library/Special Collections/ court.html> 2/13/2005

Ohio History Central, "Bison."
<http://www. ohiohistorycentral.org/ohc/nature/ animals/mammals/bison.shtml> 1/29/2005

______________. "Simon Girty," <http://www. ohiohistorycentral.org/ohc/history/h_indian/ people/girtys.shtml> 2/12/2005

______________. "Historic Indian Lifestyles…" <http://www.ohiohistorycentral.org/ohc/history/ h_indian/life/f&a.shtml> 1/16/05

"Pittsburgh and North West Virginia Papers" (from DraperMss.).<http://www.lynn-linn-lineage-quarterly.com/Draper/page_51_of_Bauer_ Transcription.htm> 6/29/2005

Pitz, Marylynne. "Descendant Makes a Case for Simon Girty," Post-Gazette, Dec. 29, 1999.
<http://www.post- gazette.com/regionstate/ 19991229girty4.asp> 2/12/2005

"Regulations for the Trade at Niagara" (1761). NACRG 10, v.1824,pt.1, pp.83-86, reel C01222, page 1 of 5.

"Richard Rue" (on Bowman attack on Shawnee). <http://www.oiwus.org/oiwus_web_site_029.htm> 2/21/2005

"Seneca Indian Legends."<http://www.indianlegend.com/lenape/lenape_002.htm> 2/18/2005

"Some Important Dates in Scott County History." <http://www.geocities.com/geneybeney/addington.htm?200529> 6/29/2005

StandingBear, Dan. "Buffalo, The. <http://www.affv.nu/andreasson/buffalo/ page18.htm> 9/19/2005

Stenoien, Randy. "William (Big Kittles) Spicer," May,2003.<http://www.stenoien.com/ william_spicer. htm> 1/21/2005

"Stickball Rules." <http://www.cherokee.org/Culture/CulturePage.asp?ID=54> 1/29/2005

Tankersley, Kenneth B. "Kentucky." <http://freepages.genealogy.rootsweb.com/ ~brockfamily/KYs-Native-Past-byKTankersley.html.> 1/3/2005

"Thunderbear 233" (Gnadenhutten massacre.) <http://www.workingnet.com/thunderbear/233.html> 3/6/2005

"Treaty of Fort McIntosh, 1785." <http://www.ohiohistorycentral.org/ohc/t/tfm-tr.shtml> 3/27/2005

"United States Census of 1850" (Virginia).
<http:// www.rootsweb.com/~varussel/census/1850CEN.txt> 6/30/2005

Vennum, Thomas, jr. "History of Native American Lacrosssse."<http://www.lacrosse.org/museum/ history.phtml> 1/24/2005

Walker, William. "Col. Crawford's Campaign and Death," 1857. (See Wyandot Nation of Kansas.)

Walker, William. "The Journals of William Walker." <http://www.rootsweb.com/~neresour/OLLibrary/Walker/wlkr161.html> 12/29/04

Willis, W.M. "Patrick Porter, A Family Biography" 1999.<www.globalsunshine.com/Patrick%20Porter. htm> 2/6/2002

Windwalker,Barefoot. "The Native American Sweat Lodge, A Spiritual Tradition." <http://www.barefootsworld.net/sweatlodge.html> 2/8/2005

"Woodland Indians." <http://iroquoisindians.freeweb-hosting.com/webdoc58.htm> 2/21/2005

"Wyandot Family Statue in Wyandotte Michigan." <http://www. wyandot.org/statue.htm> 2/17/2005

Wyandot Nation of Anderdon (Canada). <http://ishgooda.org/huron/anderdon/ dir_swontario1750-1850.htm> 12/20/2004

Wyandot Nation of Oklahoma. "Adam Brown." <http://www.wyandotte-nation.org/history/biographies/adam_brown.html> 12/20/2004

___________. "Wendat (language)." <http://www.wyandotte-nation.org/language.html> 10/15/2004

Wyandot Nation of Kansas. <www.kckps.org/disthistory/ftw/wyandots_ks.GED> 12/30/2004

Wyandotte County, Kansas History. <http:// skyways.lib.ks.us/genweb/archives/wyandott/history/1911/volume1/68.html> 12/23/04

~~~
~~~

Dark River Passage

Order Form

Use this convenient page to order additional copies:

Please Print:

Name ____________________________________

Address__________________________________

City________________________State__________

Zip________________

Phone (_____)______________________

Email (optional)___________@_______________

_____copies of book @ $17.95 each $_________

Postage & handling, @ $4 each book $_________

Okla. residents add 1.35 tax per book $_________

Total amount enclosed: $_________

Make checks payable to TapRootBooks.

Send to: TapRootBooks
P.O. Box 2521
Chickasha, OK 73023-2521
Contact info: TapRootBooks@aol.com

Phone: 405-222-4652